Eric,

# KRISTOFFER LAW

# THE JAGGED TREE

Keep writing, show me
how good you can dance.

Thanks,

Kristoffr

Filidh Publishing

Jacket design by Kristoffer Law & Dan Weeds

Filidh Publishing

www.filidhbooks.com

First Edition – Soft Cover
ISBN 978-1-927848-01-2

*For Shanna, Mary, Dori and Petra.*
*Thank you for all of your inspiration, love and support.*

*For my family.*
*You have always given me the bravery to pursue my dreams.*

*And for David Holmes.*
*I think he would have been tremendously proud of this.*

*I love you, and I thank you.*

*- K.L.*

---

*This novel was started on April 11, 2011*
*and completed on January 6, 2014*

---

*"Misery loves chaos.*

*And chaos loves company."*

*-George F. Walker, "Zastrozzi"*

*Part I*

# I

She could tolerate just about any kind of weather or season, be it the damp promise of spring; the furtive, elegant diminishing of autumn; even the long and almost breathlessly cold nights in winter. But of all the seasons of the turning year, one thing was certain: Beverly Black loathed the dog days of summer. It wasn't the extra hours she so cherished in her gardens. It was, quite simply, the *heat*.

The air-conditioned supermarket's double doors *shooshed* open onto the parking lot, and the oppressive heat of the late August afternoon almost flattened her. The sun glared down from a vast sea of blue, but there were dark clouds building on the horizon and Beverly could smell the rains that would come in just a few hours. With a huff, she struggled out into the sunshine with her only purchase: a large, dusty tray of flowers.

Beverly was a far cry from the slender, raven-haired woman of her youth. Age and sun had dulled her hair to a greyish-brown and her long fingers, once the envy of a pianist she was acquainted with back in college, were now plump, giving her hands the appearance of something squat and unlovely. The extra pounds were not confined to her hands, however. Long summers spent refreshing herself with case after case of diet cola had seen to that; the slow roundness of her midsection and bosom rather inexactly masked by loose-fitting, breathable clothing. In winter she added a cardigan to the mix. Anything to disguise the horrible possibility that she had *gained weight*.

She re-adjusted the shoulder strap on her purse with a quick shrug, and the sound of her keys jangling as they struck the hot pavement forced a breathless curse from her lips. She squatted down, her lower back screaming in agony. *Degenerative disc disease,* her doctor had called it. Months of tests and all she'd been given were more over-the-counter painkillers. Not even prescription! She closed her eyes to the pain as her fingers scrabbled blindly for the keys. She felt her middle finger slip through the ring and then, for an awful moment, her knees betrayed her and she couldn't summon the strength to stand. *Fifty-six years old and I'm falling apart! So-called doctor won't prescribe me anything stronger than a Goddamn generic anti-inflammatory. Won't even* consider *a fucking epidural!* she thought. She squatted, beads of sweat forming at her hairline as she willed away the pain and the pressure. With measured breaths, she rose to her feet.

The heat made the fifty foot walk to her car seem like fifty miles. Sweat was pouring down her face by the time she reached it and, careful as she was, her shaking hands dropped the blooms the last six inches into the trunk with a thump. Thirty-four flowers, seventeen marigolds and seventeen irises. Grief and hope. Every year on his birthday, she added one to the number she'd bought the previous year. Both represented the feelings she imagined every mother must feel after losing a child. However, her son hadn't died; she'd lost him because of her own foolish pride. Death would have been easier; at least then she would have some lonely plot where she could mourn.

When she opened the car door, a vicious wall of heat slammed into her face, carrying with it the stagnant odour of aging vinyl. The ancient car was stifling and she cringed in pain as the scorching seat burned through her sundress. She grabbed a crossword puzzle book off the passenger seat and attempted to fan herself before reaching into her purse for a bottle of rapidly melting iced water. She uncapped the bottle and took a pull, relishing the water's biting coolness as it rushed down her throat, before twisting the cap back on and tucking the bottle between her neck and the head rest. She closed her eyes for a few moments, and when the condensing water started to drip down her neck she put the car in gear and pulled out of the lot.

The car ate up the miles slowly, each bump and pothole bringing a fresh grimace of pain. The air-conditioner had given up the ghost years ago, and the wind blew in, hot, thick and heavy through the open windows. As she pulled into her driveway the wind faded away to a standstill and the drone of the cicadas, along with the crunch of gravel under her tires, formed an uneasy harmony. Throwing the gearshift into Park, she popped the trunk and walked around to retrieve the tray of flowers.

A curtain twitching in the window of her office caught her eye. Breathless, she stared at the window, but when it didn't move again she tried to shrug off the uneasy feeling as nothing and turned her attention back to the trunk.

Resuming her balancing act, she shuffled, slow and unsure, over the flagstones leading to the verandah steps. After setting everything down on the table, she turned toward the garden that lay just past the verandah. Her throat closed and it became nearly impossible to breathe.

The garden was destroyed.

Not just destroyed. *Annihilated.* Every blossom, down to the last petal, had been torn out by their roots and flung in pieces across the yard. *Years* she had spent tending it, infusing it with all the guilt, remorse, hope and joy she felt in connection with her son. Now madness had ripped it to shreds.

"Alan...*ALAN!*" she sobbed as the tray teetered on the edge of the table before crashing to the verandah floor. She'd been gone from the house for two days. Two days! Now everything she had left of her boy had been raped beyond imagining. She almost rolled her ankle as she ran down the steps to the garden's edge. "Why?" she whispered, clawing at the broken stems. "Alan...oh, my beautiful boy...who could do this to you?"

She crumpled, and wept as the moist earth and grass stained her sundress. She wept for all the years lost. Wept for her son. She swayed a little when she rose to her feet and the blood rushed to her head. When she turned to go back to the house, she noticed a pit at the base of the gnarled old apple tree that had long ago withered and died. Faded and dried, the trunk emerged from the fresh-tossed black soil and twisted upward. A few sickly roots, clotted with dirt, crept out of the pit's wall like gnarled, dead fingers.

Heavy, slow steps brought Beverly to the edge of the pit that yawned at her until space itself fell away.

The incessant buzzing of the cicadas ceased and the silence was deafening. She tried to swallow, but her tongue felt dry and heavy in her mouth. *This isn't right,* she thought.

Her knees threatened to buckle with every stride as she ran back toward the house. Her hands flew out as she tripped on the stair in front of her office door where she squawked in surprise as the door flew open upon impact. The wind was knocked out of her as she landed hard on the floor inside.

So dark.

She'd drawn all the curtains in the office before she left and the room was drenched in hazy shadow. She had banged her elbow hard in the fall, and it muttered in pain as she picked herself up, her heartbeat pounding in her ears.

Her nose flared as it detected a faint mixture of Old Spice and Pall Mall's. She took a few deep gulps to try and get her wind back, her tongue still thick in her throat. After years of refusal, she desperately wished for a cell phone.

The heavy oak chair squealed along the hardwood as the figure sitting there rose to his feet. Her eyes were slow to adjust to the gloom, but the shadows were like a part of him. Her lips were white as she pressed them together to prevent her teeth from chattering. Through great force of will, she broke out of her paralysis and turned to flip on the light switch, but it was at least a foot beyond her reach.

The figure moved out from behind the desk toward the door, pushing it closed with an outstretched hand as she backed away from him into the room instinctively. He turned to face her, the shadows moving with him. He sidled up next to her, the scent of his cologne mingling with her fear. His gloved hand reached up to brush away her hair, in a bizarre act of comfort, and her breath caught in her throat. She squeezed her eyes shut against the intrusion, whimpering like an animal.

"No need to be nervous," the man said. "Just a question or two, that's all. Unless you've destroyed even more of that rotting mass you call a brain since the last time we talked. How many drugs *are* you taking these days?" Lightning–fast, he grabbed a huge handful of her hair, bending her back in an obscene tango-like dip. An explosion of pain erupted in her lower back and her mouth broke open in a quivering wail. The shadows blew apart and his face was distinguishable for the first time. In the gloom, his countenance could not be mistaken and he grinned, showing two huge rows of nicotine-stained teeth. "Did you miss me?"

*     *     *     *     *     *

*All you have to do is endure,* she thought behind shut eyes. *This is just like all those years ago. Just do what he wants, let him have his fun and it will all be over. It doesn't matter how much he hurts you, eventually he'll leave and eventually you'll heal.* She recoiled from the curdled coffee smell that oozed from his lips. There was another smell there, too; a sweet smell she didn't recognize. An unnameable sick. *This is what insanity must smell like.* "What do you want?" she breathed.

He laughed without smiling. "I want what's mine, you drugged-up bitch. The money. *My* money!"

A wave of nausea slithered through her and in her mind she teetered on the edge of a precipice, felt reality plummeting away into oblivion. With enormous difficulty she opened her eyes to look at him again. "I don't know what you're talk..."

He let her go without warning, growling in frustration. Off–balance, Beverly collapsed to the floor, a jumbled mess of arms and legs. She cracked her head hard against a filing cabinet, and her vision swam for a moment. Muttering under his breath, he paced back and forth. He stopped mid–stride and looked down on her, a slight smile on his face. She was still trying to un–knot her legs when he crossed over and pulled her up by the hair again.

"Don't lie to me," he said. Her eyes rolled in her head a little as she tried to collect herself, and a rivulet of blood seeped out of the corner of her mouth from where she'd bitten her tongue in the fall. She licked the blood from her lips, grimacing at the taste of stale iron. That sense of overwhelming wrongness filled her again, threatened to suffocate her.

"Why arryoo doin thsss?" Her words were thick.

"Do I have to spell it out for you?" He waited for an answer he knew wasn't coming. "Yes. I suppose I do. You and the old lady were close, like peas fucking in a pod. I know she had piles of money, and you know what she did with it. Or rather, who she left it to. I know she's dead. I found that out from her fucking doorman. Nobody even bothered to call her only son and let him know she'd kicked it. Can you believe that?" She was fading, and he gave her head a light shake. She squealed and more blood seeped out of her mouth. A warm smile traced his lips. "Tell me the truth, now. Where's my money?"

She concentrated hard. "Sh'...may me prom..." Her tongue filled her mouth as it swelled, made talking more difficult. "Sh' may me promusss naw tuh tell en'wuhn." Her chin quivered as she wept in silence and her tears cut a path through the blood that streaked down her chin.

"Did she? Well, now." He let go of her hair a second time and she hit the floor with a bang. He reached into his jacket pocket and pulled out a syringe filled three-quarters full with a clear liquid. She watched him with mounting fear as he removed the cap with one hand, a smooth, practiced motion. Her eyes followed the arc of liquid as he depressed the plunger a little and squirted some into the air and onto the floor.

"Bleach," he said, regarding the syringe. "Common household bleach." He turned his gaze back to her. "I'm gonna fill you up, Bee. Fill you right up with bleach." He flashed that speckled smile again. Beverly edged away from him, but there was nowhere to go. His tone was conversational. "It'll burn, y'know. I read somewhere that it's a very painful way to die. Not that you'd die right away. With a dose this size, it could take you up to three days. And you'll suffer. Oh, Bee, how you'll *suffer*." He straddled her body at the waist, crushing her left wrist under his knee. She cried out in pain, a terrible gurgling sound that forced fresh tears from the corners of her eyes. He seized her by the throat with his free hand while waving the needle in front of her face. Her eyes followed its every move. "Always wear gloves while cleaning with bleach, right?" he continued. "It can be *so* corrosive. Just eating away at your flesh. Bit by bit, your arm will...fall apart, meat off the bone. It'll be interesting to see how long you can withstand the pain before you pass out." He flicked the needle at her face and she flinched. He laughed a rich, deep good-natured laugh. *We're just having a grand time, friend,* that laugh said. "I give you two minutes, tops." With sadistic glee, he slid the needle into the crook of her elbow and watched her face as she saw the liquid empty into her.

There was no burning. Instead of blinding pain there was a sensation of...untethering. Of disconnection. She tried to speak, tried to move, but her body lay prone and unresponsive. Her vision narrowed to pinpoints and the precipice she lingered on seemed to crumble away. Images from times long past flashed across her mind. A kaleidoscope of blurred faces, of phantom chatter. A thumping bass line. Of her kneeling on a floor next to a coffee table. Lines of powder sat on the table in front of her, and a nameless face prodded her; goaded her. "Do a snort, man!" the face said. She bent her head, stuck the tiny plastic tube into her nose, pinched the other nostril shut, and sniffed hard. The sensation then was identical to the sensation she experienced now – instead of the overwhelming feeling of euphoria and power she'd grown accustomed to with cocaine, she felt a frightening dissociation as her body grew unresponsive. Unhinged. The nameless face laughed at her as she crumbled to the floor, its voice echoing as if inside a stone cavern. "Special-K!" The voice thundered in her head. "Fuckin' awesome, innit?"

There was a not-so-distant rumble in the greying skies outside. Her mind disengaged completely on the floor of her office, and she thought no more.

*     *     *     *     *     *

He threw her down by the gaping hole in the garden. She watched, helpless, as he pulled some twine from his back pocket and tied her hands and feet together behind her back. Then he lifted her at the junction of her limbs and tossed her, face down, into the pit. Walls of dirt loomed all around her. The pallid roots of the dead apple tree caressed her cheeks, making her think of fingers on her face, welcoming her home. She couldn't move. Soon could barely feel her body under the crushing weight of dirt on top of her. Close to her face was an iris, the bloom ripped almost in half. Hope lost. *I'm so sorry for everything, Alan. I hope you find me...find me...* Her thoughts were running together now, a garbled mess inside her head. *I don't want to die don't want to love you so much Alan why couldn't I say so before why couldn't I see past myself why couldn't I why couldn't I why couldn't I love you so much baby so much so mu...* Her thoughts trailed away as one last wheelbarrow full of dirt poured down over her head and there was darkness.

She opened her mouth out of instinct to breathe and dirt, dry and bitter, crumbled inside. There was silence, thick, heavy and suffocating. Then a final muffled sound: an engine revving into life and then fading away, leaving the silence, infinite and terrifying once more. For a brief moment mindless panic burst open inside her as the blackness enveloped and began to consume her. Then there was nothing, and Beverly Black fell forever into the abyss.

## II

Alan Black placed a small decaf iced coffee on the countertop in front of his last customer. The old man reached for his wallet with a shaking hand.

"Mr. Getzel," Alan said with a raised, clear voice. "You already paid, sir." He hadn't, of course, but Alan gave an encouraging smile to the old man anyway. Getzel was the oldest resident of Shallot's Cove and the man who had sold Alan his dream. He'd long ago earned the honour of never paying for anything in Alan's shop. Mr. Getzel looked at Alan with confused blinking eyes, his chin in a constant quiver, as Alan gestured again to the icy drink. Mr. Getzel's rheumy eyes followed Alan's hand to the coffee, and he stared at it for a moment, his face a swirling tornado of wordless questions. At last he reached out a gnarled, trembling hand, grasped the cold plastic cup, and turned toward the door without saying a word. Kimberly, Alan's assistant manager, leaned her mop against a table and turned to open the door for Mr. Getzel. She watched with barely disguised sadness in her eyes as he shuffled out the door into the early twilight, mumbling to himself the entire way. Alan watched through the window as Mr. Getzel's caretaker rose from one of the patio chairs to link her arm in his and ease in alongside his halting stride as they moved toward to the intersection.

"He's getting worse," Kim said, as she closed the door.

"I know," Alan replied. The old man was a beloved member of the community. He had sold the store to Alan four years earlier, after more than fifty struggling as the neighbourhood florist. Watching his old friend succumb to the ravages of Alzheimer's was heartbreaking. Kim turned back to her mop, and Alan looked up at her from counting the till. "Go on and leave it."

"You sure? I'm just about done."

"Nah, it's good," he said. "We've both slaved enough today." She walked across the floor with the mop and put it back in the cupboard while he tossed the last of the nickels back in the drawer. "You make sure that boyfriend of yours does something nice for you tonight, like wine or a foot-rub."

"Or both!" She laughed before disappearing into the back.

Alan tucked the cash drawer into the safe beneath the counter and spun the dial. Standing up again, he ran a finger through his hair – jet-black with just a couple of grey strands at the temples – and took a moment, as he did every day, to survey the shop he'd worked so hard to build up. All the time he was growing up in Shallot's Cove this store had been a florist shop, and not a very successful one. While Mr. Getzel remained one of the most well-loved and longest-living members of the town, *Getzel's Finest Flowers* was forever on the verge of bankruptcy.

He thought back to the day of the sale and smiled at the memory of Mr. Getzel ranting in his crusty Yiddish accent that made Alan think of crumbling weathered New York City tenement buildings from the 1940s. *"This place has never earned a dime!"* Mr. Getzel had shouted at him as he pulled down his moth-eaten jacket from its hook behind the office door. Then the old man had paused, his soft hand on Alan's shoulder in a gesture of sad, almost paternal affection. He looked up at him with the same tired, watery eyes that had gazed emptily across the counter tonight. *"I'd wish ya good luck, but this place almost ate me alive."* The sale was finalized on Alan's 30th birthday. He was a nervous, unsure business owner then and a well-loved, successful and confident cornerstone of the community four years later. Mr. Getzel hadn't spoken a word in this last year, as the Alzheimer's really started to take hold, and Alan sorely missed that gritty accent.

It took him six months to convert the space into a second-hand bookstore and coffee shop. He called it *Bookends*. It seemed he'd come along with the right idea at the right time, for *Bookends* was a thriving success from the day he opened his doors. He had felt terrible guilt at first, considering how Mr. Getzel had struggled through the years, but the retired botanist gave Alan both his approval and his blessing. He smiled to himself as he looked around and thought of what he'd accomplished.

Kimberly emerged from the back with her hair fixed and her splashy woven purse slung on her shoulder. Her bright eyes followed his line of sight for a moment before she waved a hand in front of his face, breaking him out of his sightless stare. "Earth to Alan," she laughed.

Alan looked back at her with a smile. "Sorry about that."

"About what? Staring?" She smiled and flapped her hand at him. "Here," she continued, digging into her purse. "This is for you. Happy birthday." She handed him a small white envelope with *For Alan* written across the face of it in her flawless cursive.

"But my birthday..."

"Isn't until tomorrow. I know. But I'm giving this to you now in the hope that I won't see you. Maybe you'll take a day off from this place and enjoy yourself. Will you?"

Alan looked at the envelope for a moment, a smile on his face. Then he nodded. "I will. Thank you."

Kim reached out and wrapped him in a warm hug. "Thank *you* for being just about the best boss I've ever worked with." He smelled her perfume, which reminded him of endless expanses of sandy beaches, suntan lotion and children playing in the surf. She walked toward the door. "And I'm serious about tomorrow. It's your birthday, and I think you should enjoy yourself. Get some sun maybe. I've already called Sophie in for the extra shift. We'll manage without you for one day."

He nodded, already planning.

She closed the door behind her, and Alan watched her for a moment before turning off the bank of switches behind the counter. A solitary streetlight flickered into life, its garish orange light pouring in through the picture window and blanketing the floor of the shop. He strode over to the window and looked up into the night sky, watching the clouds break up and blow away after that afternoon's sudden storm. From his shop's isolated corner near the ocean, he could see lights winking on in several houses further up the avenue. He crossed over and flipped the sign on the door to "CLOSED", turned the deadbolt at the top and walked toward the back of the shop. It was Tuesday night.

\*         \*         \*         \*         \*         \*

Sunlight crashed into the room and splashed across Alan's face. Grumbling, he rolled away from the window and yawned into his pillow. *Happy birthday to me.* He had hoped to sleep in, but the sun and his own internal clock had other ideas. He burrowed his face further into the pillow and debated whether to really take the day off. He'd promised Kimberly he would, but he wondered if she'd kick him out of his own store if he showed up. A lazy smirk broke across his lips. Hell, she probably would. He half-opened one eye and stared at the wall through a sleepy haze. *Happy birthday to me.* His father had once said over a pint of beer that birthdays became less important as you got older, and for a long time Alan denied that possibility. Yet here, now, he'd be damned if his old man hadn't been right all along.

Slinking out of the shadows, Alan's grey tabby, Misfit, bared her fangs in a massive yawn of her own and then bounded from the floor onto the bed. He chuckled under his breath and scratched the cat behind her ears as she nuzzled his face. She purred deep in her throat, a thick hum that underscored the muted sounds of the ocean just beyond his property. Alan yawned again and slid out of bed. *I hate birthdays.*

Living alone, as he did, offered its own challenges. His beach-front property required constant upkeep, but he'd learned to be creative. For the big things, like building and putting up the storm-covers for all his windows, his father had come down from his house in Massey Bay to help. That had been fun. Edward Black tended to sweat like a pig and curse like a sailor whenever he engaged in hard physical activity, much to Alan's carefully hidden amusement. Despite the fact that the elder Black loved his son and bore no real animosity towards him, Edward drank and had a hair-trigger Irish temper, something which Alan learned to avoid early in life.

In a lot of ways Alan's home was a snapshot of his childhood, when there wasn't any money for luxuries. Alan had no use for television, bringing questioning looks to the faces of his friends over the years. His only real indulgences were books, and where a big-screen TV and a stereo system might have normally stood were five monolithic bookcases, filled to bursting. From the complete works of Edgar Allan Poe and first editions of Dickens and Conan-Doyle, to a hardcover collection of Stephen King's works, the greatest of the literary giants rubbed shoulders with the pop culture heavyweights. Most of the King books were signed. The library wasn't just for show either; he had read every single book on his shelves at least once.

He tossed open the curtains covering the large bay window and sat down to admire the early morning view from the window seat. Misfit hopped up beside him and then strolled over to her favourite cushion, kneading the fabric a few times before settling down with a whump. Her tail seemed to beat in perfect time to the shoaling of the waves as they crested on the shore. He decided that one of Kimberly's suggestions had been a good one, and prepared to go out and work on his tan.

He gathered a couple of beers out of the fridge and put them in an insulated cooler bag before going into the bedroom to grab a pair of shorts to put on after his shower.

Strains of *Minuet in G* floated through the air from his cell phone. He poked his head out of the bathroom where he had been hunting for his suntan lotion and glanced over at the side table next to his recliner chair. *Parissa Khorasani* flashed on the display. Parissa was a first-generation Canadian born to Iranian parents; they had met in middle school and hit it off immediately. They never dated (her parents forbade it) but they had shared a dorm in university for a time. He remembered he had volunteered her landscaping services to his mother a few years earlier, and then in the last year they'd lost contact – just fell out of touch – and now her name lit up his display screen. Alan walked out of the bathroom and crossed over to the coffee table. He pressed Answer on the touch screen.

"He-"

"-LAN! OH MY GOD, PLEASE PICK UP!"

Alan yanked the phone from his ear in pain. He fumbled for the volume control, and clicked it twice to bring her voice to a listenable level. Parissa was almost hyperventilating. "Whoa! 'Rissa? What's going on?"

Parissa's voice broke down in uncontrollable sobs. She tried to speak through them, but Alan only managed to catch bits and pieces.

"Alan...scared! I don't...oh my God, Alan..." More sobs. "Your mom...dead."

Alan's world seemed to roar all around him as the blood thudded heavy in his ears. His mind froze and rational thought fell away into a bottomless void. His mother. Dead? He struggled to comprehend it and he swayed on his feet, almost blacking out.

Confusion now, in the sobs. "Alan? Hello?"

Alan stared ahead without seeing, his mind spinning as he tried to process what he'd heard. Too many crime novels crowded his mind and, against his will, he began conjuring up all manner of different scenarios. His mother, face down in her driveway, a single bullet in the back of her head, blood and brains oozing out of the exit wound in her face. In her living room chair, a carving knife jutting out of her chest, her blouse blossoming crimson. In the bath, her neck laid open in an obscene, toothless smile, the water turning brown as the blood began to oxidize. He closed his eyes tight and willed the thoughts away, yet the images kept marching behind his eyelids. He found himself collapsed back down onto the window seat without realizing it.

"*HELLO?*" Parissa's voice cracked with fear.

He spoke without opening his eyes. "Yeah...yeah, I'm here, 'Rissa."

"You need to get down here, Alan. I'm so scared." She sniffled loudly in his ear, and took another hitching breath to get herself under control.

"Aw fuck..." Alan breathed. It felt like his brain kept bumping up against a wall. After ten years of silence, being told his mother was dead was not something he ever expected. He cleared his throat a little and felt the urge to vomit. He swallowed hard and took a deep breath. "Parissa?"

"Y-yea?" She sounded so small.

"I'm on my way, but have you called the police yet?"

"N-no...not yet."

"Can you wait till I get there to call them? Please?"

"I-I guess so. Are you sure?"

*No. But I need to see. I need to see before anyone else gets involved.* "No, I'm not. But...can you?"

"Alan, I – please hurry."

He clicked off the phone and closed his eyes. There was a faint click as the coffee-maker's pre-set timer turned on, and he rose from the window seat, swaying a little on his feet. His eyes snapped open as his head began to spin and he bolted back to the bathroom. He barely reached the toilet before he vomited, tiny remnants of last night's dinner now floating in chunks inside the bowl. He tugged on the handle, and as the water swirled away, he collapsed against the wall and wept.

## III

Guilt, confusion, indifference and resignation. Ten years earlier, Alan had walked away. He had hung up the phone on his mother and turned his back on twenty years of attempts at cultivating some semblance of a relationship with her. Now, on the heels of Parissa's declaration that his mother was dead, so many emotions (along with an unexpected and horrifying sense of relief) swirled through him in constant eddies. He had not spoken to her in over a decade. Indeed, he thought himself somehow – *finally!* – emotionally detached from all that existed between them, yet the guilt that now filled him was torturous. He had thrown up once more that morning, and then stepped into the shower, letting the hot water pour over him for what seemed like hours.

When he stepped out, naked and dripping, he caught his reflection in the mirror. Leaning on the sink, he looked at his face and saw all the stress and sadness he had pushed down inside over the years slowly rising to the surface. Behind his eyes, the roots of what would become a real bastard of a headache began to throb. After toweling off, he walked into the bedroom to dress and prepare for the ninety-minute drive to Waterford. He pulled a small suitcase out from under his bed and filled it with some clothes and a few toiletries. Misfit curled around his legs and mewled at him. He let a faint smile creep across his face, his eyes sad and crinkling, as he reached down to give her a lingering scratch behind the ears. He walked back into the kitchen, pulled down an extra bowl, and filled both it and Misfit's regular bowl with food. He did the same with the water.

Thirty years! Twenty trying to give a damn, ten of radio silence, and now this. He couldn't wrap his head around it. After his parents divorced when he was three, his mother had left the picture, moving to Waterford while he and his father stayed behind in Shallot's Cove. His father was granted full custody, and Beverly got full visitation rights, though she never bothered to utilize them. He remembered being four years old the first time she really let him down. She had phoned the house and spoken to him around Hallowe'en, promising him all the world's riches in Christmas presents. When Christmas morning came with no sign of anything from her, he remembered feeling hot shame, as if something he'd done had prevented the parcels from materializing. His father tried so hard to put a positive spin on it. "Perhaps they just got lost in the mail," Edward Black had said. "This is not your fault, Al, remember that. No matter what, your mother loves you very much." So began an internal struggle of feeling angry and guilty, yearning and hopeful, for years. Eventually he could no longer carry the burden of trying to make things work, and he had cut them both loose from the few frayed bonds that had held them together. Now she was dead, and that final threadbare knot that he could never cut away had at last been broken.

*Let's go,* a small, urgent voice in his head said. *You wanted to see for yourself, so let's go.* He hesitated only a moment more, before grabbing the spare key from its hook on the wall and walking out the door with his suitcase. The two cans of beer he'd pulled out of the fridge sat in the portable cooler, all but forgotten.

A fresh breeze blew in off the ocean and ruffled his damp hair as he stood on the deck and looked at the spare key resting on his palm. Closing his fist, he looked up and searched the outside wall for the small secret compartment he'd built. When it was closed, it was nearly invisible, but it made a perfect hiding spot. He opened up the compartment and placed the key inside.

Turning toward his road-weary silver Tercel, he held his breath for a moment as he stared inward at the edge of a cliff jutting out into the unknown. He shut down his imagination hard – he couldn't bear to see the battalion of images parade through his mind again. He opened his eyes and watched a robin bounce along the grass, putting its head close to the ground to listen for worms. Grim-faced, he tossed his suitcase into the trunk before getting behind the wheel.

First stop was *Bookends*. He pulled up in front and stepped from the car with careful, studious silence. He let his eyes roam over the unremarkable features of the brick storefront as he approached it, trying to commit to memory every nuance, every detail. He unlocked the front door and stepped into the delicate blend of dark roast and dusty, leather-bound whispers. There was a calm here that seemed to exist only for him. This was the time he cherished most: the breathless anticipation of another day. Even his footsteps were hushed as he walked across to the counter.

*Bookends* would not open today. The lingering quiet couldn't totally silence his mind, and while his task here was simple, he found it very difficult to cross the twenty-foot gap to the back office. He finally managed it, despite the way his feet wanted to drag, and he unlocked the office door and opened it. To his immediate right was a tall metal shelf, and from it he pulled down a medium-size sheet of poster paper. He took it back out to the counter, pulling the office door closed behind him, and laid the paper next to the cash register. He took a black Sharpie and, after a long hesitation, wrote *Closed Due To Family Emergency* on it.

He read back the words to himself, and then reached under the counter mechanically for a roll of twine and scotch tape. He went through the motions of affixing a length of the twine to the back of the poster paper without registering what he was doing, and then walked over to hang it on the inside of the front door. He removed the "WE WILL RETURN AT" sign that hung there by a suction-cup hook and let it drop from his hand, where it swooped away from him, skidding under a nearby table as it landed. He hung the new sign in its place.

He turned to look back at the shop one more time, his expression akin to a parent watching their child leave home for the last time. It was a look of profound sadness. *I miss you already*, he thought. He frowned, confused at the random clarity of the thought. Miss the shop? Or his mother? He had no answer. He turned the knob on the front door and walked out, locking it behind him.

As he got into his car and pulled away, he dared not look back.

He drove in silence and no matter how hard he tried, his mind kept swirling around and around in a whirlpool of horror. *Maybe she died of natural causes.* He shook his head. Beverly Black was only in her mid-fifties, and aside from her chronic back pain, there was nothing wrong with her health. *Ten years is a long time, Alan. You don't know what she's been doing. Or who. Maybe she just ended it all. Took one of her many bottles of painkillers and just upended it, open wide, down the hatch. Fell into a deep sleep, and I mean DEEP.* He took a breath and tried to stop the mental flow. *Maybe her back finally gave out. Maybe she dropped a spoon on the deck and when she bent to pick it up, her back wouldn't straighten out. Maybe the pain caused her to crumple to the deck in agony, and after a while she realized she wasn't getting back up, and the patio door was too heavy to open, and there she lay, in the fetal position, starving to death. What about THAT, Alan?* He shook his head. As gruesome as it was to imagine his mother starving in pain on her deck, he knew better. As her landscaper, Parissa was by the house far too frequently for her to be alone that long. But Parissa *had* come by, and *had* noticed something. She'd found his mother dead, and all the suppositions in the world weren't helping. The mental roiling served no purpose except to frustrate him.

A rival coffee shop came up on the right and he made a sharp turn into the parking lot without using his signal.

*MEEEEEEEEEP!* "You asshole!"

The car behind him swerved past on the left and he turned in time to see the driver flash his middle finger at him in fury as he blazed by. Alan turned his attention back toward the parking lot, apathetic. He considered going through the drive-thru, but at the last minute slid his car into a spot just outside the front entrance. Inside, the familiar hiss of espresso machines, and a few customers front-lit by their standard-issue iMacs, greeted him. Santana's "Smooth", the apparent unofficial anthem for this chain of stores, blared from the speakers and Alan had a hard time hearing the bored, gum-chewing barista behind the counter.

When he finally got his coffee, he noted with annoyance that they had written *Ellen* on the side of his cup. He got back into the driver's seat and took a moment to peel the lid off and give his coffee a blow before taking a tentative sip. It had been about two years since he last drank a coffee that hadn't come from his own shop, and the medium roast he held now was so burnt it actually pissed him off. He marveled at how, with their thousands of stores, and a massive global market share, they still managed to ruin drip coffee. "It's *burnt*," he muttered to himself. "They give it a faux-Italian name, charge $6.50 for it, and then they *burn* it. This stuff tastes like someone ran goat piss through the beans." He poured the coffee out on the concrete, earning a look of disgust from an employee washing the glass inside the cafe. He gave the cup a final shake before tossing it onto the floor in the backseat, and he tried not to look at the employee still glaring at him as he turned the key in the ignition. He found a decent modern rock station on the radio as he pulled out of the lot, his head still swirling.

Forty-five minutes later, Alan pulled into his mother's driveway. In a strange sort of way, Beverly's small single-level house mirrored Alan's, except instead of the Pacific Ocean near her doorstep, a sea of pines trailed away for several acres. A wave of unease and sadness washed over him as he noticed that very little had changed in the ten years since he'd been here. He took a moment to calm his mind – just a single, deep breath – and stepped out of the car.

He'd barely slammed the door shut when he saw Parissa running across the yard toward him.

"Alan! Oh my God!" She grabbed him in a suffocating, panicked hug. She looked up at him with wet, haunted eyes. For a moment he had to fight the urge to hightail it back into his car and make serious tracks.

"Hey." His voice was calm, which surprised him. He returned her squeeze. "I'm here. Though not willingly. Are you okay?"

She nodded too quickly, as if she was trying to convince herself more than him. "We need to call the police, Alan. And I think it's a very bad idea for you to – you don't want to look. You really don't." Parissa wiped away a tear that fell down her face, and she burrowed her face into his jacket. She drew strength from him as she wrapped both arms around his right arm while they walked. She clung to him, almost like a child, until she at last disengaged to wipe her nose ineffectually on her sleeve. When she stopped, he stopped, and he looked at her as she tried mightily to keep herself under control.

"It's bad, Alan. I went through the whole house to try and find her. Her office looks like a bomb went off. Her back garden looks even worse." She wouldn't look at him. Instead she alternated her focus between the ground and the sky and the trees. "I just came by to pick up my cheque. Normally I would have come by yesterday, but she said she had things to do earlier this week and that she'd be too busy."

Alan nodded, listening to her but lost in his own thoughts. After a moment, he began to walk toward the side yard, where he could see the edges of the flagstones that led toward the deck. In front of him sat his mother's burnt umber rust-bucket of a Skylark, a terrible leftover from the bottom of the '80's vehicle barrel.

"Sir, this is a crime scene. Turn around, get back in your car and leave."

Alan turned around to see a cop, about his height, standing next to his car. The cop had a no-nonsense look on his face and a large hand sitting on top of his standard-issue Sig Sauer service pistol. Alan shook his head at the cop as he turned to continue walking towards the back of the house. The cop ducked under the yellow crime tape and moved around to stand in front of Alan, blocking his path. When Alan made to step past him, the cop grabbed him by the shoulder. His gun was already out of its holster and aimed at Alan's gut. "Sir, I will shoot you where you stand if I have to. You need to leave. Now. Don't make me tell you again." The cop prodded Alan in the stomach with the barrel. Even through the fabric of his shirt, Alan felt the cold of the steel, and he gasped.

"Alan? Alan…are you okay?" Parissa's hand tugged on Alan's arm, and the cop blew apart like leaves on a gust of wind. With blinking eyes, Alan looked around. There was no crime scene, no tape, no cop. Nothing. Parissa looked up at him with concerned eyes. "Alan?"

He took a breath. "I'm okay. Just shaken up, that's all."

Parissa's concern didn't abate. She pointed toward the back of the house. "I won't go any further, but that's where I found her. In the garden." She grabbed his arm again, and pleaded with him, her voice quivering. "What do you hope to see, Alan? She's dead. Please, let's just call the cops, okay? *Please?*"

He fumbled for his words. "I haven't spoken to my mother in over ten years, 'Rissa. I haven't even *seen* her. After all the bullshit…maybe even in spite of it, I need some sort of closure. I don't know if that makes any sense, but…I need to see." His sad eyes searched hers, and she dropped her hand from his arm without protest. He continued toward the back of the house.

Alan froze when he saw the destruction. The mound of earth beside the gnarled, dead apple tree caught his eye right away, but it wasn't until he got up close that he saw where yesterday's heavy rains had washed away part of the earth. It wasn't until he got up close that he saw her hands, and the ropes that bound them. The tourmaline ring he'd given her for a birthday present a dozen years ago glinted in the sunlight. Parissa was right – what had he hoped to see?

*What happened to you, Mom?*

He swayed on his feet, and put his hand out against the apple tree for support. This was infinitely worse than anything he had imagined back at the house or in the car on the way down. All around him were the muted sounds of morning; the twittering of birds and the whispery rustle of leaves in the breeze. Inside him, a terrified scream echoed endlessly. He couldn't see all of her and that somehow made it *worse*, because his imagination almost cheerily filled in the blanks. Behind closed eyes, he saw his mother buried in this…this *hole*, dirt caked across her pallid, dead face. Her eyes, halfway closed and sightless. Her wrists raw and bleeding from the ropes that chafed them…

His vision swam for a brief moment when he opened his eyes again, and his stomach did a threatening back flip, ready to relieve him of more of the nothing that was in there. He took two or three slow, measured breaths, and willed his body to calm down. He looked back at the house, trying to see if there was something different about the place, some clue that might provide him with some idea of what the hell had happened. All he could see was a jumbled pile of flowers that had fallen unceremoniously on the deck, and the open door that led inside to her office. The sun lit the side of the house at such an angle as to afford him little more than two or three feet of view inside her office. He saw the corner of her giant banker's desk, and the rest was lost in shadow.

The creak of the verandah steps beneath his sneakers brought him out of his thoughts and he saw that he had walked clear across the yard without being aware of it. He reached the table below which the tray of irises and marigolds sat in a clump, and knelt down to examine them further. They didn't look too disturbed beyond the initial fall off the table, and he stood up again, knees cricking. He turned toward the office door, seeing for the first time how torn apart the room actually was. He took a step towards the door.

"Alan! *What are you doing?*" Parissa's voice was little more than a stage whisper, but in the morning stillness her voice carried loud and clear across the yard. He held up his finger to her in a "wait a moment" gesture before stepping across the threshold into Beverly Black's office.

Even with the door open to the yard, the shadows were thick and heavy inside the office. He flicked on the light and the soft incandescent glow pushed back the dark only a little. He smelled a dry, almost masculine odour, but he couldn't place it. After a few interrogative sniffs, he gave up and walked further into the room, his eyes flitting everywhere at once. The banker's desk had been shoved off-centre, and what used to be neat stacks of papers was now a mound of confusion, and several stray sheets had curled up in front of the desk. He made a cursory scan of the topmost papers on the desk without touching any of them, and saw nothing of real importance.

He turned away from the desk to check out the rest of the room. He saw the filing cabinet looming in the corner, a small dent along the edge and a handful of drying droplets of blood spatter on the floor in front of it. Near the far wall he saw a small pool of clear liquid on the hardwood, but he cringed from it instinctively, sensing somehow that it was *bad*. A tiny shiver coursed through him as he stepped over a couple of stray papers and headed back toward the door.

Shades of memories clung to the odour that still floated in the air, but each one retreated into the shadows before he could focus on any one of them. He closed his eyes for a long moment, trying to clear his mind and remember, but it was no use. The memories faded as a breeze scurried through the room from the open door, rustling the papers and chasing away the lingering aroma.

## IV

The place was soon swarming with police and medical technicians. Alan shuddered as he watched the yellow police tape go up around the property. For a bizarre moment, he found himself searching the faces of the officers who arrived on scene, trying to see the cop he had conjured up out of nowhere. Parissa was silent under his arm, looking like she couldn't decide whether to cry or throw up. A white van pulled up and he watched as members of the Medical Examiner's team piled out of it. The M.E. directed traffic as she pulled on blue nitrile gloves and headed around back, a young cop stationed at the tape pointing the way. Alan noticed the cop smirk and tilt his eyes downward as the M.E. passed. He recognized the expression instantly and traced the cop's eye line to the M.E.'s backside, noticeably firm even in rumpled powder-blue scrubs. He looked back up in time to see the cop shoot him a look which Alan had no trouble interpreting. He smiled apologetically as the cop adjusted his belt and let a satisfied smile settle on his lips. *I'm not trying to squeeze in on your action*, Alan thought. *Relax, Mr. Testosterone.* He watched as the M.E. knelt down by the tree and began unearthing the body, and he forced himself to look away. *That* wasn't a lasting image he wanted.

"Are you the people who called the police?" Alan started at the voice, and turned his eyes in its direction. The woman standing to his left carried herself with elegance, like a dancer, but her voice had an air of authority which he did not question. Her crystal-blue eyes were framed by long auburn hair and seemed to see everything all at once. He felt oddly small beneath her gaze.

"Uh, yeah. Actually, she did." Alan gestured at Parissa. A weak smile was all Parissa could manage.

"I'm Detective Naomi Wilder. I'm the lead investigator in charge of this homicide." She turned her attention to Parissa. "May I speak to you privately?" Alan lifted his arm away from Parissa's shoulders and she walked away with the detective. He crossed his arms as he watched them go and felt a tear sting the corner of his eye. He brushed it away with the heel of his palm. All the years gone by – to see it shattered in an instant was impossible to cope with. Even as the sun rose higher in the sky and held the promise of another scorcher, he couldn't get warm, and he rubbed his arms with no effect. A tiny part of him had always hoped that some kind of reconciliation might happen between him and the woman that birthed him. *No chance of that now.* He dropped his gaze back to his shoes and tried very hard not to think about anything.

Several minutes went by before Det. Wilder closed her notebook and started walking back with Parissa to Alan's car. He looked up at the sound of his name, and Parissa said nothing as she walked past him.

"I understand you're related to the victim?" Wilder spoke at last when they were several yards away.

"Yes. I'm the vic – she's my mother." A pause. "Alan Black." He stuck out his hand awkwardly and, when she didn't take it, pulled it back and stuffed it into his pocket with an embarrassed laugh. "Sorry. I don't have much experience talking with homicide detectives." Her piercing blue eyes took him all in and she flipped open her notebook.

"It's understandable," Wilder said. "Most people experience anxiety when dealing with law enforcement. I'm not your enemy, Mr. Black. I just want to talk to you for a moment about what happened. When did you get here? Do you live close by?"

"I live about an hour or so out of town, in Shallot's Cove. My friend Parissa called me right after she found my mother. I took a quick look when I got here and then we called you." Wilder raised her eyebrows. "I know, I know," he continued. "We should have called you right away, but as crazy as it sounds, I wanted to see for myself. I didn't touch anything. I know how important it is not to contaminate the crime scene. I've read too many books to…" She looked at him, her blue eyes glittering, and his nervous chuckle died quickly on the air between them. Her eyes shifted to her right, as another uniform by the dead apple tree was waving in her direction. She nodded at him and looked back at Alan. "Let's set up a time for more questions." She saw his expression change. "You're not under arrest, Mr. Black. I'm just following procedure. Can I get your contact information, please?"

## V

A symphony of colour erupted from a multitude of raised flowerbeds along Parissa's driveway. Alan marveled, in spite of everything, at how well she kept up her own gardens, despite the time she devoted to her clients. He killed the engine and turned to look at her. She was very small in the passenger seat.

"We're here," he said. She stared out the windshield at her flowers, wiping in futility at the tears coursing down her cheeks. Some of the colour was returning to her face, and she looked over at him. Her first attempt at a smile faltered, but she took a deep breath and her second try succeeded.

"I'm sorry, Alan. I just…can't stop thinking about it. I know there was a rift between you two, but your mother deserved better than this. I'm sorry. I wish I had better words than that."

There was a long silence as Alan thought about what she said and weighed it against how he felt. The conflicting stew of emotions churning inside him made grasping the truth impossible. "I don't know, 'Rissa. After all the bullshit I've gone through with her, I'm not sure what to think. I'm…disjointed. Like I'm clinging to a strip of wood out in the middle of the ocean. But…you're right, nobody deserves that. Hopefully the police can catch the son of a bitch who did this." He opened his door to get out as she released her seatbelt.

He walked to the back of the car and pulled his suitcase from the trunk. When he looked up, she was standing by his side, smiling at him. She was doing all she could to contain her emotions, a singular act of bravery he couldn't help but admire.

She took a deep breath. "Come in. Would you like some tea?"

*　　*　　*　　*　　*　　*

Alan sat at the small dining table Parissa kept in a corner of her open-concept kitchen, and watched as she busied herself with the tea. She set out everything on the counter, and then sat next to him at the table, reaching for the last tissue in a large box of Kleenex.

"God," she said. "Has it really been a year since I've seen you? I...shit, Alan..." Her face crumpled, and more tears came. Just as he reached his hand out to hers in a gesture of comfort, the electric kettle clicked off softly and she let out her breath in a rush before rising to finish making the tea. Alan watched how she moved with the same fluid grace he remembered. When she sat back down, he searched her face and saw only haunted sadness.

"What happened?" he whispered, his eyebrows furrowed in concern.

She fidgeted with a solitary crumb on the tablecloth before taking a breath and plunging in, telling him what she knew.

"I normally work two or three days a week for your mom, but she gave me this whole week off because she had doctor's appointments and stuff like that. When I walked to her house this morning to pick up my cheque, she wasn't there to greet me, which perked my ears up right away. Usually she's on the stoop waiting with a coffee or tea in her hand. The house had a very dark feeling to it." She paused to take a sip of her scalding tea before continuing.

"I walked up the steps and opened the screen door. When I knocked, the door just sort of creaked open. I walked into the little hallway and called out her name, but there was no answer. It wasn't long before I'd searched the entire place. When I reached her office…it was like a warzone. My God. The place looked like it had been turned upside down. I couldn't even begin to know if anything had been taken, though.

"When I saw that the door leading from her office to the verandah was also open, I went numb. I went outside, and that's when I saw the flowers all in a pile of dirt on the deck. Most of them were still in their little pots." She paused and closed her eyes, trying to will herself to continue. "I saw the tree…" Her lower lip trembled again and more tears fell as she got up to retrieve a new box of tissue from the sitting room.

When she sat back down, Alan was lost in thought, staring out the window as a hummingbird, a dashing little fellow with a bright splash of purple across his face, flitted from bloom to bloom gorging himself on Parissa's hanging baskets outside. The sudden *tweep!* of his cell phone brought him out of his reverie. He glanced at the display before looking over at Parissa. "My ex-fiancée." Parissa nodded in understanding, and he tapped the Answer button. "Hello, Celeste. How are things?"

"Hey, Alan. I'm just calling to let you know I've finished your new signage graphics. I'm wrapping up another small project which I figure will keep me busy until mid-afternoon tomorrow though, so I won't be able to come by your place until tomorrow night. Is that okay?"

Alan took a sip of his tea before answering. The pomegranate was doing wonders to relax his mind. "That's fine. I'm down in Waterford right now anyway."

"Waterford? What's got you in the big city? You haven't been in Waterford since...well, since..." There was a pause as she caught herself, but Alan waited patiently for what he knew was coming. "Is your mother okay?" Celeste asked.

He hesitated. How much should he tell her, if anything? "Well...not really, but I don't know much at this point." He stopped to think, hoping there wasn't too much grey in that little white lie. "I was wondering though, I might be in the city a couple of days, so would you mind looking in on Misfit for me?"

"I can, but a couple of days in Waterford? Now I know something's up. You don't leave the Cove unless there's a good reason, and good reasons rarely come. Are you *sure* everything is okay?"

Alan pursed his lips, weighing his options. He couldn't outright lie to Celeste, but at the same time he didn't want to say how he'd found his mother buried beneath a tree with dirt and bugs in her hair. "Well, yes and no. I hate to sound vague, but can I talk to you later about this when I know more about what's really going on?"

"Come on, Alan. I've known you too long for you to give me an answer like that," Celeste pressed. Even over the phone, he could almost see her right eyebrow arch. She took a breath and her tone softened. "You okay?"

"I'm fine, really. Just...thank you for taking care of Misfit while I'm gone. I promise I'll fill you in when I can."

He heard the familiar squeak of her office chair as she sat back. "Okay, I won't push. You sound exhausted," she said, her tone comforting. "Be safe and I'll talk to you in a day or two. I'll send you a text so you know I made it to your place okay, if you want."

"I would appreciate that." After hanging up, he looked back out the window. The hummingbird had left for sweeter flowers beyond his view. He let out a sigh and felt Parissa squeeze his hand. He looked her way, and felt a smile start to play at the corners of his mouth while her chin quivered the tiniest bit.

## VI

Detective Wilder stood at the perimeter of Beverly Black's property. From where she stood, she had a clear view of both the house and the garden behind it, where the victim had been found buried in the earth. Her crisp blue eyes took in everything as she tried to piece all the elements together. She was looking for what she called the "odd sock" – something that didn't fit. Burying the woman was dramatic – the killer was trying to make a statement...or issue a warning. But to whom? The victim's hands and ankles had been tied together, which made sense if the vic was alive while being buried. The bindings would have made it next to impossible for the victim to dig her way out. Not that digging herself free would have been much of an option anyway. With all the dirt on top of her, and the awkward position of the hands, she would have had a very difficult time. Wilder hoped that Black was dead well before burial.

Wilder had walked over to the house while she'd been lost in her thoughts, trying to see if there was something she'd missed in her initial sweep. No sign of forced entry and, according to the landscaper, nothing taken. Then things had turned sideways. The large oak desk in Ms. Black's office had been shoved towards the bookcases behind it, and there were papers strewn all over the floor in front of it. There was a five-foot tall green metal filing cabinet with a small splash of blood along its front. Wilder presumed that the blood belonged to Black, as there was a wound on the top of the victim's head.

Something didn't sit right; why would the killer take so much trouble not to leave any fingerprints, but not bother cleaning up any of the mess or the blood left behind? Rising from her squatting position in front of the filing cabinet, Wilder picked her way over to the door leading out to the garden. Forensics had already taken samples of the blood on the filing cabinet, as well as the blood mixed in with the dirt in the garden itself. Wilder turned away from the garden and looked toward the driveway.

Alan Black, Beverly's son. Parissa Khorasani, the landscaper. *Where do you two fit in all this?*

Her eye caught movement off to her left, and she turned to see the Medical Examiner, Julie Marsh, pulling off her gloves as she approached.

"What can you give me, Jules?" Wilder asked.

"Well, I can tell you that TOD occurred sometime between noon and 3 pm yesterday. I'll be able to pinpoint it further once I get her back to the lab."

Wilder nodded, but saw there was more to come. Something far worse.

"I can also tell you that COD was compressive asphyxia."

"So she wasn't..." Wilder frowned and looked off into the distance, preparing herself for the worst.

Marsh shook her head. "The blunt force trauma to the top of her head certainly didn't help matters, but it was the weight of all the dirt on top of her that prevented her from expanding and contracting her chest. She suffocated to death out here." Julie paused. "Whatever else may have happened here, she was likely in immense pain. And she suffered."

## VII

It was early evening when a brisk knock came at Parissa's door. Alan started to get up, but Parissa flapped her hand at him. She opened the door to see Det. Wilder standing there on the stoop.

"Good evening, Detective. I...uh...please, come in," Parissa gestured, with a clumsy sweep of her hand.

"Thank you, Miss Khorasani." Wilder stepped into the tiny foyer as Parissa offered to take her jacket. "No, thank you," the detective gently waved away the offer. "I don't expect to be long." She nodded in the direction of the kitchen doorway, where Alan now stood. "Good evening, Mr. Black."

He nodded. "Detective. Any updates?"

"Why don't we go have a seat in here, Miss Khorasani?" Wilder answered, gesturing toward the sitting room just off the hall.

Both of them were thrown by Wilder's take-charge attitude, but Parissa crossed over into the room without protest. Alan watched the door click shut with an odd twinge of confusion and sadness. He turned and went back to his coffee in the kitchen, listening to the murmur of their voices as they drifted in from behind the door.

"How do you know the victim, Miss Khorasani?" Wilder was calm. All business.

"I'm her landscaper, Detective. I've worked for her almost ten years now. Alan recommended me, actually. Ms. Black would never admit it, but her back was bad even when she first hired me and she couldn't keep up with the yard work anymore." Parissa fidgeted with her hands while Wilder jotted some notes.

"Where were you between noon and 3 pm yesterday?"

"I was here all day. Wait, no. I went out to get some groceries around 1:30. I saw the rain coming and decided to run out. It was a short trip, just there and back again."

"Can anyone verify that?"

"I'm sure someone at the store can. I know most of the staff there. It's a place I've been going to for years. It's called *Shop'N'Rite*."

"And while you were here?"

"I live alone, Detective. I'm sorry."

Wilder made a note, and then looked back up. "Did Ms. Black have any enemies? Somebody she had a conflict with? A neighbour, maybe?"

Parissa thought hard, gnawing lightly on the tip of her thumb. "Ms. Black lived by herself and didn't entertain guests at all, Detective. She didn't like the idea of socializing. She just…well, there *was* something. About five years ago, I was seeing a guy named Noah Lofton. We dated for about a year, but ultimately broke up because of his moods. Beverly made me get a restraining order against him because he kept showing up unannounced while I was at her place working. I remember Beverly tried to chase him off with a broom. When that didn't work, she called the cops. She pressed charges and everything, saying he was trespassing and violating the restraining order. That's when he had the meltdown, right there in the yard. It took five cops to get him under control and into the back of a cruiser. I'd never seen him like that before in my life. It was terrifying." Parissa pursed her lips, trying not to cry. "Noah sat in jail for a week because of that."

"Do you think he could have done this?"

"God...I don't know. I don't *think* so. I mean, Noah only slapped me once. I'm not trying to justify anything, but it's not like he beat the shit out of me on a regular basis either."

"Can you think of anything else?" Wilder asked, jotting down Lofton's name.

"No. Working for Ms. Black was very routine. Mondays and Wednesdays on site, and then pick up my cheque on Thursdays. The only change was this week, when she called on Sunday to give me the week off."

"Did she say why?"

"She had doctor's appointments. She'd organized them together over a couple of days because they were easier to manage that way. Her back was getting so much worse. She had to put her hand on the wall some days as she walked, just to keep her balance."

Wilder made a note in her pad and circled it. Then she closed it and stood up. "Thank you, Miss Khorasani. I may need to speak with you again, but we're good for now."

Alan looked up from his cold coffee as the two women came back into the room. Parissa squeezed his shoulder as she moved past him to the kettle.

"I need to see you now, Mr. Black."

*    *    *    *    *    *

Alan took his seat on the couch, and the detective sat back down in one of the wingback chairs. She took her notebook out and flipped it open to a fresh page, pulling her pencil out from inside the spiral at the top.

"I'm sorry if I seem a bit brusque, Alan. You can understand this is not a social call."

Alan nodded. "I understand. I'm here to help however I can."

Wilder looked at him with her fierce crystal-blue eyes for a moment, and then began. "You said earlier that you hadn't spoken to your mother in ten years. Can you elaborate?"

Alan sighed. "There isn't much to tell...she was never around very much. My parents divorced when I was practically still a baby, and I lived with my dad full-time after that. My mother wasn't very...maternal. Don't get me wrong, we did spend a little time together as I grew up, but the time we *were* together was superficial."

"What was the last thing you discussed before you decided to stop talking to her altogether?"

"In our last phone call, I made an off-the-cuff remark about..." He fell back against the cushion, frustrated and hurt. "She never called, Detective. If we talked – which was rare, by the way – it was always on my dime. I mentioned that it would be nice if she phoned *me* occasionally and like usual, she got all offended and over-dramatized the whole thing. That's when I realized that, no matter how hard I tried, things were never going to get any better between us. Mom was the Queen of 'I'm-not-to-blame'. We haven't spoken since."

"Do you know if she had any enemies?"

"As in, was there someone who wanted to kill her? No, Detective. Believe me, I've gone over that question a thousand times in my head since this morning. As far as I remember, my mother lived alone and pretty much kept to herself. I mean, sure, she and I had our personal differences, but if she had similar problems as far as getting along with other people...that I can't say. The type of person my mother is – was – I can't imagine anyone actually killing her."

"What about Miss Khorasani?"

"Parissa and I go back a long ways. We've known each other for almost twenty years now. Wait, you're not suggesting..."

"No," Wilder countered. "I'm just trying to gather as much information as I can so I can solve this murder and bring your mother's killer to justice. Is Miss Khorasani a suspect? Everyone's a suspect at this point." The silence that followed her words was flat and imposing. Then finally: "Where were you between the hours of noon and 3 pm yesterday?"

Alan didn't hesitate. *Bookends*. I was there from open to close. That is to say, from 8am to about 8pm."

"*Bookends*?"

"I own a small coffee shop and second-hand bookstore in Shallot's Cove." He let a smile surface on his lips, and the quirky playfulness of it caught her off-guard. "I'm a bit of a literature nut," he continued. "And I love my coffee. In my teens I used to drink coffee until the wee hours, just so I could read one more page. Drove my dad crazy, especially on school nights. One day I sat down and developed the idea of marrying the two things I love most and trying to earn a profit doing it. *Bookends* is the best thing I ever did, even if at the end of some days I'm past the point of exhaustion."

An avid book-lover herself, Wilder was unable to resist. "A coffee-shop and bookstore? But you can't be more than..."

"Thirty-three – actually, thirty-four. I keep forgetting today is my birthday." Alan chuckled. "What can I say?

I've always been pretty good with money, even though I don't have a lot of it."

Wilder nodded, still smiling a little. She glanced at her notes again. "Can anyone vouch for your presence there during the time in question?"

"Absolutely. My assistant manager, Kim, was with me from 9am till close. We were slammed, too."

Wilder took a few moments to finish writing in her notebook. After a pause, she looked up at him. "One more question, and then I think we're done," she asked. "Do you know a man named Noah Lofton?"

Alan leaned back on the couch and thought. For a long moment he drew a blank. Then out of nowhere a light bulb blinked on in his head. "Wait. He was dating Parissa for a while. Odd fella. I only met him a couple of times, but I remember he was smart. Like, scary smart. He had lots of issues, though, including an inferiority complex a mile wide. Parissa kept coming to me, asking me to help with their problems. I tried once, but honestly, I'm no Dr. Phil. I think they tried couple's therapy, but in the end Parissa broke it off with him. It was a messy business. A messy business..."

Wilder sat back a little and closed her notebook. After a moment, she stood up. "I know this is a difficult time for you," she continued. "But I'm going to need you to stay in town a little longer. Can you do that?"

Alan pressed his lips together. "I can try, Detective, but I have a business to run." He gauged her expression before continuing. "Ah...but it shouldn't be a problem. I'll call Kim and see if she'll cover while I'm here."

Wilder nodded. "That's best. Thank you, Alan. I appreciate your co-operation with this. Oh, and despite the circumstances, happy birthday." Wilder turned to leave and he saw her out. After latching the door shut, he turned to see Parissa walking down the stairwell, her eyes wide. When he reached the newel post, she stopped and looked at him, silent and fearful.

"'Rissa," he said at last. "What happened between you and Noah?"

## VIII

Alan sat back on the couch, and Parissa joined him, leaning her head on his shoulder.

"Noah…" she breathed, and for what seemed like ages, that's all she said. With old habit he thought long dead, Alan began absently stroking her hair with his left hand as she sat there resting against him.

Finally, she spoke again. "There's not much to tell that you don't already know, Alan. He hit me, and I left him. Your mother insisted I get a restraining order against him. He would show up at your mom's place all the time when I was there, trying to 'patch things up,' as he would say. I wanted nothing to do with him. Your mother was a lot more vocal about it than I was, though. One day he showed up – I was in the side yard, weeding – and Beverly screamed at him, 'GET YOUR ASS OFF MY GODDAMN PROPERTY!' It was awful. She chased after him with her broom, but she fell and hurt her knee trying to catch him. Despite that, he wouldn't take the hint, and he lingered near the front of the house until she called the police. He was arrested and he spent a week in jail."

Alan stared at his feet, trying to understand. "Is there anything else?" he asked.

She shook her head. "I haven't heard from him, directly, since. The only information I get is what Mina tells me on occasion. Sad thing is, according to her, not much has changed. She's got him wrapped around her pinkie pretty snug. She does with him as she pleases, but he's willing to go along with it, because it's Mina. His old issues are still there, though, if not somehow worse."

Alan thought about Parissa's twin sister Mina, flaunting her sexuality to achieve whatever objective she desired. Her usual method of wrapping a guy around her finger involved little more than wrapping her legs around...he closed his eyes and thought again of Noah. "Do you think he'd hold a grudge against my mother for throwing his ass in jail? I mean, despite the fact that he was in the wrong and he probably knew it?"

Parissa sat up a little, considering the possibility. "There's no way Mina would ever be a party to murder. My sister is many things, Alan, but that...there's no way. If he murdered your mother, he'd have to keep Mina in the dark about it, and you know as well as I do that that's next to impossible."

Alan nodded his head, as he considered his question and her response. "That's so odd," he muttered. "Could being tossed in jail for just a week give you motive enough to murder?"

She sat up fully on the couch. "Noah did go into one of his rages – though I'd call it more like a meltdown – when they arrested him at your mom's house. It took five cops to hold him down and cuff him before throwing him in the back of a cruiser." Alan opened his eyes in surprise. Noah only stood about five-foot-eight and barely weighed 140 pounds soaking wet. He opened his mouth to speak, and Parissa nodded. "*Five.*"

Parissa put her head back on his shoulder, and concentrated on a lock of her hair, twisting it around and around her fingers. The silence continued for several moments before she broke it once more. "I don't think Noah did it. I'll be the first to admit he had near-crippling insecurities, not to mention serious anger problems, and I'm certainly not making excuses for him, but underneath all his problems he's a nice guy."

"A nice guy who raged and hit you," Alan said.

"Only one time." She paused. "Okay, maybe I *am* making little excuses for him, but I really don't know that he'd go so far as to kill…"

Parissa closed her eyes and would say no more.

## IX

Shadowy faces fighting; black and white nightmares. A man and a woman, screaming at each other. Between them, a baby squalling. Terror struck him as his nose twitched at the same scent he had noticed back in his mother's office. This time it was clear; he knew what it was. He woke in horror, expecting the owner of that smell to lunge at him and strangle him where he lay. His heart trip-hammering, he saw the room was empty, and in a mad confusion he panicked at why Misfit wasn't in her usual spot at the end of the bed. Parissa's crystalline soprano carried a delicate melody up the stairs and slowly his breathing eased. His heart calmed, and the smell of coffee and bacon pulled his feet from under the covers.

"Hey you," Parissa chuckled at him as she flipped an omelet. "Nice hair."

"Ah well," Alan teased. "I can't be ruggedly handsome all the time. It's hard work." He smiled at her, but it was difficult to put the nightmares out of his head. He poured himself a large cup of coffee.

"I've known your secret for a long time, Mr. Black." She looked at him from the side of her eye. "We lived together, remember?"

"The university," he said, shaking his head. "You've got a good memory." He stole a piece of bacon off the giant mound she had on a plate, and then went to make a quick call to his assistant manager. Kim was concerned about the *Family Emergency* sign in the store-front window, but she maintained her professionalism, which Alan appreciated. The call was really just a formality, Kim knew the business inside out and made a better cup of coffee than anyone else, even Alan. "Stay closed for today, but go ahead and open as usual tomorrow," Alan said. "I'll be back in the Cove in a few days." Parissa set down a huge plate filled with pan-fried potatoes, a mushroom omelet and toast just as he hung up.

*     *     *     *     *     *

A short while later, while Alan was trying to get the last of the water out of his ears, his cell phone rang.

"Good morning, Celeste," Alan answered with a smile. "Thanks again for taking care of Misfit. I really appreciate it."

"Anytime, Alan. I'm just *so* excited about waiting hand and foot on Her Majesty." She laughed.

Alan took a breath, decided to change the subject. "I said I would give you information about what's going on when I had it, and now I do. I know it sounds cliché, but are you sitting down?"

"Oh." Celeste suddenly sounded very unsure. She took her own hesitant breath. "I…I guess so. Are you sure you want to tell me? Maybe now isn't the best time."

"It's best to keep you in the loop. If nothing else, I've always been able to confide anything to you." He swallowed hard. "Celeste…my mother was killed."

"What?!" Alan heard a faint *psssh* sound and an accompanying squeak which told him she had sat down in her chair, hard. *I wasn't kidding, Celeste*, he thought.

"Yeah..." His voice was weak. "The police are investigating, but they've asked me not to leave the city for a little while. I hate to ask you, but would you be able to stay at my place for at least the next few days?"

"Of course! Oh God, Alan...I don't know what to say."

"I'm trying not to think about it, but so far I've been mostly unsuccessful."

"Jesus…is there anything I can do to help?"

"Not really. Just help take care of Misfit. If something comes up, I'll let you know, but at this point there's not much you can do."

"All right. I don't know how you're keeping it together. I wish I could be there to give you a big hug, though. You do sound like you need one. You're okay?"

"I'm dealing. Beverly and I never had the best of relationships, but to be honest this whole situation kicked me in the nuts. As much as we disagreed, I never expected this." Alan paused. "Thank you so much for what you're doing. I promise you a nice dinner out when this is over."

"Don't worry about things like that. I have a million questions, but I know now is not the time. I just really hope you're okay. Please let me know if there's anything else I can do. I'll talk to you later?"

"Yeah. I'll call you, probably tomorrow. Give kitty lots of love for me."

"I will. And Alan?"

"Yeah?"

"Be safe."

A thick blanket of silence crept in around Alan after he disconnected the call. He closed his eyes and held his elbows in his hands as a shiver took him from out of nowhere.

*Things are going to get far worse before it's all over.*

# X

"FUCK YOU, YOU PIG COCKSUCKER! GET YOUR FUCKING HANDS *OFF* ME! I KNOW MY GODDAMNED RIGHTS!" Det. Wilder looked up from her paperwork in surprise as Detectives King and Morris brought a very vocal Noah Lofton into the bullpen at Precinct #9.

King kept his eyes pointed stonily forward, the right one already bruised and swelling. Morris was the one to offer up some choice words for Lofton.

"Shut up! You're damned lucky I haven't thrown you in lockup already for resisting arrest and trying to punch out my partner, you piece of shit!" spat Morris. Lofton opened his mouth to say something back, but he caught the menace in Morris's eye and thought better of it.

"Guys! GUYS!" Wilder was already out of her chair and halfway across the 'pen. "What's going on?"

"This," King said through gritted teeth, "is Noah Lofton." Lofton struggled to break free and hollered when Morris cinched his arms up behind his back. "We'll keep him safe and cozy for you in #2."

"Uh, yea…" Wilder replied, trying to play catch-up. She stood aside as the two detectives wrestled Lofton across the bullpen and threw him unceremoniously into Interrogation Room #2. The door shivered in its frame as Morris slammed it shut.

Both detectives took up position on either side of the door, Morris breathing hard from the exertion. Wilder collected her things from her desk before walking up to the pair and looking with interest at King's face.

"Nice reflexes," Wilder smirked. "It's almost like you *let* him hit you." King looked back at her with his good eye and snorted heavily through his nose, the trace of a smirk on his lips. Wilder continued, "What happened?"

Morris spoke first. "Guy bolted as we approached to bring him in. King caught him before he could make it half a block. During the struggle, the little wriggler came up with a lucky left."

"Too bad for him," King spoke up. "Now, no matter what happens in there, we get to book him for assaulting a police officer." He let his smirk widen. "It's a damn shame."

Wilder smiled back. "Let's see what I can get out of him first. Get yourself some ice while I cool this guy down."

Wilder opened the door to Interrogation Room #2 and found Noah Lofton pacing up and down like a caged animal. Calmly, she walked over to her side of the table and sat down.

"Have a seat, Mr. Lofton." Wilder gestured to the chair across from her. Lofton scowled at her, his hands opening and closing into fists over and over again. Wilder observed this reaction and jotted it down in her notes with a passive look. She looked up at him again. "Trying to assault a police officer after being asked to come in for simple questioning isn't what I would call wise, Mr. Lofton," Wilder continued. Lofton scowled again, but didn't make eye contact.

"You've got one violation of a restraining order from over five years ago on your rap sheet." Wilder said. "But you weren't in danger of violating that order when my officers approached you. So why'd you cut and run?"

Noah planted his hands hard on the table and leaned into Wilder's face. "You think I'm gonna talk to you?" Lofton growled. "You're wasting your time, cause I ain't involved!"

Wilder didn't even blink. "Oh? That's interesting, as I haven't told you why you're here yet, Mr. Lofton." She paused, and gestured to the chair again. "Have a seat."

Lofton stopped and considered her for a long moment, and then yanked the chair out and spun it around, straddling it. "Fine. Why don't you fill me in then, *cop*?"

He was baiting her, and she knew it. But ten years of experience in homicide cases kept her from nibbling. "I'll ask the questions, Mr. Lofton. How about I start with this one: Where were you Tuesday between noon and 3pm?"

"Not anywhere you might think I was."

His defiance was starting to piss her off, but she didn't let it show. "Mr. Lofton, I'm conducting a murder investigation. Part of that is to question those who had a connection to the victim. Now drop the macho act and answer me! Where were you Tuesday between noon and 3pm?"

"I was in bed."

"That's not much of an alibi. Can anyone corroborate your story?"

"Yeah," Lofton sneered. "My girlfriend. We weren't exactly sleeping, you know?"

Wilder jotted the information down in her pad. "What's your girlfriend's name? Because you know I'm going to check."

"Her name's Mina."

"Does Mina have a last name?"

"Khorasani." Lofton said. Wilder's eyebrows rose a little in recognition of the last name. Noah flipped the chair around. "And she's a knockout, cop. *Much* better looking than you." He folded his hands behind his head and looked at her smugly, craning his eyes to see behind her side of the table. "Although, you do have a pretty sweet ass."

Wilder tossed down her pencil. "Do you really think it's a good idea to antagonize me, Mr. Lofton? You're in way over your head if you think you can intimidate me. Here's the deal: the victim in my murder investigation? Her name is Beverly Black. And guess what? You two have a history. Now I want to know if you're involved. So, we can do this the easy way, where you co-operate and give me the answers I need, or we can do it the hard way, where you spend some time down in lockup until you figure out if you want to play ball. I can legally detain you for twenty-four hours, so the choice is yours. Me or lockup? You're lucky...there's only two meth-heads going through withdrawal down there today."

All the bravado seemed to drain out of Noah's face. His eyes darted around the room as the name registered with him. *Beverly Black.* He looked up at Det. Wilder, his eyes widening a little. "What are you talking about? Ms. Black is dead? And you think...oh no! No WAY! I got nothing to do with any murder! I swear it!" Fear started to etch into his features. "I don't understand what this is all about."

"Let me help you out. Beverly Black was murdered Tuesday afternoon," Noah's face went white as she continued. "You had a run-in with her a few years ago. After repeated requests for you to stop coming onto her property, she slapped you with a restraining order. Not long after, you violated that order. I looked at the report of that incident. It took five cops to subdue you during your arrest that day. Five. You're strong for a slim guy, Noah. So you spend a week in the can, it's enough to start you thinking about payback. You spend some time thinking about how it could be done, and then what, Noah? Am I getting warm?"

"I didn't kill anybody! I swear to God I didn't!" Noah leaned forward, searching Wilder's face intently with scared eyes. "Look, yes...a few years ago I was dating Mina's sister, Parissa. She was Ms. Black's landscaper. After we broke up, I kept trying to patch things up, you know? Tried to fix things, 'cause I figured I fucked up bad. Not long after, Black and Parissa slammed me with some bullshit restraining order and then BOOM! They had me fuckin' arrested. After that, I took the hint and stayed away. I hooked up with Mina about a year ago, and moved on. Please believe me, Detective. I wouldn't kill Ms. Black. I *didn't* kill her. Please, you gotta believe me!"

Wilder looked calmly at Lofton as she tapped her pencil on the open pad in front of her. Her eyes never left his. After a long moment, she rose from her chair. "I'm going to get a cup of coffee, Mr. Lofton. Do you want one?" Noah sat staring at his hands, but didn't respond. Wilder collected her things, and walked out of the room. Only when the door had latched shut did Lofton look up at it. All the fear had left his eyes and he was smiling. He was confident.

Back out in the bullpen, she turned to Morris. "Find his girlfriend. I want her in here. Now."

## XI

It was still early enough in the afternoon that Parissa had raised her eyebrows at his request for a glass of the half-empty bottle of Glenfiddich she kept hidden in a cupboard. He poured it neat with no measuring, and it was his hope that the alcohol would deaden the nightmare that still haunted him. He sat in the living room, cozy in a sunbeam, and tried to work out what had happened.

Nothing about his mother's murder made any sense. She was an isolationist at heart, and perhaps a little too fond of the prescription painkillers she kept insisting she needed. She kept to herself, even when she went out to run errands. To be murdered in the manner that she was – hell, to be murdered at all – someone was trying to send a message...but to whom? What did anyone stand to gain from her death? His mother wasn't wealthy, a result of not being able to work due to her back problems. A murder of passion? That made less sense...who would murder a woman who led a chaste, virtually xenophobic lifestyle?

He thought back to the last conversation they'd had. Nothing out of the ordinary: her neighbours down the way had been pestering her to cut back her honeysuckle because the smell was overpowering everything else. She'd refused on the grounds that it was her goddamn property and besides, she liked the smell. She had then gone on to complain that her back had been giving her a lot more trouble lately, and she just couldn't keep up with the gardening like she used to. Alan remembered throwing Parissa's name out, as she was a long-time friend and a talented landscaper. Beverly had bitched about how much it would cost, but after a minute or so of indecision, she'd relented and asked for the number. The conversation then turned sour as she complained – again! – that she never heard from him anymore. He shot back with his now infamous comment about how she could maybe call him instead of the other way around sometimes. She had blown up about it, and...

And what? Now she was dead, and he too felt suffocated, buried under a lifetime of guilt. He stared at the smooth gold of his scotch, the aroma that had chased him into his nightmares still vivid in his mind. He had recognized it at last, hadn't he? Not right away, but in the end it was too obvious to ignore. But what to do about it?

A loud knock on the door jarred him out of his thoughts. Then a familiar voice rang out.

"Parissa! Let me in!" the voice cried. The door thundered in its frame once more, but before Alan could get up off the couch, Parissa had come running down the stairs to deal with the commotion.

Mina burst into the hall the moment Parissa opened the door, flustered and frantic. "Have you heard from Noah? He isn't answering his cell! One of his friends that was with him earlier said he'd been taken downtown by the police for questioning, and then I got a call from some detective wanting me to come and answer some questions too! You have to help me, sis! What do I do??" She stopped to breathe, and her huge brown eyes, so much like her twin sister's, bulged in fear.

"Well..." was all Parissa could manage. Mina was a constant volcano of emotion, and her sudden appearance at the house had stopped Parissa's ability to speak dead in its tracks. She fidgeted her hands together and looked toward Alan as he stepped into the hallway from the living room.

"Hello, Mina." Alan kept his voice calm, a deliberate contrast to the breathless panic that Mina had brought into the house.

Her head snapped in his direction and her eyes blazed. "What the hell are *you* doing here?" she demanded. "Wait, you know what? I don't even want to know." She raised her hand at him with an appalling air of dismissal and turned her attention back to Parissa, who was now staring intently at the floor.

Alan ignored Mina's rude gesture and spoke again. "If they brought Noah in for questioning, then it makes sense that they might want you to come in for questioning as well."

Mina rolled her eyes as she turned to face him again. "Why?" she demanded.

He sighed as he weighed his options carefully. "Well...my mother was found murdered yesterday."

"WHAT?! Bee is dead? I...I don't believe you!"

Alan glanced at Parissa, who looked as though she wanted to find a dark corner and hide until Mina had left and the house was safe again. Alan glanced down at his scotch glass and made a mental note to go later and buy some more, and then answered her. "Parissa found her body. The police have already questioned both of us. Now it seems they've questioned Noah. Maybe questioning you is the next logical step for them, if only to corroborate his story."

"Logical? You wouldn't know logical if it bit you on the ass, Alan!" Mina spat. She turned to her sister. "Why would they take Noah in for questioning? It's not like he could have murdered Bee. I mean, he's had...episodes...but *you* think he's innocent, right?"

Parissa looked up at last from her hands, her eyes sad and brimming with tears. "I don't know whether Noah is guilty or innocent," she said. "However, let's not fool each other, Mina. We're both very well aware of what your darling boyfriend is...*capable*."

Mina reacted as if she'd been gutted. "FINE!" she raged. "You want to condemn him? I'll go answer their stupid questions, and I'll prove to *BOTH OF YOU* that my Noah is innocent!"

The slam of the door echoed throughout the house, as Parissa and Alan both looked at each other, too stunned to say a word.

# XII

Mina fidgeted with her hands as she sat in Interrogation Room #1, waiting for Det. Wilder. She alternated between chewing on her lower lip and picking away at little flakes of nail polish on her hands, all while looking around like a rabbit deep in enemy territory. She picked up her phone to check the time for what seemed like the millionth time, and then let it drop back onto the table with a dull thud.

After twenty minutes, Det. Wilder entered the room and strolled over to the table, though she made no effort to apologize for keeping Mina waiting.

Mina's nervousness instantly turned into anger, and her face flushed. "Hey! This is bullshit, keeping me waiting for almost half an hour. You do realize I have better things I could be doing right now?"

Wilder gave Mina the faintest of smiles, and tapped her pencil on her notepad without saying a word.

"Well?!" Mina demanded again.

"Where were you Tuesday between noon and 3pm?"

The only sound was of the ticking clock above the door. Mina looked away from Wilder with a petulant look on her face.

"Miss Khorasani?" Wilder said.

A minute or two ticked by, and with no answer forthcoming, Det. Wilder flipped closed her notebook and rose to leave. "Well," she continued. "I expected that after your boyfriend Noah came in and told us his story, you'd be eager to help us and maybe corroborate what he said. Sometimes I get it wrong." She shrugged. "It happens. Maybe you just need more time to think about how best you want to cooperate with my investigation." She grasped the doorknob. "I'll be back in half an hour to try again."

She had one foot out the door when Mina spoke up. "Wait." Wilder paused and looked at the girl. "I was with Noah Lofton," Mina said.

"Uh huh," Wilder said, moving back to the table. "What were you doing?"

"I...we..." Mina looked away feeling very uncomfortable. "It's personal."

"I need a better answer than that, Miss Khorasani."

Mina made a face like she'd swallowed something bitter. "We...were sleeping together."

"The entire time?"

Mina flushed. "How is *that* any of your business? I know you're just 'checking my story,' but if I say 'it's personal' then it's personal!"

Wilder nodded. "So you didn't do anything else during that time?"

Mina's dark eyes flashed with anger. "Holy fuck! What part of 'sleeping together' don't you understand, Detective? Yes...*the whole time!* Does your entire department share your idiocy, or is it just you? If you want my co-operation, you'd better come up with an appropriate line of questioning." Mina leaned back in her chair and folded her arms across her chest, fuming.

Wilder took it all in stride. "This isn't some tea party, Miss Khorasani. This is a murder investigation, so let's get one thing absolutely clear. I'll be the one to determine what's appropriate and what's not. I can make things very easy for you, or very difficult. The choice is really up to you. Noah was full of arrogance and swagger when he first came in, but he realized that playing ball *with* me was the easiest way to go. You answer my questions now, and worry about whether I'm being inappropriate later." Det. Wilder sat back in her chair, and adopted an expression that had won her many a late-night poker game.

Mina's eyes widened, and her lips all but disappeared. "You know what I think? I think you brought Noah in for questioning regarding Beverly Black's murder, and you tried to get him to admit that he was guilty."

*Identical in appearance only,* Wilder thought. She didn't mean to be antagonistic, but Mina was trying everything to push her buttons. "Is he?" Wilder asked.

Mina sat upright in her chair, beyond incensed, and looked Wilder square in the eye. "HOW DARE YOU!!" She screeched, flying to her feet. "Noah's innocent, and so am I. So, unless you've got something you can formally arrest me *or him* with, *FUCK YOU*. I want my lawyer."

## XIII

Mina was silent after lawyering up, and although she wouldn't let it show, Det. Wilder was beyond frustrated with how things were shaping up. Finally, Mina's lawyer, a tall fellow with tousled hair and capped teeth, showed up to collect both Mina and Noah from the precinct. As they walked by Wilder's desk, she stood up and told the couple not to leave the jurisdiction. All she got in response was a scowl from Noah and the finger from Mina before they were hustled into the elevator and the door shut them off from Wilder completely.

After they left, she sighed and sat back down at her desk, running her hands through her hair in agitated frustration. *Spin, spin, spin,* she thought. She'd hoped to hear back from Julie down at the morgue regarding any potential information about the victim, but her phone was quiet on that front. With no forensics, she had nothing to go on. Meanwhile, her killer had either just walked out the front door in plain view or they were off the grid completely without even a fingerprint to connect them to the crime. With the total lack of evidence, it was as if a ghost had dug the hole and dropped the vic in. Damn! She hated spinning her wheels.

She started organizing and re-organizing her desk as she went over the facts she had in her head when her phone rang. The M.E.'s face lit up the screen on her smartphone, and Wilder snatched it up. "Wilder."

"Well, someone's had a rough day." Marsh said. "Am I calling at a bad time?"

Wilder tried to focus. "No, it's fine, Jules. Please tell me you have something for me."

"You know I wouldn't call you unless I had *something*, but you're not going to like it."

Morris and King strolled by Wilder's desk. King made a drinking motion with his hand while Morris thumbed towards the elevator. Wilder shook her head at them and turned her attention to a paperweight on her desk.

"Well, whether I like it or not, your something is better than my nothing."

"It might be best if you came down to the lab then. What I've got is more of a show than a tell."

Wilder was already halfway to the elevator, glad to being doing something other than sitting in the bullpen trying to conjure up a killer out of thin air. "I'll be right there."

## XIV

Crews were tearing up the road outside Precinct #9 when Wilder stepped out the door, and when she saw the street full of idling vehicles with no end in sight she decided to hoof it. By the time she got to the M.E. building twelve blocks away, the 30-degree weather had ruined her blouse as well as her mood. She paused under the shaded canopy outside and tried to fix her hair using the window reflection, but most of it was plastered to her head and beyond salvaging. She gave up and strolled inside, wiping the goofy grin from the temp's face at the desk with a flash of her badge and service piece. The air-conditioning prompted a bout of shivering as she stood at the elevator, and the dampness of her blouse made the slightest movement uncomfortable. The temperature dropped a further ten degrees as she descended the two floors down to the autopsy labs. In this heat, there were times she envied her friend.

"Let me guess. Traffic?" Marsh said when Wilder walked through the double doors.

"They're ripping up damn near the entire intersection outside the 9th. Cars are backed up almost to Hedger Street, so I walked." Wilder ripped a paper towel out of the dispenser by the door and blotted her forehead. "What have you got for me?"

Dr. Marsh walked over to a small bar fridge in the corner and pulled out a bottle of water. She tossed it to Wilder. "Here. You look like you could use it," she smiled. "I have stronger stuff, but it's industrial strength and it would probably kill you."

"Thanks."

Marsh walked back over to where Beverly Black lay on the autopsy table, the tops of the ugly Y stitching poking out from under the hospital linen that covered her. "First of all, I narrowed the time of death. Our vic died about 2 pm Tuesday afternoon. She didn't die with grace either. A laceration on the back of her head, contusions on her neck and shoulders...that's not to mention the contusions and bleeding on her wrists and ankles from where she was bound with ropes. I stand by my initial COD as compressive asphyxia, however. She died *after* burial."

"No signs of a struggle?"

Marsh shook her head. "Nothing that would have contributed directly to her death. All these injuries are relatively superficial. But see here?" She pointed to a single isolated bruise in the crook of Black's left elbow. "Tox reports won't be back for a while yet, but there's a decent chance she was drugged before being buried. I won't know for sure until the reports come back."

"Well, that's efficient," Wilder muttered.

"It gets better," Marsh continued. "Your killer was good. Very good. I had my boys do a thorough sweep of the vic's house, and there was not a single trace of anything that could link us to who did this. No fingerprints, no DNA. Nothing. I didn't even find anything on the vic's body or clothes. Something wasn't sitting right for me, so I had them sweep a second time."

Wilder cocked an eyebrow. "And?"

Marsh shushed her. "All in good time, Detective. I was spinning my wheels as much as you, until I found this." She picked up an evidence baggie off the desk and handed it to Wilder. In it was a single hair. The detective's eyes glittered. "I did some DNA tests on it, to try and figure out whose hair it is. And here's where things get interesting."

Wilder looked up from the baggie to her friend. Interesting, in this business, was almost never good, and she said so.

"I found it partially threaded into the weave of her dress," Marsh said. "The size of the hair and the colour match against the fabric made it next to impossible to find. DNA testing proves that it's not the vic's. I ran medical records and it's not Alan Black's either. But the system did come back with a match, and *that's* why you're here."

Marsh walked over to the computer and nudged the mouse to turn off the screensaver. A mug shot of a clean-shaven man blinked onto the screen. Wilder stared at the face, shaking her head. "You son of a bitch," she whispered.

## XV

It was just after midnight when the headlights of Celeste's blue Mini Cooper cut the darkness as she parked in Alan's driveway. The deck light didn't come on as she expected, so she turned off the engine and then turned the key one click further to keep the headlights on. Stepping out of her car, she started to walk towards the rear to get her suitcase and laptop, and decided against it. *Go check on Her Majesty first,* she thought. The beams from her car threw only so much light in the direction of the house, and she cursed Alan under her breath for forgetting to turn on the porch light. She picked her way up the deck stairs and fumbled her hand along the wall for the secret hinged flap that housed Alan's spare key. Not able to find it by touch, she dug into her purse for a small flashlight and took it out, shining it on the wall. She found the compartment and shone her light into the recess. The key was missing. She stepped back a little, shining the light on the deck, trying to see if it had fallen out. There was no sign of the little key anywhere. *Shit,* she thought. *What the hell did he do with it? Don't tell me he took it with him when he left. Or left it in the house. Goddamn it, Alan.*

Adding to the fun, Misfit had spotted her from her seat on the kitchen windowsill and had begun miaowing to beat the band. Switching the flashlight to her left hand, she reached back into her purse to grab her cell phone. *Maybe he knows another way in that I don't,* she thought.

"Misplace something?"

Celeste spun around on her heel and almost fell on the deck. An outstretched left arm pointed in her direction, with the missing spare key pinched between a gloved thumb and forefinger. Her car's headlights cast an aura around the figure, throwing the front into shadow. She opened her mouth to cry out, but the right hand shot out, a flash of white between the gloved fingers, and clamped onto her mouth and nose in a tight grip. The left hand reached behind her head to keep her from pulling away, and the spare key dug painfully into her scalp. Celeste's nose filled with a pungent, sickly sweet smell and she felt herself untethering. She dropped the flashlight and it scattered its light before winking out on the deck. Within seconds, her eyes rolled up into the back of her head.

Then her world cut to black.

\*     \*     \*     \*     \*     \*

Celeste woke up lying on her stomach, with a nagging pain in her shoulders and knees. She tried to blow a few stray strands of hair out of her face, but the cloth gag in her mouth put a stop to that. She tried to scream, but all that came out was a muffled groan. As the fog in her head lifted, she realized she was in the backseat of her Mini, and the pain in her joints was from her wrists and ankles being bound together behind her back. She closed her eyes and exhaled through her nose as she tried to shift her body a little to relieve the pressure. The attempt was futile, and a bolt of pain shot through her right shoulder, pushed too far outside its natural range of motion.

Her purse was on the floor, next to her head. Even in the dim light thrown from the deck (*it wasn't on before!*), she saw that her purse was empty. Her cell phone wasn't amongst the little bit of road trash strewn on the floor, either.

*You couldn't use your cell phone right now anyways, girl. Not with your hands all twisted up like a pretzel.* Without thinking, she tried to blow the same strands of hair out of her face again and growled low in her throat at the gag.

Taking a moment to focus, she tried to remember how she got here. She remembered trying to find Alan's key, and then being ambushed. The overwhelming scent of what might have been chloroform or ether. Then…nothing, until she woke up here in the car, bound seven ways to Sunday. Suddenly, she raised her head in alarm, squealing as the pain bolted down her arms at the movement.

*Where'd they go?!*

As if in answer to her question, she heard the porch door slam, and the sound of footsteps walking down toward the car. She heard the familiar click of the driver's side door being unlocked remotely and the shadowy figure, dressed in a long black oilskin, slid into the driver's seat. Its right hand shot up into view, and Alan's spare key bounced off her forehead into her open purse, neat as you please. Celeste squealed in protest, and the hand reached up to adjust the rear-view mirror. Eyes hidden by sunglasses stared back at her. Then it spoke, its voice dry and oddly sexless.

"You're awake. I would suggest keeping quiet and doing as I say. A word of advice: stay on my good side if you want to stay above ground. Clear?" With that, the same hand that had drugged her turned the key in the ignition. Celeste's wide eyes never left the back of the head in the driver's seat.

*Beverly Black's killer is in my car,* she thought wildly. *I'd bet my life on it.*

As the Mini gently lurched into motion, Celeste closed her eyes and a solitary tear coursed across the bridge of her nose.

She was trapped like a rat, and she was in bad, bad trouble.

## XVI

Alan's cell phone rang again about forty-five minutes after midnight. The display read *Celeste DuMont*, and he answered it sleepily. "Hey, Celeste. How's Mis-"

"Do you know who killed her yet?" the voice whispered. Alan's blood ran cold while confusion flooded his brain.

"Who is this? Please, just tell me who this is." Alan tried to keep the fear out of his voice.

"Oh, Alan. And take all the fun out of it? No, it's better this way, at least for a little while. You'll get to know me soon enough. That I promise you."

Alan sat bolt upright in bed, his mind racing. *I'd asked Celeste to check up on Misfit...is he...?* He found his voice. "Are you in my house?" The question woke Parissa in her room down the hall.

"Alan? Is everything okay?" She called out.

In Alan's room, everything was very much not okay. No, sir. Not at all.

The voice spoke again. "No. No I'm not. I *was*, but that's beside the point. However, I did bring back a little souvenir. Say hello to your friend, my blonde beauty!"

Alan heard the sound of Celeste's hitching sobs. "He-hello, A-Alan..." There was a pause and then a drawn-out sniffle. "I was ambushed at your house, Alan, I..."

There was a loud *CRACK!* in Alan's ear, and Celeste screamed, then burst into tears.

"CHATTY CATHY! I told you to say 'Hello', not tell him your life story!" All semblance of calm in the voice was gone; in its place was a vulgar, unchained lethality. This was a man on the edge of an abyss, plummeting down into the heart of a demonic fury.

"Leave her alone! What have you done to her?" Alan yelled, his voice ugly with fear and aggression. The rational part of his mind understood he needed to stay calm if he was to get Celeste out of this predicament, but he couldn't help himself.

In an instant, his caller's calm was back. It turned Alan's blood to ice. "Oh my, nothing yet...but don't push me, Al. You'll regret it to the very end of your days if you do. Clear?" Celeste was still sobbing in the background. Alan swallowed hard, as he tried to keep his wits about him. That voice...

"Be quiet, you little bitch!" The man snarled. "Typical fuckin' woman. Can't handle a little physicality." Alan could hear Celeste struggling mightily to stifle her cries, but he could hear that she was careening out of control toward a full-blown hysterical meltdown. *Come on, Celeste. Keep it together, babe.* "Listen carefully, Alan," the man growled, all business. "You have something I want, and I'm prepared to eliminate everyone you hold dear in order to get it. I will start with your lady friend here, if you're not prepared to deal."

Alan tried to think. "I don't understand what you're talking about! I really don't!"

The voice chuckled, and slipped back into a sea of unfettered calm. "Oh, Al. Your mother said the same thing to me, 'I don't know what you waaaant!' But she knew. Oh yeah, she definitely knew. Knowing and not acting on her knowledge is what got her killed. Did you know that? Here's a life lesson for you, Alan, free of charge. Women will say whatever they think they can get away with in order to protect their own best interests. But when that woman defies me? That's a *bad* idea. You understand that, don't you Al? You understand that defying me is a *bad idea.*" Celeste's sobs escalated, and the voice pulled away from the receiver a little. "Goddammit, I said SHUT. THE FUCK. UP!" The voice grew in strength again, and Alan detected an undercurrent of absolute insanity in the tone now. "Geez, Alan...don't you see? A good business man always knows how to negotiate with anybody, even those who won't listen when they're asked to do something."

Alan heard what sounded like the hammer of a gun clicking, and his panic kicked into overdrive. "Jesus! No! Whatever you're thinking of doing, please don't do it! I'll listen! Dammit, I'll listen to you and do whatever you want!" He started to babble, and was horrified to discover that he couldn't stop. His eyes grew wide as the gaping black maw that stole his sense of rationality the morning before roared open in front of him once more. He stood helpless, on the edge of that terrible abyss that both beckoned to him and threatened never to release him.

"Oh, my dear Alan. My dear, dear boy." The even, sexless tonality was back; the roller-coaster of emotion had disappeared without a trace. "I know *you'll* listen. Your lady friend? Not so much."

There were three sounds in rapid succession: the crack of flesh striking flesh, a single gunshot, and Alan screaming.

## XVII

Parissa bolted into Alan's room when he screamed, and had to hang onto the doorframe to hold herself up, as her legs suddenly felt very weak. Alan just sat there in bed clutching the phone in his hand, his own eyes bulging.

Alan stared at his phone. Silent tears streamed down his face.

"Alan...?" Parissa whispered. "Please tell me..."

"Mother's killer...on phone. Shot..." His voice cracked, and he gulped a little. "...shot Celeste."

Parissa's hands flew to her mouth in horror, and Alan hurled the phone across the room into a chair, where it ricocheted out and onto the carpet before coming to rest in the corner. He howled in agony, and his sobs seemed to rip his body apart.

*       *       *       *       *       *

Red eyes stared at the wall, as the ring of the gunshot slowly faded in his ear. Beside him on the bed, Parissa leaned against him stroking his hair, her own face wet with tears. The ticking of the clock on the side table slowly penetrated his senses as his grief turned into a grim resolve.

*The man that killed my mother has now killed my former fiancée,* he thought. *The woman whom I loved and remained friends with even after we broke off our engagement is dead.* Alan set his jaw. *I have to stop him,* he resolved. *I owe that much to Celeste, and to my mother.*

Parissa reached for his hand just as he sat up, with a barely whispered "Excuse me" falling from his lips as he got out of bed. He pulled his jeans on, and grabbed his jacket from the chair before leaving the room.

"Alan?" she called.

But he was already down the stairs and out the front door.

\* \* \* \* \* \*

Alan sat outside the Precinct, fingers drumming on the steering wheel, wrestling with his inner torment. He wanted to find this guy himself and make him pay for everything he'd done. But he knew that Det. Wilder and her team were handling the case as quickly as they could, and he'd read enough crime fiction to understand that going out on his own, in an act of vigilantism, well...the legal beagles called that *Obstruction of Justice*, among other things. Any way you sliced it, it meant possible jail time. He bowed his head. He also knew that letting this thing remain in the hands of city officials was a huge mistake. Deep down in his guts he just knew it.

His cell phone rang. Blocked ID.

"Hello, Alan." The same whispered voice.

"What do you want?" Alan could barely control his voice.

"What are you doing outside the police station?"

Alan opened his mouth to reply, but then snapped it shut when he realized *the piece of shit was watching him.*

"Talking to the police...not very creative, Al," the voice continued. "And a *bad idea.* I would advise against speaking to them at all from here on out. That is, unless you want more of your friends and family dead."

"Where are y-?" Alan asked, but the call was disconnected. "FUCK!" He shouted. An elderly lady walking her Shih Tzu on the sidewalk in front of the Precinct turned towards the sound of his voice in shock before collecting the dog in her arms and scurrying off, almost falling over a stray construction sawhorse just around the corner of the building. He threw the phone on the seat and stared at the front door of Precinct #9.

The echo of the gunshot rang again in his mind. He squeezed his eyes shut at the noise, and something deep within him finally broke. *This has to end. I can't stand idly by while you kill and kill again. I just can't.* "Sorry, Detective," Alan spoke aloud, turning the ignition key. "But with all due respect, I'm going to have to ask you to go fuck yourself. This is personal."

# XVIII

The door slammed and Alan stormed up the stairs to the guest room, not noticing the pain in his left foot when he planted it wrong on the stair. Parissa trailed him like a shadow and emerged in the doorway as he started to pack his overnight bag.

"Alan? What happened?" No answer. "Dammit, Alan! Please...say *something!*" Her voice filled with tears.

He spoke without looking up from his packing. "I'm going after him. He called again. Said that the only way to prevent more deaths was to stop talking to the police."

"Going aft...but...the police!"

He stopped packing long enough to turn on Parissa in barely restrained anger. "Damn it all! Two people are *dead*. First my mother, and now Celeste. Who's next? Me? YOU?" Parissa cowered, reacting as if he'd struck her. He zipped up the suitcase and turned to leave. She cringed against the door frame as he shouldered his way past her towards the stairs. He had taken one step down when she found her voice again.

"Stop!" She stood at the railing and looked at him, her rich, dark eyes level with his. "Please don't leave, Alan. I don't want to be left here alone." Her cheeks were wet with tears. It seemed like all she had done the past two days was cry. "You're not the only one who's terrified..." she breathed.

Alan sighed. The last thing he wanted was to have someone with him as he went on his manhunt. But she had a point. Leaving her alone was like offering her up as a sacrifice to this monster. He reached out and caressed her cheek, watching her close her eyes to his touch. "I'm so sorry for blowing up at you like that. This...it's risky, what you're asking. You must understand that I won't be able to come back to this house for a long time…what about your clients?"

Parissa shook her head. "I have no other clients. Your mother paid me enough to afford…"

Alan looked into her eyes for a long moment, before nodding in silent understanding. She moved around the banister to meet him on the stairs and hugged him tight, eyes shut, while he quietly hated the nightmare they'd both been plunged into.

She pulled away after a few moments and looked deep into his eyes, stroking his cheek. "It's late," she said. "Let's get some sleep first, okay? Get a fresh start on this in the morning."

She kissed his forehead and almost felt his stress crumble away a little, just a little. He nodded without speaking and moved quietly past her to the guest room, giving her one last, sad look before he closed the door.

## XIX

He looked down at the smoking gun in his hand. He pulled the blindfold off Celeste's head carefully, almost lovingly, and regarded her for a moment. Her long blonde hair fell down in front of her face like a curtain, and he reached one gloved hand out to caress the back of her head as it drooped forward. He smiled. Everything was going just as he knew it would.

Just as he had been told it would.

It was brilliant, how easy it had all been. The best plans were always so simple. He looked back down at the girl, his eyes sliding over the swell of her breasts; down further to the way her legs spread apart, the skirt almost revealing its secrets. He felt a pulse in his jeans. For a brief moment he considered taking her, warm and inviting, right on the chair…

He pushed the thought away. There was so much to do.

Turning on his heel, he tucked the semi-automatic into the seat of his jeans and grabbed his jacket from the table. His body was filled with adrenaline, and it only took a few steps to cross the fifty feet to the warehouse door. On the threshold of the exit, he turned a final time to survey the windowless room. Smiling with intense satisfaction, Noah Lofton shrugged on his jacket and strode outside, locking and dead-bolting the only door behind him.

*Part II*

## I

All she had to do was what I asked and I would have left her unharmed. More importantly, she'd be *alive*. A few simple questions and I would have walked out of her life to claim what was rightfully mine. But she had to play dumb in *my* time of need, so I had to make some hard choices. Goddamn woman thought she could get away without paying the piper. Okay, yeah, tearing her office apart and torturing her a little was *fun*. Dare I say...*cathartic*? But when she looked up at me as she lay on the floor in front of her filing cabinet, playing the fool, I mean...hell, I couldn't just leave her there – what kind of message would *that* send? So I pumped her full of ketamine and sent her on the best trip of her life. I wish she'd been there as I tore up her precious garden she cherished above everything and everyone else. Wish that she'd been able to watch as I tore out every last one of her prize fucking flowers by their prize fucking roots! She woke up and looked up at me while I buried her too. Oh man, that was the best part. Her eyes rolled up towards me, soaked with fear and pain and questions. When I had finished, and the dirt completely covered her, I turned my face up to the rain as it started to fall and smiled. Then I patted the back pocket of my jeans, making sure the document I'd discovered in her office was still there. *Beverly Black's Last Will & Testament*, where she'd left my money – MY MONEY! – to her bastard kid, Alan Black. Money that was supposed to be mine was now bequeathed to a whore's filthy seed, someone who no more deserved it than a toothless bum begging for nickels on a street corner.

Watch yourself, Al. I'm just getting started.

## II

Adele Watkins leaned forward in her chair and picked up the piece of paper sitting on her desk again.

"You want me to do what?" Her green eyes were hard, but they possessed a glimmer of intrigue.

"You heard me the first time, Miss Watkins." Noah Lofton reached into his jacket and pulled out a pack of Pall Mall's. He tapped one out and stuck it in his lips.

"I'll toss you out of this office if you light that," Watkins said, glaring at him through a curtain of jet black hair. Lofton held her gaze steady for a moment, almost daring her to follow through, before yanking the cigarette out of his mouth and fiddling it with his fingers. "This is a Last Will and Testament, Mr. Lofton," she continued. "Unless your name is Alan Black, and obviously it's not, then what you're asking me to do is illegal. The fact that you *have* this is probably illegal. I don't know what you've heard about me, but there are limits to what I'll do, even if it's off the books."

"Perhaps you don't understand, Miss Watkins. If I ask you to do something, I expect you to do it. No questions asked, no demands made...if you don't appreciate by now that I'm a dangerous man, then you've got some hard lessons to learn." He leaned back and placed the cigarette in his mouth again. He lit it and took a deep drag. Adele wrinkled her nose at the plume of acrid smoke that poured out and he smirked when she didn't follow through on her threat to evict him. He pulled his semi-automatic out and aimed it casually at her. She made a move to reach under her desk for the silent alarm and he pulled back the hammer in response. "Don't be fuckin' stupid. I've already killed two women this week, Miss Watkins. It wouldn't put me out to make it three." He paused. "I don't understand what the problem is. You come highly recommended because you've done this sort of work before. This should be no different. That is, unless you have a problem with *me*. Is that it, Miss Watkins?"

Adele finally found her voice. "I won't do it for free."

"No, of course not. You charge five percent for work like this, don't you?"

"It's twenty, Mr. Lofton. I always work for twenty."

The rage within him started to bubble. In an office building full of suits, he debated whether he'd kill her if he got angry. He pursed his lips and kept the gun aimed steady.

"Twenty percent, Mr. Lofton. Or I won't do it," Adele repeated, setting her jaw.

"You'll do it for five." She opened her mouth to protest and he cut her off. "And if you insist on more, you'll go back to that miserable Australian back country you come from in a body bag. Clear?"

Adele looked at Noah for a tense moment and then back at Beverly Black's *Last Will & Testament*. Five percent? She'd never worked for so little, except once. And she'd considered *that* a very noble cause. But demanding five percent here only served to piss her off. With a gun in her face and a threat of death over her head, however, she backed down. She hated herself for it, but she backed down anyway.

"I don't have all day to sit here and watch you gawp at that piece of paper. I will kill you if you won't take the job, if that helps your decision-making along at all. Be a good girl and give me an answer now."

She nodded slowly, gritting her teeth, and pushed the paper back across the desk towards Noah. He placed the gun back in his jacket and then reached for the Will. He folded it carefully and tucked it into his inside pocket and stood up. "Smart girl." He smiled easily, and tapped the desk with his knuckle before leaving the office. Adele forced her own smile, but it disappeared as soon as the door latched behind him.

*    *    *    *    *    *

She glared at the door. Her scowl deepened as she heard him make an easy joke with the receptionist outside. She allowed herself to relax only when she heard the bing of the elevator and her clueless receptionist had giggled a goodbye to him.

"'Australian back country'...I'm from New Zealand, ya bloody chuff-monkey," she growled through her teeth. She wheeled her chair out from behind the desk and went to the window. The lingering aroma of his cigarette made her crave one of her own, but she was trying to quit. She watched him strut out of the building and hop into his car, a smart blue Mini, and drive away. *Ass!* she thought. *You arrogant, bloody ass!* She crossed over to her desk and yanked the bottom drawer open as far as it would go. She dug her hand way into the back and fished out her smokes, the pack slightly crumpled. The cigarettes were bent. She didn't care. She lit one and took a tentative first drag and coughed, almost retching. She leaned against the edge of the desk facing the window, her eyes watering as the smoke curled around her face.

Her telephone intercom buzzed. Clueless had a voice that sounded like she sat sucking helium all day, and it grated on Adele's nerves like nails on a chalkboard. She wished she had been allowed to hire her own secretary, but corporate had gone ahead with what amounted to little more than a cattle call of potential hires. Kaylee had what Adele's boss called "a winning attitude" and "an approachable, upbeat personality." Adele saw her for what she really was: an airhead with big tits that served as eye candy for the bigwigs. She hesitated before pushing the talk button.

"What is it, Kaylee?"

"Mr. Abrahams is here to speak to you about his life insurance policy!" Kaylee chirped. God, how she hated that voice.

Adele glanced at her watch before closing her eyes. "Can you have him reschedule? Something has come up and I'm going to be taking the rest of the day off."

"No problem, Miss Watkins!" Kaylee cheered into the intercom before clicking it off. Adele shuddered. *Please, just shut up. Why couldn't he have turned his gun on you, instead of cracking asinine jokes? Sometimes there's no justice.* She took another drag of her cigarette. The old familiar nicotine calm was starting to flow through her and ease the shake of her hands. He had rattled her, that's for damn sure, but she wasn't stupid. All she had to do was figure out a way to get her client money that wasn't legally his. Already a plan of action was forming in her mind before she even realized it.

She butted out her cigarette. Old habits died hard.

# III

Noah Lofton pulled the Mini up just outside the abandoned warehouse. Now that his big errand had been taken care of he could take care of the other, smaller problem that sat inside the building. He reached into the glove compartment and pulled out a pair of brown leather gloves. This was serious business, and he wanted to make sure he did it right. He left the engine running.

The gravel crunched beneath his feet as he walked toward the warehouse. He fished the keys for the deadbolt out of his pocket and unlocked the door.

*       *       *       *       *       *

The room was empty.

Noah uttered a cry of confusion and stepped forward. From behind him, the chair that Celeste had been sitting in whistled through the air and caught him hard between the shoulders.

"AUWUGGGGH!" Noah cried. The blow staggered him. Another strike, this one to the top of his head, cut his scalp and blood began to flow down the back of his neck. Part of the chair back splintered, and pirouetted into the air. Quick as a cat, Noah dropped down and rolled to his left, narrowly avoiding a third blow. The chair cracked against the concrete and all four legs broke away from the seat. He looked up at Celeste, who was panting with exertion, and he swung his leg out in a wide sweep that cut her legs out from under her.

*Thwak!* Her body smacked hard against the floor, and the air left her in a wounded howl. He reached his hand up to touch the back of his head and brought it back in front of him to see his palm dripping crimson.

"YOU CUNTING *WHORE!*" he bellowed. He staggered to his feet, blistering pain throbbing all along his spine. "I'LL KILL YOU!" He kicked her in the ribs and she barked in pain. He grabbed her by the hair and yanked her to her feet. He was reaching into his jacket for the semi-auto when her fist pushed through his nose from the left. His mouth opened in a silent scream, and he crumpled to the floor in a fetal position, clutching his face.

"Cocksucker!" Celeste screamed at him. "Fucking *cocksucker!* Yeah, hurts doesn't it? You piece of shit!" As she straddled his chest she reached inside his jacket to retrieve the gun and aimed it at his face. Noah stared back over his hands, which were still clutching his nose. "Kill me?" she said. "You should have done *that* when you had the chance, you miserable pile." She rested the barrel of the gun between his eyebrows. Her hair fell in untidy platinum and crimson snarls in front of her eyes. She tossed her head to flip them aside, and huffed a breath from her exertion.

"Yoo boke by dose, yoo fuckig *bitch!*" Noah warbled.

"Yeah? I couldn't tell by the blood pouring out of your face like a fountain." He raised his hand to swat the gun away and she drew the hammer back in response, shoving the barrel against his forehead. "You so much as *twitch* and I will fan your brains out across this floor! After what you did, don't think I won't. Give me my car keys, asshole."

"Th-they're id the car. I left it rudding. You were subbosed to be tied ub..."

"Maybe you should have been a Boy Scout. Jesus, I'm a graphic designer and I can tie a better knot than you." She rose from her kneeling position over him, taking care to keep the gun trained on him, but her hands were starting to shake as the adrenalin starting really pumping inside her. Once on her feet, she looked down on him as he struggled to prop himself up on his hands. Her size 7 trainer suddenly whistled through the air and connected hard with his testicles. She could actually feel them spread apart through his jeans and across her instep. *One for the money, two for the show*, she thought. A nervous giggle burst through her clenched teeth. Noah wriggled on the floor in agony, his mouth opening and closing in a mad attempt to get his air back. He made no sound, but his eyes were already blackening and the tears running down his face went unnoticed. His fingers clawed at the concrete uselessly. "I don't know who you thought you were dealing with," Celeste continued, "but if you cross me again, I will end you. See if I don't." She hoped her voice didn't betray her and reveal how truly frightened she still was.

She removed the clip from the gun and tucked it in her back pocket with a shaking hand. She took a deep breath to steady herself and then aimed the gun back at his face. Noah brought up a trembling hand in a pitiful attempt to shield himself. She squeezed the trigger. There was a small, but audible *click!* as the hammer fell but Noah jumped anyway, squeezing his eyes shut and screaming. She tossed the spent gun on the concrete, where it clattered and spun once lazily, the muzzle coming to rest against his nose.

"I guess you were right. A woman *will* say whatever she has to in order to protect her own interests. Too bad for you." She opened the door to freedom. Noah tried to speak, but only managed a raspy cough. He hawked once and spat a clot of bloody mucus onto the concrete. She considered him before speaking again. "I can only hope that the next time you decide to be a misogynistic asshole, you'll be a better judge of character first."

Noah propped himself up on one elbow as the door slammed shut. Gravel sprayed as the car drove off.

"Fuck," he wheezed, before passing out.

*IV*

"Is there any way to talk you out of this? I mean, what are you going to do if and when you find this guy? Just walk up to him and ask him to stop or you'll turn him in?" Parissa had been silent in the passenger seat for most of the trip back to Shallot's Cove, but the tension in the car had been palpable.

"I don't know what I'm going to do," Alan said. "Except that I can't sit around waiting for the police to 'complete their investigation' while this guy is out there, murdering my family and friends. I'm scared. I'm angry. He said I have something he wants, but I haven't got a fucking clue what he means. I can't imagine what I could possibly have that someone like that could want. Or my mom, for that matter. He spoke about that, right...right before he killed Celeste. He went on about how my mother knew about what he wanted and still she defied him and that's what got her killed."

She shook her head and looked out the window. "Insane. How can you possibly expect to reason with someone who's insane? Especially someone who's insane *and* kills on a whim?"

Alan turned the Tercel off the main road and into the parking lot at *Bookends*. He killed the engine and looked out at the darkened windows. "That's odd..." he said.

"What?" Parissa asked.

"It's after ten in the morning. We open at eight. My A.M. should be here, but this place looks dead as a tomb." He yanked the keys out the ignition. "Wait here."

Alan got out of the car and closed the door behind him. He took slow, deliberate strides up to the back door of the building. He pulled the big deadbolt key that he kept on a separate ring out of his jacket and slid it home into the Krieger. He turned back to look at Parissa one last time before slipping into the darkness.

The little hallway that led from the main body of the store to the parking lot was almost pitch black, save for a sliver of daylight that seeped in under the door separating him from the front of house. He flicked the light switch, with no success. *"What..."* he whispered, flicking it repeatedly like an imbecile. He pulled out his phone and activated a little flashlight app, enough for him to navigate past the giant burlap bags full of coffee beans and other assorted stock. He aimed the phone at the ceiling and saw the bulb, clean and intact. Even the filament inside wasn't broken.

So dark.

He opened the door to the shop.

*       *       *       *       *       *

The light from outside lit the shop well, even though several more flicks of a bank of light switches behind the till proved just as futile as in the stockroom. A sense of danger crept into his bones, and he wondered if this was how Parissa felt as she walked through his mother's house. There was a dark feeling here; nothing felt right. And where was Kim? The store should have been opened already, busy with customers. What the fuck was going on?

"Hello?" he called out. Nothing.

He knelt down behind the counter and spun the dial on the safe. Inside, the till drawer was safe and sound, as were the little coin and cash bags. He slammed the door shut and spun the dial again, securing the safe. He stood up and did a quick inventory check to make sure nothing else was out of place. He walked out from behind the counter, unsure of anything. He crossed over to the front door to make sure it hadn't been compromised. The handmade *Emergency* sign was still hanging on the glass. Where the hell was Kim? He knelt down by the door latch to inspect for any signs of forced entry. There didn't appear to be any sort of damage. He stood up, tracing the line of the door up to the deadbolt near the top. He jiggled it and it was solid.

He screamed as a knock on the glass startled him half out of his wits. He had been so focused on the inspection of the door that he hadn't seen the old man come shuffling up to the entrance of the shop, all by himself.

"Mr. Getzel?" Alan shouted through the glass. "What..." Getzel rattled the door knob, his attitude becoming more and more agitated. "All right, all right! Hold on..." He unlocked the door and Mr. Getzel pushed his way inside, muttering incoherently. "Mr. Getzel," Alan called over his shoulder as he closed the door. "Where is your caretaker? Mr. Get..." He watched with worry as Mr. Getzel shuffled around in a sort of circle, mumbling louder and louder. Alan walked over to the old man, who appeared to be suffering some sort of delusion brought on by his Alzheimer's.

"Assa! Hababa! Aaaagalala!" Mr. Getzel exclaimed. "HASSA!" His sunken eyes glared up at Alan, an almost accusatory expression on his face.

"Mr. Getzel! It's me, Alan! Remember?" The senior shoved feebly at Alan's chest and shuffled off toward the back office door. He started shaking the doorknob, his agitation escalating. "Wait! Whoa!" Alan said. He had no idea how to defuse the situation. Where was his fucking caretaker, Ms. Peachey? *What the hell was going on?* He was halfway to the door where Getzel was when he heard the muffled screams.

*       *       *       *       *       *

He got the door open and Mr. Getzel shoved past him and into the bathroom, slamming the door. Before he could really register what was going on, he heard a small *click!* and the old man had locked himself inside. But there was a bigger problem than Mr. Getzel and it lay near his feet.

"Kim? What the fu--?" She looked up at him with terrified eyes and he saw immediately why her screams were muffled. He pulled the cloth gag out of her mouth and started to work on the knotted rope that bound her hands and feet.

"We have to get out of here!" she cried. "Was that Mr. Getzel?"

"Afraid so." Damn, these knots were complicated. Behind the closed bathroom door, Mr. Getzel ranted and raged in his delirium. "What happened?"

"I'm...not sure." Kim said. "I came in this morning through the back entrance to open up and was attacked just after I walked into the shop. I think he drugged...OW!"

"Sorry. These knots are tight."

"It's okay, just hurry. Whoever it was drugged me, I think. When I came to, I was here, lying on my stomach, all tied up. I could hear someone moving around in the stockroom, shifting things back and forth...hey, I think you got it." She moved her wrist around within the loop of rope that bound it and, indeed, the knot was loosening. Alan saw that once one knot was undone, the rest came away quickly. Kim was able, at long last, to extend her arms and legs back to their natural positions.

"Can you walk?" Alan asked.

"I...ooooh. I might need your help a bit. My legs are a little stiff." He helped her to her feet and she stood, unsure of her balance and weight. "What about Mr. Getzel?" The old man was eerily quiet behind the door.

"I..." Alan began, and as if on cue, Mr. Getzel came out of the bathroom, armed with a plunger. "Mr. Getzel?"

Mr. Getzel shuffled past them, silent as a ghost, back out into the main shop. Alan and Kim exchanged worried glances but quickly followed.

"HASABA!" Mr. Getzel shouted, before shuffling toward the stockroom, shaking the plunger in front of him. Alan started after him, but Kim held him back.

"Wha-?" Alan said.

"We have to *leave*. I don't know what the guy that attacked me was doing, but I heard him say something like, 'This will surprise him! Everyone loves a fireworks display!'"

Alan's brain tried organizing everything into a logical order. "I can't just leave Mr. Getzel behind, Kim. Wait by the front door, and we'll head out together, all three of us. Once we get outside we'll have a chance to work out what to do next from there."

Kim nodded and walked to the door. Alan went into the stockroom.

Even with the door partway open, it was still very dark inside the stockroom. Dark enough that Alan had to turn on his flashlight app again in order to see. Mr. Getzel had gone quiet again, not even moving in the small space. "Mr. Get..."

"Shhhh..."

Alan turned to his left, shining the flashlight into Mr. Getzel's face. The old man was looking at him with eyes that were clear and comprehending. He raised a bony finger to his lips in a shushing gesture, and Alan heard a sound that made his blood run cold.

*Ticktickticktickticktick.*

Getzel, his eyes burning with intensity.

"Go," Getzel said.

Alan ran.

\*     \*     \*     \*     \*     \*

Parissa was fidgeting with a loose thread on her dress when the concussive force of the explosion blew out the windshield and windows in Alan's car. She squeezed her eyes shut as glass shards flew at her in a deadly rain. The car rocked on its springs and a hail of rubble came clattering down on the roof. One larger piece of the brickwork landed with a thud on the hood, denting the metal. She opened her eyes and saw a smouldering ruin where *Bookends* had stood. Her ears were ringing so loud that she couldn't hear anything, and when she shook her head to clear it, a shower of glass fell from her hair. She looked down and saw a blanket of glass covering her lap. She had several small lacerations on her arms from where the glass had struck when she raised them to protect her face. Tiny tendrils of blood seeped from the wounds. Shaking her arms free of a few stray shards, she reached for the door handle and pulled.

"Alan?" Her voice sounded muffled and close. She yelled louder. "ALAN!?" She had no idea if he could hear her, if he was even still alive. She staggered from the car, her legs weak and unsteady. Glass tumbled from her dress and crunched under her shoes as she moved toward the shop. Smoke, acrid and sour, reddened her eyes and forced agonizing, wheezing coughs from deep in her lungs. She called again, the effort nearly doubling her over as his name lost itself in the fire. She stood there, shell-shocked, while in front of her eyes, *Bookends* burned.

# V

When the cab pulled up in front of her four-storey walk-up, Adele slung her laptop case onto her shoulder and dragged a briefcase full of paperwork out behind her with her left hand. She handed the driver a few bills and checked the sidewalk both ways, like she would on a street corner, before walking toward her shitty apartment complex. Young trash-mouth skateboarders often practiced outside the complex without regard for anyone, and she had learned to look before stepping out of or into the building. A wino clung to the brickwork just outside the door like a barnacle – hard, grasping, but immovable. She hated this dump, but she understood its necessity. When your side gig was obtaining large sums of money for questionable people, and charging a fee for your efforts, it was important not to draw attention to yourself. She could afford a penthouse in one of the high-rises deep in the downtown core, but to any of the over-spent Average Joe's who walked through the glass doors of the biggest bank in Waterford, she was a mere clerk, and the fewer questions asked, the better. The downside was, this place wasn't quite Skid Row but it was damn close.

She side-stepped a week-old dog shit that sat on the third floor landing, and walked down a hallway that in its better days had threadbare carpeting and peeling wallpaper. The odour of rancid beef, Indian curry and Chinese take-away seemed to leach right out of the walls, amplified by the August heat wave. A minor earthquake a few years earlier had misaligned the framework of the entire building, so when she turned the key in the lock of her apartment and gave the door an extra shove at the midway point, it barked in protest and the noise set off a bout of crying from a crack baby in the apartment across from her, an unfortunate soul who rarely knew real peace.

The interior of her apartment was an extraordinary contrast to the filth and decay that threatened to seep in just beyond the door. Something tried to scuttle in from the hallway, but she crunched it underfoot just on the threshold. No bugs here, thank you. It was bad enough that the filth in the rest of the building was almost a grasping, living thing, trying to overtake and dominate all in its path. In here, the cupboards were filled with cleaners and scrubs of all kinds. She kept the place as sterile as a surgical room because she would go insane otherwise.

She set her briefcase down on the dining table and the laptop case in an adjoining chair. She went to open the window at the far end of the room and had her hand on the clasp when she thought better of it, her hand dropping back to her side. As hot as it was, she couldn't bear to breathe in the stench of the alleyway. She turned back to the table and clicked open the briefcase.

Alan Black.

She thought back to the office where she'd stared down the barrel of a gun and agreed to the demands of a well-dressed lunatic. According to the Will, Alan Black was the sole beneficiary. She wondered who Noah Lofton really was and how he knew Alan. In order to keep above ground in this game it went without saying that what you didn't know wouldn't kill you. Questions were the enemy. But this was something different. Something she had never tried before. On the surface, a Last Will and Testament was legally watertight, and she knew when she nodded and pushed the paper across to Lofton that she would come up against roadblock after roadblock in her attempts to get him what he wanted. She pulled out a stack of paperwork from the briefcase and snapped it shut. She pushed the case to the far end of the table and opened her laptop.

She absently reached into her purse to grab a cigarette before remembering the pack was still in the bottom drawer of her desk at the office.

Old habits.

*Fuck.*

She ran a shaking hand through her hair and stared at the laptop as it started up. She thought about Alan Black and who he was, how he knew Noah Lofton…*if* he knew Noah Lofton, and what he was doing in the midst of all this. She opened her web browser and typed "Alan Black" into the search field. The website for *Bookends* came up first and she clicked the link. Her breath caught in her throat.

Alan Black's name was unknown to her. Yet, his face…

*     *     *     *     *     *

The clock on the wall chimed the next hour as she stared out the window into the alleyway, not really seeing the hobo with the grocery cart scavenge whatever seemed remotely edible out of the dumpsters. *That face,* she thought. *I know that face.* But how? An only child born in Christchurch, New Zealand, she'd moved here on her own ten years ago. *But there it is,* she thought, looking back at the computer screen. Alan smiled at her over his giant, almost cartoonish, mug of coffee as he stood outside of a packed shop. She looked out the window again and shivered. The hobo was taking a piss in the back corner of the alley, hands behind his head, as he stretched out his back. So many questions! She cracked her neck and decided on a plan of action.

She picked up her cell phone, dialing the number on the screen. In her ear, the phone buzzed as it tried to connect to a line that no longer existed.

The sound of sirens wailing up the street brought Alan out of the clutches of unconsciousness. The fog in his head was tremendous, but he became aware a bit at a time of the pain, and soon he was coherent enough to discover he was doubled over a hedge that sat fifty feet in front of his shop. He was impossibly lucky; a foot to his right and he would have been impaled on a piece of rebar that jutted out of a cement median.

The sirens were louder now, swelling as they approached the intersection, as he tried to peel himself off the hedge. Everything hurt, especially his guts, and there was a ringing in his ears that he couldn't understand. He stood up gingerly and tried to gain his bearings. He turned and watched as a black Bomb Disposal Unit truck roared into the lot opposite and several men in flak jackets piled out of it, heading toward what was left of the shop. *Like a clown car*, he thought, with no humour. He turned away to stare up the street, trying to collect his wits, but trying not to think about anything. A fire truck growled in behind the BDU and he watched with helpless detachment as firemen started pulling equipment and hoses off the truck.

A few minutes later a police cruiser pulled in and wiggled past the BDU truck to where he was and he raised a hand to shield his eyes as its windshield reflected the sun right in his face. A young officer jumped out and ran over to him, hand on his service piece. He was about to reach out and touch Alan on the shoulder when someone hollered at him. The cop turned away at the last minute.

The officer's partner was already over by the shop, shaking his head at him. "Party's over *here*, Holby," Officer Patterson said. "The ambulance will be here in a few to check on him. We have to wait till we get the all-clear from the BDU. Come on."

The minutes ticked by, until the first of the disposal unit came through what remained of the front door. "All clear!" he said, as a cluster of them left the building.

Officer Holby stepped out of the way as some of the members of the task force pushed past him to the open back doors of the truck. A fresh round of sirens signaled the arrival of the ambulance. In his confusion, Alan suspected that every resource the town had was here at *Bookends*. His chin quivered.

There was a brief tussle between the BDU truck and the ambulance as they both tried to negotiate the small turn-in lane into the lot. The ambulance made a beeline for Alan, and again he had to raise his hand as the sun blazed off the windshield. The ambulance had barely stopped when the young man in the passenger seat was out the door. He took three long, easy strides to reach Alan. The driver, slightly thicker and sporting two day's growth on his jaw, jogged past Alan on his right. Alan was about to answer the paramedic's first question when he was interrupted.

"'Cesco, over here. Code 5," The older medic huffed.

Alan turned at the voice and started to move toward it when he was held back by 'Cesco.

"On it, Andres." He turned to Alan. "Sit down, please, sir. I'll be back in a minute."

He was still out of it enough to acquiesce immediately, and he moved to the cement median and sat down slowly. Sitting down didn't stop him from looking over to where the two medics were, just behind the hedge. Didn't stop him from seeing one of Kim's ballet flats resting upside down against the front of the hedge. And his hearing had come back enough that he was sure he heard one of them – 'Cesco, as it turned out, judging from the admonishment the young man got – step away a foot or two, lean over and vomit. After a moment, his curiosity got the better of him and he rose slowly to his feet, his knees protesting the entire way. He took a few shaky steps and peered over the hedge and instantly regretted his decision.

Kim was lying halfway into the ditch, face down in a pool of muddy water. But lying face down in a ditch was the least of Kim's worries now, because on top of the large pool of blood that had begun mixing into the drain water, was a large piece of brickwork where her head should have been.

\*      \*      \*      \*      \*      \*

He tried to scream. Was sure he had, in fact, but all that came out was a strangled warble. The driver of the ambulance looked up and saw Alan, and nudged 'Cesco towards him.

"Try not to throw up on that one," Andres said. 'Cesco shot him a dirty if still mostly squeamish look. Alan had stumbled backward a few steps and smacked the back of his legs against the median. He made to sit down but the rebar jabbed him in the ass and he jumped up again, straight as a poker. His face had gone white.

"Sir? I need you to come over here, okay?" 'Cesco said. Alan nodded silently, and walked over to the ambulance with him, as agreeable as a docile old man. *Mr. Getzel...*

"Wait!" Alan said. He looked towards the shop for the first time and saw the destruction. Plumes of smoke were billowing into the sky as the firefighters blasted water at the ruined husk of the shop. Alan walked around the front of the ambulance and saw what remained, which was very little, and began to cry. Torn scraps of paper and chunks of books littered the ground along with piles of rubble and broken glass. *My shop...my baby...* he thought in anguish. *Mom...Celeste...my shop...Kim... He's taking everything. He's taking everything away from me! But WHY?* He stopped and stared without seeing, and felt whatever joy he had left in his life drop out of him. He staggered back a bit, suddenly very weak, but 'Cesco was there to catch him and bring him to the back of the ambulance.

He accepted the oxygen that was offered to him, and sat down on the bumper of the ambulance. From here he could see the interior of the shop clearly and his body shook at the sight of four years of his life, decimated in as many seconds. Whatever had been in that stockroom had been enough to damn near level a city block. Mr. Getzel had come in, ranting and raving. However, in that final moment he had clarity and whatever illness had been eating at his brain seemed to vanish, like it had never been there to start with. He had saved Alan's life. How had he known? He thought of Kimberly. Kim, the sweet, cheerful blonde who had worked so hard to make Alan's life just a little bit easier the past three years. Now she, too, was dead - another victim of some maniac's desire to tear Alan's world down around him.

"Alan...?"

He looked up toward her voice. At first he couldn't believe what he was seeing, but as Parissa came staggering toward him, glass in her hair and blood on her dress, he couldn't help but smile. 'Cesco looked up from checking Alan's vitals and he quickly handed off the blood pressure pump he'd been holding to Andres and jogged over to help her. Alan reached out his hands to her. She was here. She was alive.

"You look terrible," Alan whispered, his smile broken. And he hugged her hard, sobbing into her arms.

Parissa stroked his hair as he cried, rocking him gently as the sobs wracked his body. She looked over his head at the jets of water spraying into what little was left of *Bookends* and tried to hold her own tears back as she saw the destruction of her friend's livelihood. The medics left Alan and Parissa, and moved off toward the hedge.

"M' Lord in Heaven! What 'appened 'ere?" Alan and Parissa both looked up toward the tiny woman as she struggled to step over the fire hose that stood between her and the ambulance. "Alan? Are ye...naw, I can see yer not okay just by lookin' atcha. And th' shop! What in th' world?"

Mr. Getzel's caretaker, all four feet ten inches of her and originally from Dublin, stood near the back of the ambulance with her hands on her hips, staring at the aftermath. The colour was high in her cheeks and she was breathing just a little bit heavily, no doubt from power-walking to get there. She shook her head in disbelief and turned to Alan, who was trying to dry his eyes. The paramedics were moving into view, and they caught her attention as they tried to bring Kimberly's covered body discreetly up out of the ditch. She watched them for a long moment, a million questions on the tip of her tongue, but she bit every one of them back before asking the one question that seemed most important.

"Ye haven't seen Mr. Getzel around 'ere, 'ave ye?"

Alan pursed his lips and looked away from the caretaker, back towards the shop. The waterworks had stopped blasting, and some of the firefighters were beginning to gather up the equipment, while three of them stepped into the shop to assess the damage. The silence was so pronounced and Alan's stare so fixed that it wasn't long before she put it all together and pointed a shaking hand at the building.

"He…" she began. "'e's in there? But how? Yeh couldn't save 'im?" Her voice was brittle and sad.

Alan found his voice and spoke. "Ms. Peachey, I…Mr. Getzel saved my life." Both Parissa and Ms. Peachey looked at him with open mouths. "I came in to see why the shop was still closed, and he came up to the door, all agitated. I didn't see you with him and I didn't know how to calm him down…" He went on to describe how Mr. Getzel had marched into the stockroom and how the Alzheimer's seemed to disappear in that final moment between them. He explained the ticking sound and how Mr. Getzel spoke to him – actually said the word "Go," how Alan and Kimberly barely made it out the front door before the explosion happened, and how the force shoved them clear across the parking lot toward the hedge. He paused, looked over at the hedge for a long moment, and couldn't continue.

Ms. Peachey and Parissa were both dumbstruck by Alan's story, but in the end only Peachey could summon up the will to speak. This time her voice was soft. "I woke up dis marnin' t' foind the front door bangin' away in the breeze like a judge's gavel and Mr. Getzel nowhere t' be found. O' course I panicked, but even dese days 'e was a fierce creature of 'abit and I thought the first place 'e'd likely go was 'ere." She looked up at Alan with a gentle smile on her face. "'e did love ye so much, Alan. But wakin' up, like ye said, from 'is Alzheimer's? An' speakin'? Tha's unbelievable. God truly does work miracles."

She squeezed his hand before strolling away, leaving the two of them to watch her go before turning their attention back to the shop.

## VII

Three miles. Three miles of walking in thirty-degree heat, with a useless Glock tucked into the seat of his jeans. Although walking would be considered a generous term. What he did was less like walking and more like a combination of staggering and shuffling, with his legs spread apart and his back hunched over, bruised and sore from the beating he'd taken. He'd tried sticking his thumb out a couple of times when he'd first started, but with his eyes blackened, the blood in his hair and beneath his shattered nose starting to congeal, the few cars that did pass him did so with a slight pick-up in speed as they blew by.

So Noah Lofton walked the three miles back to town.

He had a real motherfucker of a migraine by the time he put his key into the lock of his apartment and turned it. He could hear voices inside, voices that trailed away at the sound of the door latch in the frame. He turned to go into the bathroom, but stopped himself. He wasn't ready to see the damage that little bitch had done to him just yet. He pulled the Glock out of his jeans and tucked it into the drawer of a little side table next to the door. He tossed his jacket on the floor next to the closet and suddenly felt ten pounds lighter.

"Noah?" Mina called from the other room. "Noah, is that you?"

"Yeah. Yeah, it's me. Who's in there with you?" His voice carried an old, weighted tone of jealousy in it.

Noah turned to step into the living room and saw Det. King stand, his blazer parted so Noah could see his badge.

"Holy shit..." Det. Morris muttered behind his partner. All three reacted to his face.

"Noah??" Mina started towards him, and then cowered back a little when she got too close. "Noah, what *happened?*"

"Miss, please step back." Det. Morris stood and held her arm with his hand. Surprisingly, she offered no resistance.

"Turn around please, sir." Det. King made a twirling motion with his finger. Noah's first instinct was to run, to fight, but his broken body had nothing left. He wasn't going to win this fight. Not today.

"Hands behind your back," King continued, as Mina started to cry and protest against Morris's hand. The cold click of the handcuffs bowed Noah's head as King began to speak again. "Noah Lofton, you are under arrest for the murder of Beverly Black. Anything you say can and will be used against you in a court of law. If you cannot..." King's voice was drowned out by Mina's wailing sobs, as she ripped her arm out of Morris's grasp and ran into the bedroom, slamming the door behind her.

*       *       *       *       *       *

Even Naomi Wilder, who had witnessed some pretty grisly scenes in her ten years in Homicide, did a double take when she stepped into Interrogation Room #1. Defeated and dejected, Noah sat with his hands folded neatly in front of him on the table, the glint of the steel casting a short line of light on his face. For a moment, Wilder felt enormous sympathy for Noah. Gone was the brazen, arrogant beast who had tried to frustrate her the last time he was here. Gone too, was the fear. In its place was a deep melancholy, a sadness that seemed impossible to fathom. She took a long, slow breath and continued into the room, remembering why she was here, and why he had been arrested. She pulled back her chair and sat down, dropping the evidence baggie with his hair in it on the table in front of him.

"Look what I found, Noah." She gestured to the baggie. He looked at it in disdain for a moment, and then looked away, closing his blackened eyes. She took a moment to assess him, now that she was closer. Noah looked like a prizefighter on the end of a ten-fight losing streak. "What happened?" she asked.

"Caught me by surprise," he mumbled. "Broke my fucking nose." His voice rose a little as he continued. "Which I'd like to get looked at, by the way. You have no idea how much this fucking hurts."

"Caught you? Who caught you by surprise?" The question hung on the air with no response. "Noah?" He sat in the chair and turned his face away, sullen. Wilder tried a different tack. "I found this hair on the vic's clothing, Noah." He looked up at her again. "It's yours."

"So?"

"*So?* It places you at the scene, Noah. You think I had you arrested just for the hell of it?"

"You brought me in for questioning last time just for the hell of it." His eyes narrowed, accusatory. "Didn't you?"

Wilder leaned in, pointing her finger at the baggie but not taking her eyes off Noah. "You really don't get it, do you Noah? This is *your hair*, which we found threaded into the victim's sundress. That means *you were there*. That means you were in physical contact with the victim. And if you weren't, I would like you to explain to me how this got on her dress."

He lifted his right hand to scratch delicately under his eye, and sighed as his left hand followed. He paused a moment more before he spoke. "No. Because *I wasn't there.* Get it through your stupid head. I don't care *what* you have in that baggie. I want my lawyer."

## VIII

The isolated location of *Bookends* proved both a blessing and a curse, in the end. The blast had sent pieces of brickwork flying out into the middle of the nearby intersection, some 100 feet away, but no other businesses or private residences were damaged at all. One elderly lady declared some of her prize bone china had been shattered in the percussive force of the blast, but there were no other casualties.

The questions the solitary officer asked Alan and Parissa were cursory, but polite, and after being given the okay from the paramedics, he offered to give the two of them a lift back to Alan's house.

"Just here if you can, Officer." Alan said. He pointed to the side of the road just before his driveway. The officer nodded, smiling, and pulled over gently to the shoulder. Alan reached over and offered his hand, wincing a little as a flash of pain flared up from his abdomen. The officer grasped his hand and shook it gently, a look of concern at the pain in Alan's face.

"You gonna be okay, Mr. Black? I can drive you right up to your door, if it's easier."

Alan shook his head. "No, thank you. I'll be fine." He looked back over his shoulder. "How about you, 'Rissa? Are you okay?"

"I just need to lie down, that's all. Thank you." Parissa whispered from the back seat.

Officer Holby nodded in understanding and got out of the cruiser along with Alan and Parissa. He tipped his hat at them and wished them a speedy recovery. "And I'm terribly sorry about your shop, Mr. Black," Holby said. "Me and the rest of the boys are not going to like having to go someplace else for coffee." His expression was downcast and, before Alan could say anything, Officer Holby slipped back into the driver's seat and pulled a neat U-turn back toward town.

Alan took Parissa by the hand and they walked up along the driveway to the house. After all they'd been through, conversation was not necessary. Before they'd left the shop, Alan had walked around with Parissa to assess the damage to his car. It was, of course, a total write-off, but it still shocked him. He couldn't believe she'd been sitting in there when the place went. He couldn't believe she'd survived. He'd circled the car, marveling at how the glass had blown out on all sides and the absence of glass outlining where she'd been sitting in the passenger seat. He was thankful, however. If he'd parked close to the shop instead of at the back of the parking lot, she'd be dead.

He felt a light squeeze on his right hand, and looked up from where he'd been lost in his thoughts. Looked up and saw the blue Mini. He ripped his hand out of hers and clapped it over his mouth, screaming through his fingers. *He WAS here! He was here and he…*

Alan crumpled to the ground and bowed his head, crying into the dirt.

*     *     *     *     *     *

Parissa managed to coax him into the house, where Misfit mewled and encircled his legs, almost tripping him.

"Hey youuuu…" Alan said in relief, scratching the cat behind her ears. "God, I missed you." He knelt down and began snuggling the cat, who seemed beside herself with joy now that Alan was back. Parissa patted him on the shoulder and excused herself to the bathroom. The door had barely latched shut when the sliding door that led out onto Alan's side yard slid open. He heard the light smack of flip-flops on the laminate in the dining room, and tensed.

"Oh my God..." Celeste said, dropping the bucket of blackberries from her hand where they scattered across the floor. Misfit started at the sound, but soon trotted over to sniff at the purple flecks of juice some of the berries left in their wake.

Alan looked up and saw her standing there, wearing the goofy hot pink "Talk Nerdy To Me" baby tee that he'd given her as a birthday present once, and did something he would never do again. He slouched onto the floor in a heap, unconscious.

*    *    *    *    *    *

He woke a short time later, looking up into two concerned pairs of eyes. He was on the couch in the living room, and Celeste was adjusting the cold, damp cloth on his forehead while Parissa held his left hand in hers.

"Heh...what happened?" Alan muttered, and then looked intensely at Celeste. "I thought you...?"

"Shhh..." Celeste gently restrained him from sitting up too quickly. "First things first. You...fainted. And from the look on your face, you want answers. But first..." She dove on top of him and hugged him fiercely. "I'm so glad you're safe!"

Alan pulled in a pained breath from the strength of Celeste's embrace, and then responded in kind. He tried mightily to keep from crying, but one or two tears strayed down his face nonetheless. He thought back to the sound of the gunshot deafening him the night before, and how terrified and powerless he'd felt.

"How did you…? I mean, you're alive, but how?" It was all he could manage. Celeste pulled away from their embrace and he felt relieved that her own cheeks were wet with tears.

Celeste sat cross-legged on the floor for a quiet moment, thinking of how best to start. "First of all, Alan, I don't know what is going on, but whatever it is, it's some *scary* shit. I got here last night…God, it feels like years…but it was just past midnight, and I couldn't find your key."

"But I left it in the…"

She flapped her hand at him. "Yes, I thought so too, but it wasn't there when I got here. And while searching for it, someone attacked me and I was drugged. The next thing I remember, I was tied up…"

"…and lying on your stomach? With your hands and ankles tied up behind your back?" Alan interrupted.

"Y-yeah…how do you know about that?" Celeste's eyes narrowed a little.

"I'll explain after," Alan said. "Sorry I interrupted."

She cleared her throat and continued. "So I was tied up seven ways to Sunday and then this guy wearing all black got into the car and tossed your spare key in my face. He also said something about staying on his good side, if I wanted to live. Just the way he said it, I was sure it was your mother's killer, Alan. Oh God, I was so scared…" She took a quick moment to calm the shake in her hands.

"You want anything to drink?" Alan asked.

"No, no…I'm fine. It's good to get it out," Celeste said, looking better for the few deep breaths. "We left here and drove for a while. I'm not sure how far, I couldn't see very well. But it was probably close to an hour. When we did stop, he put a big blindfold on my face, but not before showing me this gun he had. A semi-automatic, like a Sig Sauer or a Glock. I couldn't tell in the dark." She checked their confused faces and rolled her eyes subtly before explaining. "I did a job for a guy a while back who was advertising his shooting range. It looked interesting enough that I did a little research into different types of guns and so on. Anyway, after he blindfolded me, he cut my bonds and then knocked me out with more of that shit he had." She chuckled nervously to herself. "And I thought chloroform only worked like that in films..."

Alan and Parissa exchanged worried glances at each other, which went unnoticed by Celeste who was focused on something just outside the bay window.

"Anyway," she continued. "Next thing, I come to tied to a chair, and I still had no idea where I was, except that it was kinda echoey. Hollow, you know?" Alan nodded. In his panic at the moment, he hadn't noticed. But now, separated from it a bit, he thought he could remember a bit of an echo during the conversation. Like the caller was in a cave or something. "Then, the phone call," Celeste said. "I was so *scared*, Alan. He was talking so crazy and angry. And I couldn't *see*. Then he slapped me, and fired the gun. I was so worked up and it was so *loud*...I just...fainted."

"I thought he killed you!" Alan blurted out. "The call was disconnected right after, so I didn't know any different. God, when I heard that I...I thought I would..." He cleared his throat, and sunk into chagrined silence.

She reached for his hand. "I know." There was silence in the room for a moment before Celeste continued. "I don't know how long I was out, but when I did wake up, I could see. He had taken the blindfold off and left. I took a look around, tried to figure out where I was. Best I could tell, I was in an abandoned warehouse-type place. There were no windows. But here's something funny...in a morbid kind of way. By my feet was my phone. *With a bullet in it*. He'd shot my phone, Alan. *That's* what you heard. I think he only wanted you to *think* I was dead. I have no idea why, but whatever it was he was thinking sure didn't work out for him."

"What do you mean?" Parissa asked.

"Well, while he was gone I managed to untie the knots that bound me to the chair. Easy peasy stuff, too. I bet Misfit could have tied a better knot, and she lacks opposable thumbs." Misfit turned from her perch on the window-seat at the sound of her name, and purred deep in her throat before returning to whatever she was watching outside. "Once I was free, I grabbed the chair and waited for him to come back. I waited a while, too, because I dozed off. But when I heard the gravel crunch outside, I grabbed the chair by its back and got ready." She smirked.

"What happened?" Parissa's eyes were huge in anticipation. Alan thought she looked just like a little kid hearing ghost stories around a campfire.

A smug look settled on Celeste's face. "He came in. And I kicked his ass."

"What!" Alan and Parissa spoke in tandem, and then stifled giggles that came from nowhere. Alan spoke alone:

"How?"

"The chair came in handy. That self-defense course you bought me for a Christmas gift back a few years ago really helped also. He got a shot or two in, but then I got up and broke his nose. Actually, *crushed* might be a better word. He won't breathe the same way for the rest of his life, I shouldn't think. Anyway, by lucky fluke, I managed to snag his semi and while he was down I planted him right in the nuts...sorry, Alan." Alan had visibly winced. A memory of Celeste kneeing him in the same place once while they were play fighting came to him and he remembered how much it had hurt. He could only imagine the agony if she was deadly serious about it.

"The long and the short of it? I got my car keys back from him at gunpoint, removed the clip and gave him his gun back. And I drove straight here from Waterford." She pulled the clip out of her back pocket and held it out to Alan, like a trophy.

Alan and Parissa sat in stunned silence for a few moments, absorbing what Celeste had said. Finally, Alan spoke up.

"Waterford? Celeste...what did he look like?"

"Hmmm," Celeste said. "He was...about your height, Alan. Maybe a little shorter. Really wiry. Thin, but strong. Short, dark hair. Angular nose, or at least it was before I happened to it. Actually, Parissa...now that I think about it, he looked an awful lot like..."

"...Noah Lofton." Alan and Parissa said together.

# IX

The apartment was deathly silent after the two detectives took Noah away in handcuffs. Mina lay on the king-size bed, her long fingers dug deep into one of the pillows as she clutched it to her chest, tears streaming down the sides of her face. Her Noah. *HER NOAH!* A killer? It seemed so, but she found it impossible to believe. She threw the pillow aside. She felt hurt, confused, horrified...and betrayed. *Of all the people! How did they manage to nail you to this crime, Noah? I refuse to believe you're guilty of whatever they're accusing you of doing. I REFUSE!*

She got up and started pacing the room, holding her arms with her hands and shivering uncontrollably. There hadn't been any incidents like those that her sister had once described in the entire time she'd dated him. Besides, if he got huffy she always had the perfect remedy for such...lapses. Some women would find it uncomfortable, even disgusting. For her, angry sex was the most thrilling. And he'd never hurt her, not once. The animalistic side of him scared her, but that uncertainty was something she reveled in. Feeling that power throb within him...*within her.*

She opened the door of the bedroom and stepped into the hall. She had to find out what was going on, and how to stop them from nailing Noah to the nearest tree. She walked down the hallway toward the front door, her mind racing to try to think of something, some *way* to prove him innocent.

She saw his suit blazer lying in a heap on the floor, and stood there frowning at it. *Why can't he hang things up like normal people? Always toss, toss, toss. Men!* She knelt down to examine it, not sure what she was looking for, but searching just the same. The outside pockets held nothing.

She almost gave up when she noticed a small inside pocket with a dark blue envelope sticking out of it. She pulled it out, and opened it. What she read made her stomach churn.


*Last Will & Testament*
*Of*
*Beverly May Black*


She stuffed the Will back into the envelope before she could get past the first fold. So it was true. Noah *was* involved, and deep from the look. Her mind started filling in the blanks. *The only way he could have gotten this was if he was there, Mina. And if he was there, then he must have had time and opportunity to kill Bee. This proves it.*

Her hands shook and her defiance took over. "This proves NOTHING!" she shouted to the empty apartment, her voice echoing slightly. "NOTHING!!" she screamed again, to cement the idea inside her. Despair and anger fought inside her for supremacy, but anger was winning. She let the envelope fall onto the side table by the door. Then she noticed cold black sitting inside the drawer.

She pulled it fully open and saw the Glock. Despair made a sudden leap from nowhere and staggered her. She tripped over a pair of heels she had kicked off near the door the week before, and caught the handle of the linen closet door before she fell. Once she was sure on her feet, she turned and ran into the bathroom, fearing the worst.

She was kneeling in front of the bowl when the landline in the bedroom rang.

*Don't answer it.* DON'T *answer it!* Her mind screamed at her.

"I must," she whispered into the porcelain. "What if it's Noah? What if he needs me?" *What if I'm his one phone call?*

She pulled herself up from the floor, checked herself once in the mirror and saw a haggard, pale face staring back through eyes ringed with running mascara.

*RRRING!*

"Yeah, yeah...I'm comin'," she muttered, as she walked into the bedroom.

She picked up the phone.

\*     \*     \*     \*     \*     \*

"Hel--?" she began, before a voice, hard and cold, cut her off.

"Noah! If I wanted that little French bitch left alive, I wouldn't have had you bother grabbing her in the first place. I gave you very specific directions and I expected you to carry them out. Now we have a problem, all because you have no balls and couldn't – or wouldn't – do what I asked of you. The problem is she's talking to Alan Black, which means complications. For you."

Mina clutched the phone to her ear, her eyes wide with fear.

"However, I'm not an unreasonable man," the voice continued. "And I'm prepared to give you one more chance to fix the problem that you created. And this time my directive is simple: Find her. Kill her. Put a bullet in her brain and walk away. Do you understand?"

Mina was frozen, hardly breathing. The silence was thick until the voice cut through it, razor quick.

"NOAH! DO YOU UNDERSTAND ME?"

She tried to give her voice strength, but she only managed a whisper. "Who is this?" she said stupidly.

"YOU!" Then, unexpectedly, a chuckle slithered into her ear. "You're his little Iranian cunt, aren't you? Mina..." She nodded slowly, mindless of the fact that he couldn't see her. It didn't matter, because he continued anyway. "All you're good for is fuckin', and eye candy." There was a stagnant pause on the line. "Oh yeah. And turning up dead. Maybe it's time for Mr. Lofton to...prove his loyalty."

*Click.* The buzz of the open line droned in her ear.

Mina's arm dropped to her side, and the receiver clattered onto the floor with a crack. Her brain was overloaded with fear, and she didn't know whether to cry, scream, faint or run, so she just stood there, blinking blindly into the terrible black void that opened up before her.

# X

Adele sat on the couch, while the purr of the phone ringing in her ear seemed to go on forever. She checked her watch again and then looked over to the website to where the Hours of Operation were listed. Three more rings and she pressed End on her cell. It was so odd, she thought, that the store wouldn't be answering at this time of day. She checked the website again. Hours of Operation: 8am-8pm, Monday through Saturday. Sundays off. It was close to 1pm – lunch rush – so they might just be hopping busy, and not able to hear the phone.

She tossed her phone on the couch beside her and clicked her way through the site. Nothing fancy, but attractive. A cozy, down-home story in the About section, and a mini-online store where one could buy some of the second-hand books the shop carried. *So you sell coffee and books? You're more interesting by the minute, Mr. Black.* She clicked a few more links and then decided to check on the store's location. She picked up her cell again to enter the information. 1578 Shallot's Cove Road, Shallot's Cove. She smirked. *When you're naming whole streets after the name of the actual town, you know you're tiny.* She checked her watch again. Maybe tomorrow she'd be up for a little road trip.

She closed the laptop and set it aside on the couch. She dropped her phone on top and scooted the hassock closer, plopping her feet down upon it. She leaned her head back on the couch and closed her eyes.

\*       \*       \*       \*       \*       \*

When she woke up four hours later, the sun had dipped down behind the building next door and the room

135

had darkened considerably. She picked up her phone and checked for messages. There were none. One nice thing about having a ditz on the desk, Kaylee rarely had enough forethought to call her for anything, ever. She brought her hand up and rubbed it along her forehead. Fucking cigarette had given her a headache. She sat up and grimaced a little. Check that. A headache and a bit of an oogy tummy. She hesitated on the edge of the couch, legs poised to launch her towards the bathroom. Closing her eyes helped as she willed her stomach into behaving itself. This was one of the worst side effects of quitting smoking, the pain and nausea that came with even a temporary relapse. The minutes ticked by and she felt the flips and flops in her guts lessen, while the throb behind her eyelids seemed to pick up the slack.

She stood and crossed over to the kitchen to grab a glass of water and a couple of Tylenol. She washed the white pills down in one go, feeling the water hurt her teeth as it always did when it was too cold, and placed the empty glass on the counter next to the sink with a clack. She kept her eyes closed for a moment more, thinking about Alan Black, and the Will, and the gun that had been pointed in her face, and craved another cigarette, no matter how awful it made her feel.

She let a long, hissing breath out through her teeth, and went back to the couch. *What's on the idiot box*, she thought, reaching for the remote. She flipped over to the news, where a tidy young man in a light grey pinstripe held a microphone in front of him, while police and firefighters milled about both inside and out of a building that used to be.

"That's right, Melanie," the young man said. "This coffee-shop behind me, or what's left of it, appears to have been the target of some sort of bombing earlier today." Adele sat bolt upright on the couch. The young man continued. "I'm not clear on the details just yet, but I'm told that this was a very popular spot for the locals here in Shallot's Cove. What I *can* tell you is that there was reportedly only one person inside when the incident occurred, but that person's name has not yet been released. Also I understand the owner, a Mr. Alan Black, was on site, but fortunately not inside when the explosion happened. He was treated for his injuries and has since left the scene." Adele's jaw dropped open at the sight of *Bookends* blown to pieces, and the destruction stood in marked contrast to the idyllic village setting that surrounded it.

The tidy young man kicked it back to the cheery blonde in the studio (although her face bore a sad expression deemed suitable for whenever buildings blew up in tiny towns), but the rest of the newscast faded to nothing in the background as Adele sat there absorbing what she had seen. *That's why the phone kept ringing with no answer*, she thought in horror. *The place was already gone.* She opened her laptop and brought up the website for *Bookends* again. Definitely the same place. She ran her fingers through her hair, trying to think of what she would do. The Will, Noah Lofton, *Bookends*...all roads seemed to lead to Alan Black. She wondered how long it would take before she saw his face on the news, identified as "recently deceased."

The sun sank further down toward the horizon, washing the walls of her apartment in the early blues of dusk. A gurgle in her stomach reminded her that the only thing in her fridge was week-old sushi that was probably in the early stages of colonizing the shelf on which it sat. She snapped the lid of her laptop closed, and slipped it into its case as she grabbed her jacket from the back of the chair, turning off the television as she did so. She picked up her keys from their hook by the door, took a reinforcing breath as she always did before leaving her apartment, and then stepped out in search of a decent restaurant.

## XI

The conversation quickly turned to the beginning, two days prior, from the panicked phone call from Parissa to the incident with Parissa's sister Mina, and ending with the explosion of the shop.

"That's what that was?" Celeste exclaimed. "I heard the explosion but I thought it was just teenagers blowing stuff up out in the limestone quarry by the railway tracks. Oh God, Alan. Was it bad?"

"The whole place is gone," Alan answered. "I...I don't want to talk about it." He got up and left the house through the sliding door. There was an awkward silence between the women as they watched Alan through the bay window, walking down toward the ocean.

"Christ," Celeste said. "That shop was his life. All the time he invested. Every nickel he had went into that place. Christ..."

"I can't believe we survived, honestly," Parissa said quietly. "My ears are still ringing. And that poor old man."

"What old man?"

"Alan said some old man came into the shop, just before the explosion. Told him to get out of the store. Alan said it was like he knew what was going to happen or something. What was his name? Gillis? Gettle? I wish I could..."

"*Mr. Getzel?*" Celeste cried out. "But that's not possible. Mr. Getzel has Alzheimer's, he can't even function on his own without his caretaker, let alone speak. Are you *sure?*"

Parissa nodded.

Celeste pressed her hand over her mouth. She turned to look back out the window. Alan had disappeared.

*      *      *      *      *      *

He found a log washed up on the beach and sat down, burying his feet in the sand in front of him. The ocean lapped lazily at the shore a few dozen feet away, and he stared out across its expanse without really seeing it. In his mind he was trying to be everywhere at once, trying to figure out what had happened, what *was* happening, and why. He took in a deep breath, and discovered with some relief that the pain in his abdomen was fading.

Good.

He glanced around his feet, trying to find some decent skipping stones to throw. He slowly gathered up a few and stood, dusting his pants free of sand before walking down to the water's edge. He tucked three of the stones he held into his pocket while lightly bouncing the fourth in his right hand.

"THIS IS FOR MY MOTHER!" he shouted through clenched teeth, and fired the stone flat across the water. It smacked the surface some ten feet out. *Skip skip skip skip skip.* He smiled to himself a little. *Five skips? Not bad for a guy who's rusty.* He palmed the second stone, feeling its cool smoothness in his hand. He tossed it in the air, straight up, and caught it again, testing its weight. "THIS IS FOR MY SHOP!" The stone flew across the water in great arcs before finally cutting through the surface and sinking to the bottom. He'd lost count, but he guessed somewhere in the teens. Even better! He reached into his pocket and pulled out a third stone, a large flat beauty that fit perfectly in his palm. He raised his arm to launch it, but a muscle near his ribs protested, and the rock tumbled out of his hand into the wet sand. A wave licked it, turning it from a dusty grey to a shining gunmetal, and he grabbed his side, grunting in pain. *Bah,* he thought, as he fell back onto his ass on the beach.

"All signs point to you, Noah," he said after a moment of contemplation. *But why?* He thought back to the only time he'd seen Noah mad. It was during what Parissa had half-jokingly called "their family counseling sessions." Alan had been in the middle of making a point when Noah slammed his fists down on the table and stormed out without saying a word. *He gets like that*, Parissa had tried to explain. *It's best to just leave him alone until he calms down.* He remembered asking how long that would be. Her answer surprised him. *Two hours, maybe three*, she said. He was surprised at her answer, yes, but also tremendously sad because of how she seemed to accept it. He remembered the look on her face as she gazed out the window at her hanging baskets. It was an expression of resigned apathy. How he hated Noah for that. Hated him for how he made Parissa feel.

But to kill his mother? And abduct Celeste? What madness drove him to *that* point? What had misfired in his brain so badly that he was possessed to do such terrible things? He lay back and closed his eyes in the shade of a willow at the edge of the beach.

"Alan!"

He turned to see Parissa walking down the beach toward him. She was wearing one of Celeste's tees, and she had a large towel wrapped around her waist.

"Hullo," he said. "Cute shirt."

She looked down. *Coffee Drinkers Get Roasted,* it read. "I found it in your closet. Celeste tossed my clothes in the wash. I hope you don't mind." She sat down beside him on the sand. The sun had just started to dip below the horizon, spearing the darkening blue of the water with a dagger of molten gold.

Alan shook his head. "It's fine. Mi washer es su washer." She laughed and hugged him.

"That's terrible. Didn't you take a Spanish course in university? Didn't you *ace* it?"

"Yeah, but with nobody to practice with I've forgotten most of it." He shrugged. "Jes' anudda gringo, *señorita.*" He smiled as he put his arm on her shoulder and hugged her back, watching the sun sink even further past the horizon. In the far distance he thought he could make out the twinkling lights of a passing cruise ship.

Parissa snuggled closer to him, shivering a little. Once the sun went down, the ocean winds cooled things off a fair bit. "Come inside? Celeste saw your fridge and went to get some take-out for us. Something about you being a typical bachelor?" She stood and held her hand out for him.

*     *     *     *     *     *

Dinner was pizza from Mama Leoni's just a few blocks away, and Alan served each of them a glass of Stella Artois to go with the pie. Parissa tried a couple of sips, but couldn't quite bring herself to finish it, and she handed it to Alan.

"I never could develop a taste for beer," she said, smiling apologetically.

"I said the same thing myself, until this one introduced me to Stella," Alan said, tilting his glass a little toward his ex-fiancée. Celeste responded in kind by smiling back at the both of them as she raised her own glass to her lips. "But to each their own. I have some wine in the kitchen if you'd prefer." Parissa nodded a little, smiling.

Alan walked out into the kitchen and opened the tall cupboard where he kept his wine. "White or red?" He called over his shoulder. "What goes best with an everything pizza?"

Parissa laughed a little. "White is fine, thank you."

Alan brought back her glass and handed it to her. He took a bite of his pizza before falling into silence. The two women talked for a minute to each other before realizing that Alan was sitting there, chewing so slowly as to not be chewing at all.

Celeste waved a hand in front of his face. "Halloo? Wakey wakey, eggs and bakey." She frowned. "Alan?" She turned to Parissa. "I know that look."

Parissa put her hand on his. "Alan?"

"Hum?" His eyes turned to hers, losing their faraway stare a little at a time.

"You were on vacation in the Bahamas there for a second, I think," Celeste said. "Whatcha thinkin' about?"

"I was just thinking...you're sure it was Noah that abducted you?"

Celeste nodded. "It's been ages since I last saw him, but I'm pretty sure it was him. Why?"

"Just thinking." His eyebrows furrowed. "Let's see. It was the day before yesterday when my mother was killed. Or at least when you found her, 'Rissa." He turned and looked at Celeste. "Now, I talked to you yesterday and asked you to come by here and take care of Misfit." Celeste nodded, dabbing a bit of tomato sauce from the corner of her mouth. Parissa remained silent.

"And somewhere in there you were abducted."

"Right. I was taken from here to Waterford." Celeste nodded.

Alan nodded, before taking another bite of his cooling pizza. "And he took your car."

Celeste nodded again.

Parissa spoke up. "He would have had to. Noah has never owned a car."

Alan nodded at that and threw the idea in the hopper as he tried to work everything out. "What time did you get here the first night?"

"Um...it was late. Really late. Around midnight or so."

Alan checked his watch. It was 4:30pm. They'd been here about four and a half hours. He steepled his fingers together in front of him and tapped his nose with them. Something didn't add up. "What time did you get back here today?" He finally said.

"A little after 10? I heard the bang around an hour after I got here."

"Which means you would have had to leave Waterford by no later than eight-thirty." His brow furrowed even more.

"Yeah, that's about...yes. I remember looking at the dash clock in my car as I left the warehouse. It was 8:23am."

He picked up his beer and drained it before reaching for Parissa's. "It's possible that Noah left Waterford sometime after he brought you to the warehouse, and took your car all the way here to Shallot's Cove with enough time to set up a bomb and ambush my assistant manager before she had time to open up the shop at eight this morning. But there's no way he could have done all that and still managed to get back to Waterford in time to get his ass handed to him by you." Celeste let a small smile tease her lips. Alan went on. "That's assuming he's the one behind everything that's happened up to this point...and I don't think he is."

"What?" Parissa whispered.

"Well, think about it. He ambushes Kim around eight this morning, and she told me that it wasn't until after he tied her up that she could hear him setting things up in the stockroom, which means he probably didn't *leave* here until at *least* eight-thirty, maybe even closer to nine. And, let's be honest...how adept at bomb-making do either of you think Noah is? Hmm?"

"So..." Celeste said, puzzled.

"So, there's a second man," Alan said, and finished his beer.

## XII

"Well," Celeste said, carefully breaking down the pizza box and putting it in the recycling bin by the door. "I think I should be heading home."

"Oh, whoa!" Alan replied, a deep look of concern on his face. "After what happened, I would rather sleep on the couch and let you stay here in one of the beds than…"

"Than what? It's okay, Alan. Really. I've got projects due and I can't keep clients waiting." She looked at him with warm affection. "I understand how you feel, but I can take care of myself. I promise."

Alan knew the look she was giving him and relented. "Okay. I don't like it, but I guess you'll do what you'll do, right?"

Celeste nodded and picked up her purse from the end of the table. She rose, and Alan and Parissa stood with her. Celeste wrapped her arms around him and squeezed tight. "Thank you for caring," she whispered. "I'm glad you're okay."

Parissa opened her arms to Celeste as she moved past Alan. The girls hugged each other warmly. "Good to see you again," Parissa said.

"You too," Celeste agreed. She opened her mouth to invite Parissa down to *Bookends* for a coffee soon, but snapped her mouth shut before she could breathe a word. She looked at Alan with an apologetic look in her eye, and it puzzled him.

"What's that look for?" He asked.

She flapped a hand at him. "Nothing," she said. "Nothing at all. Goodnight, Alan. Parissa." With that she turned and walked out the door to her car. Alan stood staring at the door for a few moments, scarcely breathing

146

even when the purr of the motor broke the silence as she started it up.

"Come on," Parissa said, touching his arm. "She'll be fine. You *know* that. Remember what she did to Noah? Relax."

Alan nodded and went to the fridge for another beer.

*    *    *    *    *    *

She left him alone on the back deck at his request, and he kicked back in one of the reclining chairs with his beer and watched the night sky come alive with stars. For a little while he entertained himself by trying to pick out various constellations, but soon gave it up because he only knew Ursa Major, Cassiopeia and Orion. He had deliberately not told the girls all he knew at the dinner table earlier. He had mentioned his suspicions of there being a second man, but would not elaborate. Now, with a gentle breeze pulling at his hair as he took a pull of his Stella, he thought more clearly about his theory. Of course there was a second man. The more he thought about Noah, the more he sympathized with the poor bastard. In his mind, Noah was a pawn. Nothing more.

He drained the bottle and put it on the little wooden table beside his chair. Had it just been a week since he sat in this same chair and stared into the universe watching the meteors race each other across the sky? In the dark, he felt very alone for the first time in a long time. He picked up his empty beer bottle and tipped it, trying to get the very last drops out of the bottom. He put it back on the table without looking and caught the edge; the bottle fell to the deck with a dissonant *clank!*

He brought his head up, and his nose flexed. The same smell that had been in the office wafted on the air from his left, and he glanced in that direction with narrowed, suspicious eyes. Then it was gone, gone so quickly that it was easy to think that maybe he imagined it. *Stress*, he thought. *You're so fucking stressed.*

Footsteps, this time from his right.

"Alan? Are you going to stay out here in the dark all night?" Parissa asked in a quiet voice. He reached down over the arm of the chair and grabbed for the bottle.

"No. I was just coming in," he said. But as he rose, he cast one final glance to his left. The air was fresh and carried no strange secrets.

# XIII

Good food was one of the few indulgences Adele allowed herself, and she let a little smile play on her lips as she was guided by the host toward a private table near the back of *La Festa*, an Italian restaurant she frequented. She ate here often, as she'd been granted near-VIP status by the owner whom she'd bailed out of a financial jam and because the food was incredible. Still, she always felt a little guilty for bypassing anyone that waited at the front for a table, so when she was seated she reached into her purse and handed the young man $50 for his trouble.

"What is this? I..." He stammered and flushed, and Adele thought he looked severely cute, flustered as he was.

"That's yours, as a thank-you. Can you let the waiter know I'll have a glass of Pinot Gris, please?"

"O-of course, miss. I...th-thank you." He made a clumsy attempt at a bow and left the alcove, his reddening face clearly visible even in the candlelight.

She smiled to herself as he departed, and then turned her attention to the menu. She had made it halfway down the list of appetizers when the owner, Mr. Abbatelli, brought her a glass and a bottle of Pinot Gris in an ice chiller.

"Miss Adele! My darling!" He bowed slightly with a flourish. She smiled as he took her hand and kissed it, his dry lips pressing lightly against the skin of her knuckles. He pulled the wine from the ice, ran a bar-towel over it with a fluid motion, and uncorked it with ease. After pouring her a glass and replacing the bottle in the chiller he sat down in an adjacent chair, his brows furrowed. "Can you say why my newest hire is standing near the end of my prep line trying like hell not to cry?" His tone was quiet, concerned. Adele looked at him with wide eyes.

"I...gave him a tip?"

"Yes, I saw. A fifty. He's very grateful, but he's perhaps...how you say, *unaccustomed* to such generosity. That is why I am here. To explain, and to serve you personally. You are too kind. My staff and myself, we are all grateful to you."

Adele regarded the owner for a moment, the candlelight dancing in her eyes. "It's I who should be grateful, Mr. Abbatelli." She turned her attention to the ice chiller. "And *you're* too kind. I only ordered a glass."

"It's the least I can do for you," Abbatelli said, rising. "Now, perhaps I give you more time to see the menu? Or have you decided?"

Adele had been eyeing a couple of things on the menu, the fettuccine alfredo being a particular favourite. In the end she closed the menu and handed it to Abbatelli. "Surprise me," she said.

*       *       *       *       *       *

She was on her second glass of wine when her entrée came. She'd downed her first before the appetizer – a plate of bruschetta – even arrived. Mr. Abbatelli presented her with a modest dish. She had just opened her mouth to inquire when Abbatelli spoke.

"Chef thought to prepare you something not on the menu, Miss Adele. Although, it looks so good I am unsure it doesn't belong on the menu. Perhaps as a special? I leave it to you to decide." She leaned in a little and inhaled.

"It smells exquisite, Mr. Abbatelli."

"Such praise," the owner said, clapping his hands. "It is fettuccini with smoked salmon, and a spicy creamy tomato sauce. I hope it is to your satisfaction."

Adele took another sip of wine. "I have no doubt that it will be excellent. Thank you, Mr. Abbatelli."

The little man bowed and left the alcove. Adele raised the glass to her lips again and then stopped, the glass trembling. She'd spent the last hour actively trying to *not* think about what her brain had for some reason dubbed The Alan Black Affair. Everything about this job was wrong. Shady business deal after shady business deal and none of them were like this one. She'd never had a client stick a gun in her face before today, for a start. The circumstances surrounding it were another. *"I've already killed two women this week, Miss Watkins. It wouldn't put me out to make it three."* That was what he said. And she looked into the best poker face she'd ever seen and folded her cards.

Then there was the website for *Bookends* and Alan's smiling, almost cheeky, face looking back at her. Something about him seemed so familiar. Then the newscast about the bombing. And the Will. Everything about this job was wrong.

She picked up her fork without realizing it and started poking at her food, the desire to eat totally gone. There was more to this deal than what Noah Lofton had told her. *WAY* more. Alan Black stood to gain a substantial sum of money. And then somehow his shop was blown up? And he was *there*; he was treated for his injuries according to the news reporter. Someone was trying to get Alan out of the picture. It wasn't *just* about the money. It was about eliminating him as well.

Mr. Abbatelli came by to check on things, but as he approached the alcove he saw the faraway look on Adele's face and thought better of it. He knew from experience not to disturb her at the best of times, especially if she ate alone in his restaurant.

Adele pulled out her laptop and set it on the table. *La Festa* was one of the few restaurants in town, other than the fast food joints, to offer free Wi-Fi and she took full advantage of it most times she was in here. This was also one of the reasons she preferred the private alcove to the open seating of the main dining room – less chance of intrusion. She opened up the website for *Bookends* again; maybe there was something she missed. Her adopted father had told her once, "Always check your maybes." It had served her well at both her legitimate and her...well...other jobs.

She reached for her fork to eat some of her meal before it got cold, and the smoked salmon was almost to her lips when he stepped into the alcove.

## XIV

The lawyer entered the Interrogation Room with stifling arrogance. His tousled hair and immaculate suit made him seem out of place inside the starkly lit room. He pulled up a chair and held his hand up in Lofton's face when Noah opened his mouth to speak. His eyes never left the detective and, even with all her experience, she couldn't hide the light shiver as she felt his eyes roam over her body. He smiled a little at that, the corners of his eyes crinkling.

"Detective," he said. "This is the second time inside a week I've been inside your taxpayer-funded junkie trap. Mind telling me why you're harassing my client?"

She'd danced this dance before. Lawyers were slippery, always looking for the out. "Your client has been arrested for murder, Mr...I'm sorry, I didn't catch your name?"

"Shore. David Shore. Name partner of Braun, Johnston and Shore. Originally from Massachusetts...ah, but we're not here because of me." He paused to fish a business card out of a silver card-holder and tossed it carelessly on the table. "I'm interested in making sure you stop harassing my client." His eyes rested shamelessly for a moment on her breasts before he looked back up into her eyes. "And I always get what I'm interested in."

The silence hung for a moment between them. Finally Wilder took a breath and broke the stalemate.

"Your client murdered someone, Mr. Shore." The lawyer never blinked as he looked her in the eye, the tiniest of smirks on his face. "So whatever you're hoping for here, isn't going to happen," she continued. "I don't care *how* good you think you are." Noah sniffed a little and grunted in pain under his breath.

"You claim he murdered someone," Shore said. "He confessed as much to you, did he?" The lawyer's eyes stared unsmiling at Wilder, waiting for an answer. When none came, Shore looked over to Lofton and nodded before returning his gaze to the detective. "Ah. Well then. My client and I are going to leave now, but being an upstanding member of the community, he would like to give back what's yours." He gestured at the cuffs. "If you wouldn't mind."

"He's not leaving. This time I've got evidence."

"Oh?" Shore said. "What's that?"

Wilder showed him the baggie with the hair in it. "We found this on the victim. It's a match to your client. So unfortunately for you *and* him, he's not going anywhere."

Shore turned to Noah with an expression that said, *See what I have to deal with?* Noah smiled at the lawyer and pushed his chair back a little. "That's all you've got, Detective? One hair?" Shore let a small grin play over his capped teeth. "That's circumstantial evidence at best and you know that. You have rookies fresh out of the academy working in this precinct that know that. One hair would never convict my client, even if it went to trial...which it won't." He rose and reached for his valise while Noah sat staring at Wilder with his hands outstretched. "I'm disappointed in you, Detective," Shore said. "I can tell you're scrambling, but I expected better than a weak bluff from you."

"He's not going anywhere, Mr. Shore," Wilder said. "Sit." Her face was firm, but her eyes told the story. She'd lost.

"I'll make sure he doesn't leave the jurisdiction, Detective. Just in case you find more…*concrete evidence.* In the meantime, get the cuffs off him. We're done."

*     *     *     *     *     *

Noah turned to Shore in the elevator as it headed down toward the lobby, his eyes red and exhausted.

"Thank you, Mr. Shore. I appreciate what you did back there." He sniffed again and moaned a little in pain.

Shore considered his client for a moment before returning his gaze to the closed elevator doors. "I think you should come to my office and sign a sworn statement regarding your innocence," Shore said. "Just in case they decide to harass you on your doorstep again."

Noah tried to wipe away a lone trickle of blood and winced, the pain in his nose flaring even at the slightest touch. "Thanks, Mr. Shore, but I think I'm going to go see a doctor about this first."

The two men parted ways on the steps outside the precinct, and Noah headed off down the street toward a walk-in clinic. He was halfway across the intersection when his cell phone rang. He fumbled and almost dropped it as he tried to pull it out of his pocket, before managing to flip it open.

"Hello?"

"Noah." The voice on the other end was warm, almost fatherly. "It's me. There's something we need to discuss. I'm concerned that you're not living up to the arrangement we have."

Noah thought about speaking up in his own defense, but changed his mind. It was better to listen. He had learned that lesson the first day. It was always better just to listen.

"But I have an idea," the voice continued. "Something that will definitely prove your loyalty, and ease my doubts. Do you want to know what it is?"

"S-sure," Noah said.

"Well first maybe you need to sit down, my boy. This idea is that good."

Noah found a bench on the sidewalk and sat down. It took him some time, but he managed it. *Damn, she almost crippled me*, he thought. "All right. I'm sitting."

"Okay, here it is." Noah could hear a note of muted excitement in the voice now. "The French bitch can wait. Your girlfriend? Mina? She's become a liability. She'll threaten this entire deal if we – if you – don't shut her down." A pause. "You need to kill her."

Noah felt like he'd been ripped open. For a moment he couldn't speak, and then he could only manage a whisper. "I...I can't..." He closed his eyes. "You can't be serious."

"Serious? Of course I'm serious. She needs to go, and you're just the man for the job. It's perfect. She'll no longer be a threat, and you'll show me I can count on you. You don't want to lose out on this deal, do you?"

"I...I *can't*, Mr..."

"Oh, I think you can, Mr. Lofton." From the corner of his eyes, Noah saw a man in casual clothes on the street corner facing him. A rustle in the bushes behind him, and another man made his presence known as he leaned casually against the brickwork of Our Lady of Divine Waters. Yet a third man snapped his gum as he leaned against a post box. All of them bore the same expression as they looked in his direction. *Move and we will kill you, friend.*

"You can do it, or the men you see will kill you before you get up from that bench. Now…what do you say?"

Noah closed his eyes and took a deep breath. He let it out in a shaky wheeze and nodded. "Yeah…yeah, I guess I have no choice, huh?"

"Oh come on, Noah," the voice goaded. "You always have a choice." And the line went dead.

*     *     *     *     *     *

Noah snapped the phone shut and watched as the three men disappeared down the street in three different directions. He exhaled again, hard, and was disgusted by the wheezy rattle it produced. He hawked a pink loogie out onto the sidewalk, and closed his eyes a third time, tears running down his face.

He had no recollection of actually getting up from the bench and walking, but after what seemed like minutes – but was probably closer to half an hour – he stopped dead and peered through a kaleidoscope haze. His thoughts were a jumble. Mina…the one person he knew who understood him completely without imposing her own beliefs on him; the one person who loved him without question…

*You always have a choice.*

"FUCK YOU!" he screamed, the obscenity drawing the attention of several diners inside a nearby restaurant. He glowered at them for a moment before noticing a familiar face near the back of the restaurant.

Noah went inside.

The host looked up from his podium near the entrance in surprise. "Hel–…ah, sir, I'm afraid I'll have to ask you to leave. We have a strict dress code."

Noah glared at him. "I'm not here to eat; I'm here to see someone." The host opened his mouth to protest before Noah cut him off. "And you need to find something else to do other than harass me." The finality in his tone left the host hurrying toward the kitchen. Noah ignored the shocked expressions of those seated as he brushed past them on his way toward the alcove. He saw Adele hunched over her laptop, barely touching her food. He moved into her field of vision and she looked up in surprise.

"I...Mr. Lofton?" She spoke in a stage whisper. "What on earth–"

He sat down next to her. "I'm out," he said.

"What do you mean, you're..."

He cut her off a second time. "I'm out. I'm done. What we talked about in your office? No deal."

Adele's face swirled in confusion. "I don't understand."

"Dammit! *Listen!*" Noah hissed as he slammed his hand down on the table, causing nearby guests to turn their heads toward the alcove. He looked over at them nervously and then turned back to Adele. "I can't stay, but please listen. *Please.*" He watched her nod, her eyes wide, and started to say what he had to. "First, I'm sorry. That business in your office, I can't begin to apologize for that, but I want you to know I'm sorry. There's someone else I'm working for, someone you can't know about, but they're the one that had me come to you. They're the one that wants what I asked for. But circumstances are...*different* now. Something's happened and I'm no longer involved." He paused, looking around. "I should tell you to distance yourself from this whole thing, but I need you to do me a favour."

Adele raised her eyebrows. "A favour? After what you did?"

Noah's eyes grew wide with desperation. "I'm not the same guy who sat in your office. Look at me, for God's sake! I'm begging you to do one little favour for me. Please..."

Adele looked him over. He'd been through the wringer, all right. Whoever had done this knew what they were doing. "All right," she said. "What is it?"

"Keep yourself safe, for a start. But more importantly, I need you to find Alan Black. The guy that's after him is bad news and Alan needs all the protection he can get. I beg you."

Mr. Abbatelli was fast approaching the alcove with his towering sous-chef right behind him. Neither looked pleased. The sous-chef placed a giant hand on Noah's shoulder.

"Sir, you need to leave," the sous-chef said in a low, menacing voice. "Now."

"I'm so sorry he disturbed you, Miss Adele," Mr. Abbatelli finished.

"Please..." Noah pleaded as they lifted him under his arms and pulled him towards the front entrance. *"Please..."* His face was contorted in grief and agony as he looked to Adele for some confirmation to his request.

All Adele could do was stare as they dragged him away.

## XV

It was just before midnight when Parissa knelt by the side of Alan's bed, placing a hand on his shoulder to give him a gentle shake. He moaned a little and then opened one lid halfway, his brain fuzzy with sleep.

"Whudizzit?" he mumbled.

Parissa's eyes were wide. "I heard a noise. Just a little one, but it spooked me." She took a breath to speak again and then hesitated.

Alan propped himself up on his elbow and rubbed his eyes, the fog lifting a little at a time. "It's an older house, bound to creak a bit. You get used to it."

"I know this sounds silly, and I feel like a little kid asking, but...can I sleep in here with you? I just...I can't deal with creepy house noises. Please?"

Alan looked into Parissa's eyes and then slid out of bed, pulling back the covers for her as he stood. She flushed a bit as he stood there in front her, wearing nothing but a pair of pyjama pants. "You get in first. I have to sleep on the outside, away from the wall. I hope that's okay."

Parissa nodded her head and climbed into the bed, careful not to expose herself to him. He had given her a longish tee-shirt to wear for bed, but she was nude beneath it due to the heat. Alan pulled two extra pillows out of the linen closet in the corner and fluffed them. "You can use my pillows there, and I'll use these. Okay?" Parissa nodded as she tucked an arm under her pillows.

"Thank you, Alan. I feel stupid, but the noise really spooked me."

Alan got back into bed and sunk his head into the fresh pillows. There was a faint aroma of the cupboard wood in the fabric of the pillow shams, and it made his nose crinkle a bit. He pulled the coverlet up and felt Parissa's breath on his neck as she sighed. He could almost feel her body relax next to his. He felt her hand on his shoulder, the warmth of it surprising him.

"Thank you, Alan. Goodnight." He felt her turn away under the covers.

Alan smiled a little into the pillow. "You're...good night, 'Rissa."

He lay awake for a few minutes, listening to the steady pace of her breathing. It had been a long time since he'd shared his bed with anyone and, while he'd never shared it with Parissa, having her beside him was comfortable – *right*. He closed his eyes, the smile on his face widening.

*     *     *     *     *     *

A cool breeze on her face opened her eyes, and she found she had draped her arm across his chest as she slept. Alan had rolled over onto his back, his face turned to hers, his chest rising and falling gently with his breathing. She pulled her arm back and tucked it under her chin, and she watched his face for a moment, mesmerized. She saw that she'd tossed his tee-shirt on the floor, and brought an arm over her breasts instinctively. Then, without thinking, she reached her hand back out and placed it on his cheek. He was so beautiful lying next to her, the moonlight casting its soft glow on them both. She leaned forward and kissed him, and an unfamiliar tremble coursed through her as his breath caressed her lips.

She pulled away a little, unsure of herself. She had never let herself go this far. Noah kissed her only once, but she hated how rough he was. She had never slept in the same bed as him. Had never done what her sister did...

She closed her eyes for a moment, considering. When she opened them, he was still lying there, his chest rising and falling with each breath, his face illuminated by the moon. Another fresh breeze slipped into the room and she watched, breathless, as his nipples perked up in the cool air. She flushed as she felt her own nipples pucker in response. In that instant, she knew what she wanted and she reached a hand out to him. Pulling herself as close as she could, she pressed her breasts against his arm and rested her face against his shoulder. Her hand roamed on its own and she let it, closing her eyes and just *feeling*. She kissed his shoulder softly as she slid her hand down his chest, her fingers entwining themselves in the fine spray of hair there. When the tips of her fingers came up against the waistband of his pyjama pants, her breath caught in her throat and she hesitated, nervous and trembling. Then, before she had a chance to think it over, her hand was moving again, reaching down and over him. *Hot,* she thought to herself. *It feels hot.* She squeezed him, so unsure, so afraid...and yet there was a burning inside that overwhelmed her. Propping herself up on her elbow, she looked down at her hand as she felt him swell beneath it. Her mouth was open now, and she felt heat radiate from her own centre. It throbbed once in her hand and she squealed in surprise. Alan chuckled quietly under his breath.

His hand reached up and into her hair, gently pulling her face to his. There was a moment where time seemed to stop as his mouth met hers and the tip of his tongue ran gently along her lips. She wanted him, but she was afraid, and he sensed it, pulling back a little and looking into her eyes.

"Oh, 'Rissa. I'm sorry..." His hand relaxed and he pulled it out of her hair, chagrined. "I didn't..." He gasped as she undid the single button on the front of his pants and slipped her hand inside, encircling him. "Oh!" he breathed. Her mouth descended on his as her hand stroked him, and he groaned at the softness of her hand wrapped around him.

Out of nowhere, she remembered coming home to find Noah watching a dirty movie on the television, his pants around his ankles and his hand shifting back and forth in his lap. She had stood transfixed in the doorway as the girl on the screen did all kinds of things she had never thought a lady would do. One of those things crossed her mind now and, after a final lingering kiss, she began kissing her way down his neck to his chest. Further down and she could not resist flicking her tongue against his nipple, smiling at the reaction she received. Further down until the smell of him, clean and hot, filled her senses. She pulled him out through his open fly, watching her hand as she stroked him. She marveled at how soft the skin was, yet how rock hard he felt. She looked back to him, his eyes half-closed but focused on her. She licked her lips before lowering her head. Alan turned his head and buried it into the pillow in ecstasy.

*    *    *    *    *    *

Alan woke a couple of hours later, in a spoon position behind Parissa. He smiled a little to himself as he realized she still held him snug inside her, her right leg lying on top of his. He watched her sleep for a moment, the soft swell of her breast in the moonlight making him throb a little. *She's so beautiful,* he thought. But she had been nervous also. He thought about how she had put him in her mouth and sent him over the moon with pleasure. Later, her eyes wide and her face flushed with a combination of fear and desire, she had lain back on the bed, her dark, rich eyes burning with desire for him as she looked up into his face. When he gazed down on her, she covered herself with her hand, her cheeks flushed. He had taken her hand in his, and brought it up to his lips, kissing the tips of her fingers. The smell of her intoxicated him, and he shifted forward, pressing himself against her. She closed her eyes and tensed, not quite daring to let him enter.

*Are you sure?* he had said, sensing immediately she was still a virgin. She nodded, closing her eyes as she did so. Her parents were very traditional in their ways and Parissa had always respected that, especially when Mina had not. When she shared a dorm with him in college, her parents were horrified at first, taking months to finally accept it. If it had been anyone but Alan, they never would have allowed it. So, as he knelt before her, her small hands in his, he understood her hesitation. But he also felt her passion and desire, all of those emotions in tremendous conflict. Finally, she had broken the silence.

*I want to, Alan, but I'm scared. Will it hurt?* Her voice was so small.

*Yes,* he had said, *it probably will, but only for a little while.* She had bit her lip as he pushed forward, then her eyes flew open and she took in a sharp breath before nodding gently. There was resistance at first, then suddenly everything tore away in a rush and he looked up to see a single tear slip out of the corner of her eye. She tried to breathe through the pain until at last she opened her eyes and looked down. He pulled back a little, and a tiny trickle of blood was visible. Another tear fell.

*Alan...nngh,* she breathed, pressing her fingertips into his chest. *It hurts...*

*I know,* he said, trying not to lose it all in a rush. Her grip on him was incredible – delicious, but almost unbearable. He swallowed hard before speaking again. *I love you.*

His words had brought a palpable hush over the two of them. There, in an instant, were the words he had never spoken but always wanted to. Twenty years and there it was.

She looked at him with huge eyes for a long time, then she pulled him close, and he began to make love to her.

*   *   *   *   *   *

He loved her. That simple truth he'd held inside for so long was no longer a secret, and as he looked at her sleeping, peaceful face, he loved her even more. He cupped her breast in his hand and kissed her on the shoulder before reaching down to move her leg off his. He felt a dull pressure as he extricated himself from her, and the need to urinate was immediate. He reached down to remove his pants from around his ankles and then slipped out of bed at the foot of it, careful not to wake her as he headed to the bathroom.

The moonlight pouring through the door of his bedroom provided enough light to see by in the bathroom, and Alan was grateful for that. He lifted the toilet seat and waited for relief to come. The first splash of urine as it hit the water muffled the sound of a floorboard creaking, and as his bladder emptied he closed his eyes. Had he not done so, he would have seen the shadow dart past the moonbeam shining out of his doorway. He looked down to give himself a final shake, and cold steel pressed against his temple.

He stopped breathing. For an eternity it seemed as if his body had simply forgotten how to perform basic functions and even when he heard a low voice say "Don't move," it was as if all the wind had been knocked out of him.

He tried to turn his head toward the voice on his right.

"What did I say? Don't fucking move!" the voice hissed. The barrel pressed harder into the side of his head, and Alan heard the click of the hammer being drawn back. He realized he was nude and, amazingly, he felt intense embarrassment. He started to move his hand around to cover himself and the figure grabbed him by his neck, dragging him back toward the bedroom.

"Get in there!" The figure shoved him through the door, and Alan cried out in horror. Her face was mostly obscured by a black gloved hand, but her eyes peered over the thumb, enormous. Parissa's assailant had what looked like a Bowie knife pressed against the soft skin of her neck. Her attacker seemed to be clutching her in a sort of body scissors, her arms pressed firmly to her sides by his legs. He felt a hand on his shoulder and he lost his breath for real as he was spun and slammed up against the wall hard enough to make a framed picture jitter and slant askew on its wire, almost falling. Then the gun was in his face and, in an absurd moment, his eyes crossed in fear as he tried to focus on the barrel as it wavered in front of him. Out of the corner of his eye, he saw Parissa's attacker squeeze her tighter with his legs, and she stopped struggling immediately. Alan thought her eyes might actually pop out of her head.

"What..." Alan's words were cut off by the man's forearm in his throat. Nose to nose as they were, Alan thought he could smell the same odour he had smelled in his mother's office, and his blood froze.

"You're getting too close, boy," the man whispered. Far too close." Alan gasped for air, the man's forearm pressing further into his trachea. The rancid smell of coffee oozed off the man's lips and Alan grimaced in spite of everything. Suddenly, he was released and he staggered forward, clutching at his throat and sucking in harsh, ragged breaths. The colour started to return a little to his face. Alan looked back up as the man leveled the gun at his face, a smirk on his lips. The silence in the room was thunderous.

"Prrroww?" Misfit poked her face around the side of the door, her own eyes wide. The sudden noise startled the gunman, and his arm swung as if on a pivot, firing the gun in the cat's direction.

"NOOO!" Alan screamed, sliding down the wall and toward the door in an attempt to get away. Alan's movement brought the gun back to where he had been, and another round blasted a hole in the wall. The gunman cursed at his misfire, and tracked Alan's movement to where he cowered on the floor near the door. The gunman pulled back the hammer once more and took aim, and then there was a sound, from outside. The neighbour's dog had started barking, and Alan could hear voices from the house down the way. A shimmer of relief passed over Alan's face, but then, lightning-quick, the gunman lunged at him, keeping the gun aimed at his face.

"Stay away!" the gunman breathed. "We're always here. We're always watching. Remember that, and STAY AWAY!" Then the gunman was up and out of the room, and Alan stared ahead with terrified eyes as he heard the bedsprings squeak and the man who had imprisoned Parissa followed his partner's shadow. In the ensuing silence, Alan could hear Parissa weeping softly.

From his vantage point on the floor he couldn't make out the hour, but his alarm clock ticked away about twenty minutes before he found the strength to stand. Parissa was still sobbing, burying her face in the pillows. He went to her, and at first she tried to get away, tried to scramble up the wall away from him. Her eyes held all the fear of a wild animal, and it was several long, tense minutes before Alan could calm her out of her panic. She began to shiver as he hugged her, her tears hot and wet as they landed on his shoulder.

*    *    *    *    *    *

Out of exhaustion and fear they had fallen asleep again, and when Alan woke up he saw Parissa standing near the door, her face ashen. For a brief moment he thought it had all been a dream, and then saw the bullet hole in the wall and realized it had not. He looked back towards Parissa.

"'Rissa? You okay?" He went to stand by her and looked where she was looking.

There, just outside the door, in a pool of blood, Misfit lay dead.

## XVI

He buried her in the yard beneath an enormous willow. Of everything that had happened – the shop, the apparent death of Celeste, the murder of his mother – this one hit the closest to home. Misfit, a loving, loyal companion for twelve years, as affectionate as a baby and as serene as a lake in the fall. Misfit, slung on his left shoulder for three hours as he walked around the animal shelter, talking with the lady in charge, looking around at the assortment of cages set around the converted basement in a sort of organized chaos.

He had gone there to see about another cat, a lovable bruiser named Charlemagne, but the poor boy had undergone hernia surgery the day before and was in no mood to socialize. Alan had put his hand out in a gesture of goodwill, but Charlemagne had slunk under a couch and took to growling at anything that came close. Misfit, on the other hand, stood on a high shelf and pawed the air as Alan passed. He looked up into her face, her emerald eyes looking so intently into his. He took her down from the shelf and she had settled onto his shoulder like it was the coziest place in the world, purring almost constantly the entire time. Even when he sat to sign the paperwork, she kept trying to nudge his hand. Insistence was the name of the game, it seemed. The shelter owner instructed him that it was perfectly normal for a cat to "hide out" for up to three or four days in a brand new environment. Misfit made herself scarce for only two hours, and then she was out and about, rubbing her face over any surface she could reach.

Alan could not have asked for a more doting companion than his tiny, cross-eyed sweetheart.

It took him close to an hour to dig the small hole in the earth, sweat and tears mingling together down his face. He placed her delicately in a shoebox, an embroidered cloth covering her little head. His face contorted in sorrow as he laid her to rest. Parissa hung back by the house, clutching her arms with her hands.

He was sobbing quietly as he began to fill in the hole, his hands shaking as he held the shovel. When, at last, he had replaced the last of the dirt, he tamped it down a couple of times, smoothing it out. Then he let the shovel just slip out of his hands as he knelt down beside it.

"How much more?" he whispered to himself. "How much more can I be expected to take?" He ran a hand across his nose, coating his index and thumb in a thin film of mucus. His tears began to flow in a steady stream as he looked down on his baby. "You've taken everything I am," he muttered. He looked upward. He never believed in a God, but he looked up all the same. "Why? WHY?"

Behind him, Parissa broke down.

*     *     *     *     *     *

Back inside the house, Alan's cell began ringing constantly with condolences for him regarding the loss of his shop. Mostly regulars. His part-timer, Sophie, called to ask what she should do now, and Alan didn't have a clue. Sophie was a sweet girl, 17 years old and top of her class in the local high school. All Alan could think of was to offer her a good reference should she decide to apply for other jobs. He felt horrible for suggesting it, not that Sophie didn't deserve it, but because he wished he didn't have to in the first place. Sophie thanked him and hung up.

The calls kept coming so frequently that he was obliged to use Parissa's cell to call Celeste. He was about to hang up on the fifth ring when she picked up, her voice sleepy.

"Goo' mornin'?" Despite everything, her habit of making basic statements into hazy questions when she was just waking up made him smile.

"Mornin', Celeste. How are you doing?" he said.

"Urrrnnn...fine?" she stretched and made a squeaky noise. He remembered suddenly how that noise used to drive Misfit nuts and he had to purse his lips together in a desperate attempt at composure. "Whose number are you calling from?"

"Parissa's. I had to turn my cell off for now because of all the sympathy calls coming in for me about the shop." *Although they should be calling about my cat,* he thought but did not say.

"Oh, I see." Celeste said.

"I was wondering if I could ask a favour," Alan said. "Just a little one."

"What's up?"

He looked over at Parissa, who was staring into space with an expression of desperate sadness. She looked absolutely defeated. "I was going to rent a car and go visit my dad this morning, up in Massey Bay. Tell him about what's happened with mom, and all that." He cleared his throat. "I would like for Parissa not to be alone here while I'm gone. Do you think it'd be okay if she came and stayed with you until I get back?" His voice was hopeful, even though he felt the request sounded like he was asking Celeste to babysit his child. Celeste didn't even hesitate.

"Definitely. I'm sticking pretty close to home for a few days, so it's fine. Just buzz when you get here."

"Thanks, Celeste. I owe you double."

Alan hung up and put the cell down on the table. When he looked over at Parissa, he saw that her expression hadn't much changed.

"Parissa? Hey..." he put his hand on hers. It was icy cold. "Hey," he said again, giving her hand a light shake. She looked up at him slowly, with those same empty, sad eyes.

"I'm not going away forever," she whispered. "It's just university, Mother." Her voice was distant, and she seemed to look through him with eyes half-closed.

"What?" Alan said, concern clouding his face.

"Father will kill you when he finds out you're dating." Her voice was haunted now. "Why do you always have to be like this?"

Alan rose from his chair and knelt down in front of her. "Parissa? 'Rissa, it's me!"

She looked at him as if in a dream. "I just want to go home."

# *XVII*

The cool evening air ripped through Noah's bloodied dress shirt as he limped back to his apartment complex from the restaurant. Any thought of going to see a doctor was long forgotten, as he tried to sort out in his head the best plan of action.

*Eliminate her. Kill her. Show your loyalty.*

He stumbled on the third step leading to the front doors of the complex, and almost fell. Once he got up to the door, he reached into his pocket for the key, and experienced a brief moment of panic when he couldn't feel it. Then the cool metal pressed into his palm and he pulled it out, bringing a large clump of lint along with it. Inside, he had to wait several minutes for the elevator to take him up to the 14th floor. The waiting gave him too much time to think.

*You always have a choice.*

He was dead tired as he dragged his feet into the lift.

The elevator chimed as it reached his floor, and the door whispered open onto the hall. He stepped out slowly, cautiously, muscles tensed in anticipation of...well, he wasn't sure. He stood outside his door for a long time, rocking from foot to foot, almost in a trance. Inside the front door, sitting in a drawer, was his Glock. He kept an extra clip on the top shelf of the hall closet. The whole job would take less than two minutes, three if she struggled. He closed his eyes and fought back tears. Could he really go through with it?

He still wasn't sure when he opened the door.

\*     \*     \*     \*     \*     \*

Inside was silence. Inside was uncertainty. Inside was a torrent of emotions that Noah could barely control. He looked down at the side table and saw that the drawer was open, and the gun was easily visible. He thought he'd closed it when he came in earlier. How the cops had missed it as they'd shuffled him out in cuffs was a mystery. Lady Luck hadn't completely abandoned him after all. But if the drawer was open...

"She knows," he said to himself in a whisper. He pulled the Glock from its hiding place and palmed it, feeling its weight. Two pounds of black death sat in his hand. All he had to do was rack the clip and find the girl he loved. He slid open the closet door and reached up past the board games and dusty jigsaw puzzle boxes to find the spare clip. He closed his fingers around it and pulled it down. He held it in his open palm and stared at it, horrified at the thought of what he was about to do.

"You're going to do it, aren't you?"

He spun on his heel to see Mina standing on the other side of the closet door, her eyes staring up at him, dark and haunted.

"What?" he whispered, suddenly very afraid.

"Kill me. Like that man said. 'Prove your loyalty,' right?" A single tear slid down her cheek unheeded. She just kept staring at him with those dark, dead eyes.

"I..." His voice broke and he couldn't finish. She shuffled towards him with slow, soundless steps.

"Said all I was good for was fucking and looking pretty," she said. "Is that true? Is that all I am to you? Just some pretty Iranian whore for you to show off to the world? Maybe suck your dick till you can't see straight? IS THAT ALL I AM TO YOU?" She was sobbing now, pulling at her hair, yanking out whole clumps of it with her hands.

"What..." Noah backed away from her into the living room. Her anger was edging dangerously close to madness, and he was terrified. "No! Mina...*I love you!*"

"Do you love me when I do this?" She pulled out more hair. "Or maybe when I do *THIS?*" She reached one hand down and grabbed at her crotch, rubbing it hard while her other hand tore her blouse open. She ripped her breast free and squeezed it, her nails biting painfully into the soft flesh. "You like that, huh? And when you get tired of me, you just kill me?" Her eyes blazed. "*FUCK YOU!*" She flung herself at him, enraged. He tried to fend her off, and her fist knocked the gun out of his hand. It clattered across the floor to the wall. She broke through his defenses and began beating at his chest, howling in tears.

"No no no no no no no..." he said. His guilt overwhelmed him and he pulled her to him in an embrace. She fought him at first, but was at last overcome and clung to him in anguish. He rocked her gently in his arms, her cries softening. He kept repeating 'no' in her ear as they rocked, unable to say more.

He looked down at her finally, tilting her face up to his. "I love you," he whispered. "You mean more to me than my own life." And he kissed her, a soft, full, soul-penetrating kiss, so unlike any other kiss he'd given her. Mina wrapped her arms around his neck just in time, as her knees couldn't hold her anymore. She pressed against him, her body craving his. He responded in kind, the heat of him pressed hard against her core.

When at last they broke off, the air between them seemed to hum. He held her away from him and regarded her as if for the first time. *Or is it the last?* She inhaled deeply and he saw her breast, still free of her blouse, was bleeding. Four little puncture wounds encircled her areola, and he reached for it with concern.

"Don't," she said. "Please. Don't. It hurts, but please just leave it alone." Her voice was strengthless. He pulled her back into his arms and cradled her like a baby.

His attention was caught by a white van as it pulled up on the street at the end of the alley their apartment overlooked, and the sliding door opened in a rush. Out of it piled the same three men he'd seen earlier that evening, and he watched in shock as they talked among themselves. This time they were wearing all black. This time they were armed. One of them started counting floors.

*Me. They're looking for me.*

The man counting froze his finger and Noah felt like he was pointing directly at him. The man's face broke apart in an enormous grin and alerted his cohorts to the couple standing in the window. The trio moved to the front entrance and that was enough to break Noah's paralysis. He began dragging Mina away from the window.

"What are you doing?" she cried.

"You have to get out of here. Now!"

"What? What do you mean, get out?"

He yanked her sweater off the back of the chair and thrust it in her face. He felt in his back pocket for his wallet and then forced it into her hand, all the while pushing her towards the door.

"You need to get out, get out, GET OUT!" he shouted. The look of puzzlement on her face forced him to explain. "Take the stairs. Find Alan. Find your sister. If the men come here and they catch you…"

"What men? What are you talking about?!"

"JUST GO!" He was already picking up the Glock from the floor and slamming the magazine home. "Three men are coming to kill us. First you, then me," he said as he shoved her out the door. A glance at the elevator told him they were already on 9. "And I don't intend to let them. Go!" He shoved her down the hall toward the stairs. She staggered a little before finding her footing and looked back at him, tears streaming down her face once again.

11...12...

He waved at her frantically from the doorway and she turned to run to the stairwell at the end of the hall. She wrenched open the door with her free hand and slipped out of sight.

The elevator door opened just as the stairwell door latched shut.

*    *    *    *    *    *

Noah closed the door to the apartment and double-locked it just as the first man strode off the elevator into the hallway, moving backward down the hall toward the bedroom, his breath coming in ragged gasps. He could hear them talking outside in the corridor, trying to figure out which door to try. He brought the gun up to his chest, cocking the hammer as he did so. He kept retreating, trying to keep distance between him and them.

Once inside the bedroom, he shut the door. His breath was barely audible now, his eyes bulged out in fear and anticipation. Tiny rivulets of perspiration started to slip down his temples and his shirt felt cold and clammy. There was a loud splintering noise as the front door was kicked in, and he felt the coolness of the window through his shirt as he pressed against it. He had reached the end of the line.

He closed his eyes for a moment, as if in prayer, but it wasn't to God he was speaking.

*Find Alan. Find your sister. Go. Be safe.*

He heard them as they came down the hallway, banging open doors and calling his name. He raised the gun, gauntleting his right hand with his left, aiming it at the door. He held it there, his hands shaking with adrenaline.

*You won't take her. You won't take me. Just watch.*

The three men were on the other side of the bedroom door, calling his name. The door suddenly blew inward and splinters of wood flew through the air. Noah didn't flinch. The three men burst into the room, weapons ready. For a terrible moment that spanned a lifetime, nobody breathed, and another runnel of sweat trickled down Noah's cheek.

"Get out," the man in the middle finally said. "Wait in the hall." The two men flanking him lowered their weapons and stepped over the remains of the door as they exited. The man in black cracked his knuckles and slowly moved towards Noah. "Where is she?" he said.

"Who?" Noah replied.

"Your whore. The one you were told to kill. Where is she?"

"She's safe. Safe where you can't get to her."

The man in black cackled with glee at the smug defiance the boy was showing. Defiance? Yes. But also misplaced loyalty. In a heartbeat, he lunged at Noah, wrestling him for his weapon. Noah was slammed backward against the window, and long fractures snaked out across the glass.

"Fuck you!" Noah said through gritted teeth. His body screamed in pain from a hundred different places, but he fought back, knowing that every little minute gave Mina the time that she needed. He hoped she had made it away from the building. Hoped like hell. He felt two large hands encase his as the man in black tried to both pry apart his fingers and push the gun back into his face. He heard more cracks and the fractures on the window branched off in larger tendrils. His strength was flagging and the man in black sensed it, pushing the gun a few more inches toward him. Sweat began to pour down Noah's face. It was like arm-wrestling a grizzly.

Motion, down in the alley.

*Mina.*

Down at the far end of the alley, in the opposite direction Mina was heading, was a beat cop.

The man in black shoved him a third time, and the glass finally gave way, shattering. One large shard burrowed into his back about an inch before snapping off, turning Noah's face white with agony. A fourth push sent Noah's head through the window, a jagged piece of glass slicing his forehead and narrowly missing his left eye. He looked down the alleyway toward the beat cop, who was just moving out of sight behind the building. He looked back up at the man in black, and gambled.

"Fuck you," Noah said through clenched teeth. "I hope you fucking *rot* for what you've done." He looked the man in black dead in the eye, and tucked the barrel under his own chin.

Noah waited three seconds.

Then he pulled the trigger.

# XVIII

She ran headlong down the stairs and when she reached the bottom she failed to negotiate the final turn and slammed face first into the fire door leading outside. She stumbled back a step and shook her head before grabbing the panic bar and pushing the door out. The cool air of the alley made her shiver, and the cuts on her exposed breast flared in pain. She paused a moment to tuck it gingerly back into her bra and then slipped the sweater down over her head. In doing so, she felt his wallet slip and fall out of her hand onto the concrete. As she bent over to pick it up, she heard a window smash and a shower of glass tumbled down around her. She screamed a little, and then looked up as she backed away from the building, terrified of what she might see but looking anyway.

*Please don't be dead please don't be dead please...*

She *didn't* see right away, and that was okay. But then she *did* see. And that was bad. Very bad.

Noah was hanging out of their bedroom window, struggling with someone dressed all in black. Part of the window had shattered and there appeared to be blood on the bottom part of the window that hadn't broken

*Find Alan. Find your sister. Get out.*

She ran.

\*　　\*　　\*　　\*　　\*　　\*

She flagged down a cab at the corner and flung open the back door.

"Where to, Mi—"

She panicked when she couldn't remember where Alan lived. Then it came all at once. "Shallot's Cove! I need to get to Shallot's Cove!" Her voice quavered with fear.

"What?! Shallot's Cove is over an hour's drive away!"

Mina reached into Noah's wallet and pulled out a wad of bills, mostly twenties and fifties, and waved the cash in the driver's face. "I have money! Please! Drive!" She slammed the door closed and in the instant before the driver stepped on the gas, she heard a gunshot from the direction of the alleyway.

*Maybe Noah shot him. He had his gun.*

Mina curled into a ball in the back seat.

*Part III*

# I

Hanging up the phone on her ten years ago was the most difficult thing I ever had to do. I didn't want to, but I had to. It was either that or resign myself to her bullshit in perpetuity. I remember standing in my living room staring at the phone resting on my palm for I don't know how long, torn between hoping she'd call back and knowing she wouldn't.

That was the biggest obstacle I almost couldn't hurdle, hoping for something different despite what 30 years of experience told me. I always hoped that one day she'd get it. She was my mother, after all.

But when I got the call from Parissa, my whole life shut down. The one thing I never expected to feel was what ended up suffocating me. The guilt was almost unbearable.

The guilt!

Nobody in their right mind, upon hearing my story, would ever consider guilt as the emotion that would bring me down. Relief? Definitely. Sadness? Possibly. But guilt? That came completely from left field. I'd hated her, felt sorry for her, felt sorry for *myself*... But the emotional battlefield I'd fought in for so long had at last been trampled into oblivion. All the things I hoped one day to tell her could now only be shouted into empty space. Everything I wished could be fixed between us died with her in that damp, black hole.

Then the phone calls began. Celeste. My shop. Mr. Getzel. Misfit... all the things I held dear were ripped away from me. I told Parissa I loved her, and now she sits, staring, swallowed up by an incomprehensible despair.

*Why...?*

## II

Mina stared out the window of the cab with red-ringed eyes, watching the layers of the city peel away until they reached the 'Hat, a stretch of lonely highway that snaked its way through the mountains. The cabbie had not attempted conversation with her, but he kept sneaking concerned glances in the rear-view as he drove. As she watched the sun dip down behind a peak, Mina began to realize that she couldn't remember Alan's address; in Noah's hurry to get her out of danger, all she had was his wallet – which was filled with more cash than she'd ever seen him carry in his life – and the clothes on her back. Her cell phone still sat on the dresser in their bedroom.

*Noah...*

She couldn't think about him right now. In spite of everything, she felt humiliated for bawling like a child in the backseat of the cab. She couldn't let the tears flow anymore. *Spare me more shame*, she thought. She looked up toward the cabbie and met his eyes in the mirror for an instant before he snapped his attention back to the road. She hugged her legs closer to her chest, shivering. She had never felt so alone. So *vulnerable*. She looked up at the back of the cabbie's head once more, only to see his eyes looking at her in the mirror again.

"What?" she snapped, her anger wrapping itself around her like an old familiar blanket. This time, however, she regretted her tone. Hated how hard and brittle she sounded. She wanted desperately to take back what she had said, but it was too late and the eyes that looked back at her in the mirror were weighted with sadness. She felt her heart struggle against the weight of her own sorrow, and she stared forcefully out her window again, unblinking, trying to will the pain away. This man was an innocent, and she had no reason to be angry at him. Her brusqueness did little to change his expression, and when he spoke there was an unmistakable tone of deep concern.

"I'm sorry, Miss. I do not mean to pry. Forgive me."

His words hit her hard, and her vision began to swim once more.

He did not look back at her after that, until the lights of Shallot's Cove winked brightly in the distance. Night had almost completely fallen, and with the city of Waterford miles behind her, she looked up into the sky, breathless for a moment at the ocean of stars above her.

"Miss?"

His voice made her jump, and she squeaked a little in her throat. She took a moment to collect herself and then looked towards him. "Yes?"

"We're almost there." He pointed out the lights of the town limits. "Shallot's Cove is just ahead. Do you have an address?"

She thought hard for a minute. She'd made a point to not keep in serious contact with Alan for the past several years. Her anger had seen to that. She was starting to realize there was some serious bridge-mending to be done in the next little while. She tried to remember something – anything – about where Alan might live or the name of his business. She came up blank.

"Miss?"

"I'm...I'm sorry. I can't remember." She tried to think of an alternative. A town this small wouldn't have a hotel, would it? Not even a motel. She sighed in despair as the taxi pulled over to the shoulder, the tires whispering in the gravel. The driver fiddled with his GPS for a few moments, and then spoke.

"Miss? There's a Bed & Breakfast about two miles up the road. How about I take you there? Is that all right?" His tone was so comforting. She nodded, and the taxi pulled back onto the road, its headlights piercing the darkness.

As the cab turned a minute or so later, she saw the sign for the Shallot's Cove Bed & Breakfast pass by her window, illuminated by a single globe lamp. She took a long, slow breath in through her nose and felt tears well up in her eyes again as she thought about what brought her here. She had tried to remain hopeful, but even as they'd driven through the mountains, she knew in her heart of hearts that Noah was dead, that Noah had died so her life could be saved...

*     *     *     *     *     *

She had stood in the bedroom staring into nothingness for what seemed like an eternity, the phone's open line droning like a sluggish fly from where it lay on the floor. The words the man on the phone had spoken echoed in her mind, feeding the fear growing inside her. After a long time, she had come to herself and begun to pace around the apartment aimlessly, her fear slowly dissipating and turning to a hopelessness she couldn't fathom. She had a vague memory of pulling out the butcher knife from the wooden block on the kitchen counter and holding it carefully in her hand, feeling its weight. She twisted her wrist a little, catching the overhead fluorescents on the flat of the blade and gazing at it, almost in a hypnotic trance. She held her other wrist up over the sink and brought the blade down, resting it gently on her skin. Her heart was pounding, and she could see the tiny veins under her skin pulsate against the edge of the knife. It wouldn't take long, she had thought. Just a couple of quick movements and there wouldn't be anything left to worry about.

But she had stopped herself at the last moment. She rose from the depths just enough to realize this was not a path she wanted to take. She let the knife fall from her hand into the sink, the metal clattering flatly in the basin.

She wandered back toward the bedroom then, her brain sinking down into the darkness once more. *His little whore. His little Iranian whore.* That's when she heard the rattle of Noah's key in the lock, and the sound of the door opening brought her to the edge of the hallway. He was too preoccupied with the gun in the side table, and with the closet, to hear her come up beside him. She knew then what he was there to do. It was written all over his face. But there was doubt there also. He was there to kill her, but the grey of his face and the way his hands shook betrayed his true feelings.

Then, the panicked look on his face as he pushed her toward the door. Through the door and down the hallway to the stairwell. He had held her in his arms and told her he loved her, that he loved her more than his own life. She closed her eyes then. In the back seat of the cab she bit her lip in a mad attempt not to cry. She took another deep breath through her nose, and looked up to see the cabbie turned toward her from the driver's seat with an expectant look on his face.

"We're here, Miss. Shallot's Cove." He smiled clumsily.

Mina nodded her head. She opened his wallet, the smell of his cologne wafting delicately out of the pores of the leather as she pulled out four fifties – about what she figured the trip would cost – and looked at the bills for a long time, the smell of him lingering on her fingers. He smelled like this as he held her close to his chest in their apartment that afternoon, her face hot with tears and his voice murmuring gentle reassurances in her ear. Her chin quivered. She extended her hand to give him the money, and the driver put up his hand, palm out. She looked him in the eye as he shook his head.

"No, Miss. No."

"But..." She glanced at the meter. Her eyes widened at the display, which read *TIME OFF*. "But, I must...you drove me so far beyond..."

The driver shook his head again, this time a little smile crinkling the corners of his eyes. "No, Miss. I can't accept this. When you got into my cab, you looked scared to death, like you were running for your life. I heard the gunshot. Also..." the cabbie paused for a moment, looking a little embarrassed. "Also, you're wearing slippers. No woman in a situation that wasn't life or death would run out of a building wearing just her slippers."

Mina looked down at her feet in shock. On her feet were her angora slippers, a gift from her father a year earlier. She looked back up at the driver, and tried again to give him the money.

"Go," the cabbie said, tipping his hat. "Go and be safe."

Mina bowed her head in despair and relief, barely managing a *Thank You* to the driver as she stepped out of the cab. After she gave the door a gentle shove, the driver waved at her one final time before backing out of the driveway, and heading off into the night.

She looked up at the Victorian-style house with the wraparound porch, and started walking up the drive.

The tiny foyer of the house was warmly lit by simple but elegant wall sconces at either end of the little desk, upon which sat a leather-bound register. Mina shut the door behind her cautiously, looking around to see who might be running things. *Maybe they're all in bed*, she thought. A tall, dark shape caught her attention, and she turned in panic towards it. Standing in solemn majesty in the corner was a large grandfather clock, ornate designs carved into its wooden frame and the long brass pendulum swinging hypnotically from side to side. *Tick…tick…tick…tick…* The yellowed face declared the time to be just after nine in the evening. She was trying to catch her breath and calm herself when a voice spoke, only a foot from her right ear.

"Good evening, little miss," the voice said.

Mina screamed.

"Oh, the Lord in heaven!" the voice shouted in response. Mina backed up all the way to the door before she had a chance to really look at the woman who had come within a hair's breadth of giving her a heart attack. Another voice called out from an unseen part of the house.

"What on earth was that?" This voice was male, a rich baritone, gold and silky like aged scotch.

Mina's eyes darted back and forth between the voice she couldn't see and the woman who stood before her, dressed in a simple blue blouse and a full-length tartan skirt. The grandfather clock's pendulum seemed to sway in time with her pounding heart, and her breath was shallow and shivery. She wanted to turn and wrench open the door, wanted to run out into the night, terrified and directionless like a fawn with a predator hot on its heels. The cold of the brass doorknob shocked her as her fingers wrapped around it, and broke through her terror. Slowly, she peeled her hand away from the doorknob and turned to face the woman who still stood facing her, her own face tight and frightened.

"I'm...my...I'm Mina Khorasani," she began, her voice a dry, breathless whisper. "I was wondering if I might be able to stay here tonight." Her eyes dropped in shame to the carpet, feeling that she was truly alone for the first time that she could remember.

The woman took a few steps towards Mina and brought an arm up to put around her shoulder, but Mina cowered at the gesture and the woman let her arm fall to her side after only the slightest hesitation at Mina's reaction.

"Certainly, dear," the woman said, trying to put the girl at ease with a comforting tone. "Would you come over here to the registration book with me?"

"Everything all right out there?" the silky baritone spoke again.

"It's all fine out here, Hammond," the woman called out. "No need for you to put down that confounded pipe of yours." The woman looked over at Mina and winked. "Now, Miss...Mina, did you say?"

The girl nodded.

"Well, Mina, my name is Esther. We have a lovely room on the top floor which overlooks a small duck pond. Would you like that?" Mina furrowed her eyebrows at Esther for a moment, not understanding what she asked, and then the confusion broke and she nodded.

"Sorry, it's been...a long day," Mina said. *Well, that's being very charitable,* she thought, and closed her eyes against the image of Noah tumbling halfway out of their bedroom window. *Did he fall?* She thought. *I can't remember if he fell. NO! Stop thinking about this stop thinking about it stop do you hear me it does you no good to think about*

She opened her eyes to see Esther looking at her with a worried look on her face. Mina took a deep breath and tried to focus her mind on the task at hand. She reached out for the pen sitting on the desk next to the register and she tried to sign her name on the line where Esther was pointing, but her hand was shaking far too much at first. She closed her eyes in frustration.

"Would you like a glass of water, dear?" Esther said.

Mina, who had never tasted anything stronger than coffee in her entire life, surprised herself by thinking, *I would take a shot of whiskey right now if you offered it. Anything to steady my hand and help me forget.* She opened her eyes again and answered, "Yes, please."

Her voice. So weak. Esther turned and swished out of the room, her tartan skirt whispering against her legs. Mina picked up the pen once more and tried to sign her name. This time she willed her hand to steady itself, just enough for both her name and the date, which she entered in the space just to the right. She let the pen drop back onto the desk and stared blankly at the towering grandfather clock until Esther came back and presented her with a tall glass of water, ice cubes clattering softly at the brim.

"Thank you," Mina said. Her voice was stronger now, and the tremors in her hands had all but disappeared.

"Not at all," Esther said, checking and then closing the registry. "Now, dinner finished up a couple of hours ago, but if you'd like I can make you a sandwich. Are you hungry at all, or would you like to be shown to your room?"

Mina's stomach grumbled at the mention of food, and why not? It had been at least seven hours since she'd last eaten. Esther smiled at the sound.

"Sounds like your belly has made the decision for you," she chuckled, a soft, maternal sound. "Come, this way. I'll whip you up something a little nicer than just a plain old sandwich." With that, she put an arm around Mina's shoulders, and smiled a little wider when Mina did not cower as she had before.

*     *     *     *     *     *

Mina's slippered feet made creaking footfalls on the carpeted stair as she was led up to her room and the beef stew Esther had served her sat warmly in her stomach. With the stew had come an overwhelming wave of exhaustion.

"Here you are, Miss," Esther said. "The bathroom is here, across the hall from your door. Towels and the like are in the closet here, next to it." She gestured at a tall, skinny door before continuing. "The last of our guests left yesterday, so you have the whole floor to yourself. Well, what I mean to say is you won't be disturbing anyone. My husband Hammond and I sleep downstairs, just off the kitchen. Breakfast is at eight, and if you like I can give you an alarm call first thing."

"Alarm call?" Mina said.

"Yes. On the bedside telephone. So you don't miss breakfast. Would 7am be all right?"

Mina nodded slowly. Her brain was clouding over fast, sleep was not far away. Esther patted her once on the shoulder and left the room, her tread catching every creak on the stairway.

She shuffled over to the window, her eyes barely able to focus. Outside, the moon shimmered on the duck pond in lazy ripples, and a few bulrushes waved light and easy in the breeze. She opened the window a little, and the wood frame grunted in response. She sank into a plush upholstered chair and felt the air upon her face. Somewhere in the distance, a barn owl *hoo-hooed* and she could hear the rushes in the pond rustle carefully, secretly. Here in Shallot's Cove, with the night sky drowning in stars, she felt a peace steal over her that she hadn't felt in a long time. *Years*, she thought. *It's been years since you've felt like this.* Her eyes brimmed over with tears, surprising her with their suddenness and their abundance. She tried to control it, but her cheeks were already wet with them.

She thought of Noah. Noah...dear, sweet Noah, who had given his life so that she might live. In her exhausted state, that thought did not seem as preposterous as others might think. He had seen the danger coming and in that moment thought only of her safety, of ensuring her protection. The images returned. Her slippered feet whispering on the carpet in the hall as she bolted for the fire stairwell. The sound of the door closing behind her. Scurrying down the stairs towards the exit. She reached up a trembling hand to her face and wiped away a mat of tears from her cheeks, and watched a small shadow – a duck – swim out into the middle of the pond. It floated into the middle of the moonbeam and then pushed its head under the water, its tail feathers wriggling for a moment before righting itself and shaking its head. She couldn't see it clearly, but imagined a fine spray of water erupting from around its face as it did so. Then it turned and slipped back into the shadows, just a quick midnight snack before returning to sleep.

She rose from the chair then, slowly. The breeze had stiffened her joints a little, made movement a little more pronounced. She stepped out of her slippers and clothes before pulling the coverlet back, and slipping between the icy sheets. She lay there, shivering, sleep banished for just a moment as she tried to warm herself in the expansive king-sized bed. That feeling of smallness, of *vulnerability*, washed over her again.

There was a sound from downstairs, a gruff, throat-clearing noise, presumably from Hammond, but she did not hear it.

Mina slept.

*    *    *    *    *    *

The hallway stretched for miles beyond the bedroom doorway as she stepped over the threshold, watching Noah wander toward the closet. She watched as he pulled down a small black box from a shelf, regarding it sadly as it lay in his hand. She started to walk towards him, wanting to rip that black evil from his hands. She shouted his name

*NOAH!!!*

but no sound came out of her mouth. She began to run, and the hallway seemed to telescope outward, taking him farther from her the faster she ran. She screamed his name silently over and over, as he snapped the box into the handle of the gun he held in his right hand. She looked back over her shoulder at the bedroom door, which now dwindled in the distance behind her. She was miles from where she started, but Noah was still far beyond her reach.

There was a loud, splintering crack as the front door disintegrated under the force of the kick that felled it, and three formless black shapes filled the hall just in front of Noah. She could see the glint of gunmetal in their hands; could see the blazing furnace in their eyes as they towered over the man she loved.

Noah heard the sound too late, brought the gun up far too late. The black shape in the middle, the biggest of the three, aimed its monstrous gun – it looked more like a cannon – straight at Noah's head. She put on the brakes and skidded to a stop, screaming at Noah to duck, oh please DUCK! DUUUUCK!!!!

A bullet the size of a softball rocketed out of the end of the gun

*cannon*

and vaporized Noah's head upon impact. The bullet roared past her left ear and buried itself in a wall far behind her. Noah's headless body slumped to the floor, blood spraying from his neck in an impossible jet across the walls.

She stood there, barely breathing as the forms turned their fiery eyes to her, stepping over Noah like an old newspaper as they toward her. She took a step backward and slipped in the growing pool of blood flowing out of Noah's neck

*he was right in front of me oh God why couldn't he hear me*

and she fell hard on her tailbone, cracking it. The formless evil towered over her, and she saw grinning teeth glittering like a great white shark's in the moonlight. The barrel of the gun in her face, the blackness within it reaching out to swallow her whole. The smell of burning gunpowder was everywhere.

The trigger, pulled.

*RRRRING!*

She fell on the floor with a bang, her hair wrapped around her skull and neck in sweaty, clinging fingers.

*Rrriiiing!*

She looked up over the edge of the bed towards the night stand on the opposite side, where the little white phone sat, its little dull red light pulsing in time with the ring.

*Rrriiiing!*

She looked at her watch, which told her it was seven o'clock in the morning. Her alarm call, right on time, just as Esther had said. The sun had already poked its face up over the horizon, and the few clouds in the sky had their underbellies tinged with gold. Even the breeze coming through the window crack seemed cheerful. She pulled herself up onto the bed with shaking arms and stared out the window, not daring to close her eyes. In the darkness behind her eyelids the nightmare figures would be back, and they would finish what they had started. First Noah, and then her.

The phone rang again and then fell silent at last. With trembling fingers, she pulled away the tendrils of hair that were wrapped across her nose. The smell of fear lingered on her sweat and it sharpened as she moved. She stood up and walked to the bathroom. She needed a shower.

She stepped cautiously out of her room, her large eyes even wider now on the heels of the nightmare and in the unfamiliarity of the house. She crossed the hall to the linen closet and found a stack of towels, chose two and then closed the door with a click. She stepped into the bathroom a little more quickly than necessary, as if something might reach out and catch her ankle at the last moment. She closed the door and slid the tiny bolt across, the power of the nightmare still strong enough to make her think that a bolt this small would never hold back those terrible dark figures, that they'd break down the door just as easily as they had at the apartment. She shook her head. The face that looked back at her in the mirror looked older. Looked haunted. *Hunted.*

She turned away from the sink and saw that there was no shower. Just a claw-foot tub, cream on the inside and sponge painted dark red on the outside. *How elegant,* she thought, as she turned the hot and cold taps. The sound of the water splashing heavily into the tub shook the last of her fear and her nightmare away, and soon she was lost in the scent of lavender as she slipped into the warm, bubbly water.

*    *    *    *    *    *

Esther met her at the bottom of the stairs as she came down, the treads complaining mightily under her feet. Mina felt very self-conscious wearing the same clothes she had worn yesterday, despite knowing it couldn't be helped.

"Breakfast, dear?" Esther asked.

Mina's stomach gurgled again before she could take a breath to answer, and Esther laughed, a light, bell-like sound that even pulled the corners of Mina's mouth into a smile. Mina nodded, still smiling and yet feeling hot shame at the cheerfulness Esther brought out of her. She shouldn't feel happy, not even a little, not when Noah lay dead back in their apartment or behind the building in the alleyway.

The thought took some of the light out of her eyes again, but Esther was already leading her from the foyer back into the dining room where she had eaten the night before.

"Did you sleep well?" Esther asked after setting a fluffy omelet and a fruit salad on the spotless linen in front of Mina. For an instant it all came rushing back to her: the endless hallway, the soundless screams, Noah lying on the floor, blood flowing

*sometimes I think I'd forget my head if it wasn't screwed* on

out of his neck and the formless shapes, black and towering and evil...

Mina shook her head gently, clearing away the memory of that nightmare from her mind, and looked across at Esther with what she hoped was a genuine smile.

"Fine, thank you." She watched Esther dip a piece of buttered toast into the heart of a soft-boiled egg sitting regally in its tiny porcelain cup on her plate, and then turned her attention back to her omelet. The two women sat together for a few moments, not speaking, the silence punctuated at random intervals by the rustle of a newspaper that Hammond was reading in the bedroom just beyond the kitchen doors.

Esther was mopping up the last of her egg yolk with her toast when Mina broke the silence again.

"Thank you for letting me stay here last night, and with no notice at all. You'll never know how much I appreciate everything you've done." Mina scarcely recognised her own voice, the hardness and anger were a distant memory. It was as though she had left all the bitterness and animosity behind her in her flight from the apartment. Esther reached out and patted the back of Mina's hand in quiet acceptance.

"Not at all, my dear," she said. "The look on your face last night told me a great deal. You looked like the hounds of the Devil himself were nipping at your heels. I've never seen anyone look so frightened in all my life, and I've seen a great deal, I can promise you," Esther smiled again. "But all's well that ends well." She began to collect their dishes up from the table, not speaking for a moment. Mina heard the ducks splashing in the pond outside and turned her head in that direction, smiling mutedly.

Esther said something she didn't hear. She turned back to the woman with an apologetic look.

"I'm sorry, what did you say?" Mina asked.

"I asked if you were staying another night," Esther said.

"Oh," Mina replied. "No, I don't think so. I'm actually here to see an old friend." She hesitated just a moment, and then her face brightened a little with hope. "Perhaps you can help me?"

Esther looked at her with a reassuring gaze. "In Shallot's Cove, everyone knows everyone. I think that's one of the things I love so much about living here, that sense of community. It makes one feel very secure. Who are you looking for?"

"Alan Black," Mina answered.

Esther's face darkened immediately, a look Mina didn't care for at all. *With all that's happened, please don't let Alan be in trouble too,* she thought. Esther spoke again.

"I see. I don't know how much I should tell you. Is Alan a close friend?"

Mina nodded.

"Well, we all had a pretty bad shock here in the Cove. *Bookends* – that's Alan's shop – was blown up.

Popular spot for the locals, you know. And Alan was there at the time it happened..."

Mina let out a gasp in horror. Not Alan. Not like this. Was she truly alone now?

"He's alive," Esther continued. "He was badly hurt, from what I've heard but, Lord help him, he's alive. Last I heard, Officer Holby had given him a lift back to his house from the shop." Esther rose from her chair. "I can give you his address if you'd like. Would that help?"

Mina nodded, a little sick to her stomach. She had burned with questions ever since Noah had pushed her out the apartment door, and now hundreds more piled into her brain. She walked numbly after Esther to the foyer, where the older woman was already pulling out the phone book from behind the desk and flipping through it.

"Let's see," Esther muttered to herself. "Ah, yes. Here it is." She pulled out a pad of paper and scribbled his address onto it, and then below it his phone number. She tore off the sheet of paper from the pad and handed it to Mina. "Would you like to call him? You can use the desk phone over there if you like."

Mina walked over to the phone and reached out a hand to pick up the receiver. For a long moment her hand hovered over it, and in her heart she knew that all she would hear if she called him would be a busy signal. Or it would go straight to voicemail. In either case, he wouldn't pick up. She pulled her hand back and turned to Esther, her hand reaching for Noah's wallet.

"Let me pay you for last night's stay," Mina said. "Can I ask you to call me a taxi?"

# III

Alan left the light in the bathroom off when he went to have his shower. There was more than enough sunlight coming in through the window and, oddly, the shadows poking from around tiny corners helped him to focus and think. Time was of the essence now, not to be wasted.

He bowed his head and let the water rush past his ears. He held little hope that talking with his father would help in any way, but he was obligated to let him know, wasn't he? She was his ex-wife, after all. *And ya never know,* Alan thought. *He might have some way he can help.*

Suddenly his headlong quest to find out who was behind everything overwhelmed him. As he rinsed the shampoo from his hair, he couldn't help feeling like a naïve kid, caught up in a riptide current with the shore fading away quickly in the distance. He was in over his head, and he knew it. Already the emotional wounds were festering, and the pain fogged his thinking.

He was toweling out the last of the water from his ears as he walked to the bedroom when a light knock came at the door. He pulled on a t-shirt and the pyjama pants Parissa had pulled off him the night before, and went to answer the front door just as the knock came again, light and inquisitive.

The first thing he noticed when he opened the door were the angora slippers. He blinked in surprise. Mina stood there on the patio, dark circles under her eyes and her hair hanging in untidy threads on her shoulders. He couldn't remember ever seeing her so tiny and fragile.

"Hel–" he began to say, and then she took two small steps toward him and hugged him tightly. He raised his arms, unsure of whether to hug her back, and then gently put his arms around her. She seemed to focus solely on squeezing him in desperation and breathing deeply, trying not to cry. The breathing wasn't helping, and Alan felt his t-shirt dampen with her hot tears.

"I'm *so sorry*," Mina breathed into his chest. "I'm so sorry for everything I've ever done that hurt you, for everything I ever said that was mean or hurtful to you." She released her death grip on his ribs and looked up into his face, her eyes pleading. "I'm sorry for being the biggest bitch to you when all you've ever been to me was genuine and kind."

Alan looked at her, confused. "What brought this…?"

Mina swept past him through the door, pausing just inside. She looked down at the floor when she spoke again, her fingers fidgeting together. *So much like her sister,* Alan thought. *At last, so much like her sister.*

"Noah's…" She seemed to choke on her words as she said them, and for a moment she couldn't finish. Her shoulders trembled as she took in a deep, shuddering breath, and then she tried again. "Noah…is dead." Another long pause. "Men came. Noah told me to run. And I did." She turned to Alan, her face gaunt. "But I saw, Alan. When I was in the alley behind our building, I saw." A single tear coursed down her cheek; she was beyond sobbing now. "They killed him," she whispered.

Alan felt the bottom drop out of his stomach. So there it was. He had hoped before this was all over to sit down with Noah and ask him a few questions about everything. Seemed like the list of people he could talk to was decreasing too fast for him to keep up.

"So why are you here?" As the words came out he was struck by their bluntness, and immediately felt the

204

desire to take them back. Mina reacted as if she'd been struck. For a moment – just a quick flash – Mina's face tightened in anger. Alan braced himself for the onslaught he knew was coming. *I deserve it,* he thought. *Go ahead and hit me if you need to.* But the anger didn't stay. It was there and then it was gone. *Presto change-o! Alakazam! Now you see it, now you don't, Al, my boy.* Her shoulders slumped and she looked him dead in the eye. The honesty he saw there was raw.

"This is where he told me to go. *'Find Alan. Find your sister. Go and be safe.'* That's what he said to me," she said. "So, I'm here. And I'm in bad trouble, Alan. You have no idea how bad."

Parissa stirred in her seat on the couch where Alan had led her before he took his shower. The couch squawked a little as she stood up and padded into the kitchen where the two of them stood.

"Mina...?" Parissa whispered, sounding drugged. "Mina, izzatchu?"

Mina looked past Alan to her sister, her eyes wide. "What happened?" Her eyes darted back and forth between them. "Alan, what happened to my sister?"

"I don't know. She sort of just...sank...into this state this morning. We've had a lot going on here, too." He held a hand out to Mina. "Help me bring her back into the living room, okay?"

*    *    *    *    *    *

"I don't understand," Mina said as she held Parissa's hand. "Why is this happening?"

"That's the $64,000 question," Alan replied. "It all started this week with my mom's murder. There was the whole shit-storm with you and Noah..." Mina shot him a sour look. "And then my shop was blown up, my assistant manager and the man who sold me the shop were killed in the blast, and then last night, two men dressed all in black broke in here and attacked us. I think they would have killed us if..." He trailed off.

"What?" Mina asked.

Alan chuckled, but there was no humour in it. "Neighbour's boxer down the way started barking. Her name is Pandora, I think." He paused and allowed a tiny smile to reach his lips for a brief moment. "I love the play on words. Pandora boxer. In any case, I think the sound of the gunfire started her up. The men didn't want to risk getting caught so they bailed. They killed Misfit before they left though, like some kind of fucking parting gift."

"Who's Misfit?"

Sadness watered down his throat. "It really has been a long time, hasn't it? Misfit was my cat." He swallowed hard. "I buried her early this morning under the willow outside. I think that was the breaking point for 'Rissa." Parissa sat between them, staring sightlessly at Alan's cell phone on the coffee table.

"Anyway," Alan concluded. "I was getting ready to go up to Massey Bay today, to see my dad, and then someone I didn't expect knocked on my door."

A puzzled expression broke on Mina's face. "Wait," she said. "You said men in black attacked you here last night?"

"Yea, why?"

Mina bit her lip. "I can't be sure of exactly what happened at our apartment yesterday, because Noah got me out of there so quickly...but I had a nightmare last night. A terrible nightmare." She shuddered at the thought.

"We were in our apartment, and I couldn't get to Noah. Three huge black creatures burst in, waving guns...guns like..."

"Like cannons," Parissa finished. "They were like cannons and they tore Noah's head right off at the neck." She wept as she spoke before turning to look at Mina for the first time since she had arrived.

"How...?" Mina started.

"...did I know? I don't know how. I just do. But there's something else I know that you need to hear. They didn't kill Noah."

"WHAT?"

Parissa shook her head. "He fought with one of them. He really fought, like he was..."

"...giving me time to escape," Mina breathed. "Holy *shit*..."

Parissa kept speaking. "They drove him through the window partway. He saw you in the alley, running to a cab. That's when he pulled the gun under his own chin and pulled the trigger. *You won't take me...you won't take her...*"

Mina and Alan stared at Parissa with incredulous eyes. "How...?" Mina whispered.

"I don't know! I just...saw it. Like you can see a memory. I can't explain it." She looked down at her fingers, which had entwined with Mina's. "I'm just glad you're safe. And I'm sorry about Noah. And..." she continued, brushing away some of her sister's hair. "You surprise me sometimes."

"How?"

"You were brave."

## IV

The beat cop was halfway to the next intersection when he heard the sound of the gunshot. He spun on his heel and headed back into the alley which he had just passed. His eyes scanned the garbage-lined walls and saw nothing. A rat skittered across the alley just in front of him and then there was a sound from high in the air; a shard of glass snapped and then tumbled down to the ground thirty feet in front of him. The cop raised his eyes in surprise and saw something else fall and hit the ground with a small smack. A man was hanging partially out of a window on the 14th floor. The man's head had broken open, like a crimson bloom, and blood oozed down the side of the building. He jogged toward the building wall, reaching for his radio. He stopped short, his toe barely an inch from a pile of congealed grey. It looked like raw oatmeal injected with bloody mucus. The cop gagged.

"Oh fuck. Oh sweet Jesus," the cop muttered to himself, backing away instinctively. "Oh *fuck!*" He grabbed for his radio again and almost dropped it. He snatched for it with his left hand as it slipped out of his right, the radio barking static as he squeezed it tight. He started to call it in, whatever had happened here, and he could feel eyes from all angles peering into the alley. Seems he wasn't the only one alerted by the gunfire. In the year and a half he'd pounded the streets as a beat cop, he'd never seen anything like this. Waterford was a pretty easy-going city, and the worst you might catch on the streets was a territorial dispute between a couple of vagrants who were high on whatever they could get their hands on. A few broken noses, maybe a handful of busted teeth, and that was it. He never expected to call in a (murder? suicide?) while standing three feet away from a lump of cooling brains.

"Precinct 9, this is Officer Moore. I'm...reporting shots fired in an alley behind Edgemont Apartments, near the corner of Grove and..." he paused, his mind blank. *This is no time to panic, Moore,* he thought. *Get your shit together, and fast.*

The radio crackled. "Say again, Officer Moore?"

He closed his eyes and sucked in a deep breath between his teeth. "I said, shots fired behind Edgemont Apartments, near the corner of Grove and Sherwood. Area is clear; one victim in an apartment window...thirteen, maybe fourteen floors up. Send help immediately!" He tried to replace the radio on his shoulder but missed the clip, and the damn thing fell and dangled by his right knee.

*    *    *    *    *    *

Officer Moore was standing at the end of the alleyway and making a very pointed effort not to look *into* the alley when Detective Wilder pulled up in her unmarked Crown Victoria along with King and Morris. She popped the trunk before stepping out of the car, and walked over to the shaken cop.

"M.E.'s on her way, but in the meantime I want you to go put the tape up, seal off this entire area. Tape's in the trunk." Wilder said.

"Yessir," Moore whispered before starting to jog to the car. Wilder grabbed his arm as he started to move.

"Walk, don't run," Wilder hissed in his ear. "You're a cop. Act like it. At least for the rubberneckers, hmm?" Moore nodded, looking around at the small crowd that had begun to form, and forced his stride to slow.

Wilder stepped into the alley with Morris and King flanking her, and saw the mess by the dumpster almost immediately. She glanced up and saw the body hanging out of the window, her eyes making note of everything at once. Another cop car, and then a third, pulled up near her Crown Vic and more uniforms piled out. She watched three of them start doing crowd-control, and the other three go over to assist Moore.

"I wanna get inside," she said to Morris. "Go and see if the building manager can let us in."

"On it," Morris said.

"I'll start interviewing these people, find out if they saw anything," King followed up. Wilder smiled.

"This is why I love working with you guys; you're always on the ball. Go to it."

King strolled away, passing under the yellow police tape just as Dr. Marsh pulled up in her white van. Wilder acknowledged her with a gentle nod.

*     *     *     *     *     *

The mousey building manager followed them up in the elevator, stepping out first when they reached the 14th floor. He reached into his pocket for his keys, and then hesitated in the hallway as he saw the remains of the apartment door.

"Well, I guess you won't be needing me anymore," the manager said, pocketing his keys. "That's it, though. 1406. I'll be downstairs in my office if ya need me." He scurried back into the elevator just as the doors were closing.

"I...okay..." Wilder said as she watched the number above the elevator decrease. She un-holstered her Sig and brought it up to her chest, stepping over the destroyed door into the apartment. Morris and King flanked her from behind as she walked cautiously into the hall.

"WPD! Come on out!" Wilder shouted. Morris slipped past on her left into the living room. King followed him, veering off into the dining room and kitchen. Wilder made her way down the hallway toward the bedroom. Morris and King both shouted "Clear!" as they finished checking the rest of the apartment.

"Well, someone didn't care about making a mess," Marsh said quietly. Wilder jumped half a foot into the air and brought her gun out away from her on instinct, aiming it at the wall at the last second.

"Dammit, Jules. Not when I'm armed!" Wilder whispered through clenched teeth. Marsh walked around her friend and over to the window.

"Sorry," Marsh said. "I thought you heard me. I tripped over the front door on the way in. Stubbed my toe pretty good."

Wilder checked the closet and then lowered her weapon, approaching the window cautiously. Even though the cause of death was clear from the street, she waited on Julie to confirm it anyway. Protocol was habitual.

"Well, COD's pretty obvious," Marsh said, gesturing at what was left of the victim's face and head. "Looks like a 10mm, although I'd need to see the weapon to confirm. Entry occurred here," she pointed to a small hole under the chin, "and exited near the forehead here. Disruption and fracturing of the facial bones will make him harder to identify, however." She pointed roughly to where the nose and cheekbones would be. She peered out the window, looking into the alleyway, and then back at the body. Her eyebrows furrowed. "When was this called in?"

Wilder checked her watch. "I'd say no more than ten, twelve minutes ago. Why?"

"Well, there is no doubt he's dead. Aside from the evident cranial injuries, heartbeat, respiratory, all of that is shut down. But he's fresh." She gently inserted her gloved middle finger into the blood on his face. "See? It's not even tacky." She placed the back of her hand on his neck. "And given body temp, I'd say he died almost immediately before your boy downstairs called it in. And there are definite signs of a struggle here. Did the officer who reported it see anyone leave?"

"He didn't mention it." Realization dawned on Wilder's face. "That means whoever was here with him might still be in the building!" She spun on her heel and ran face-first into Morris's chest.

"Whoa, Detective! Where's the fire? Looks like our boy there is dead," Morris said.

Wilder looked up into Morris's face. "Have any of our guys reported seeing anyone entering or exiting the building since we got here?"

"Uh, no? Why?"

"Our vic is still fresh. I want this entire building searched from top to bottom."

King stepped in. "You think whoever did this…"

"…is still here in the building? I'd say it's a big possibility. Go!" Wilder shouted, before turning back to Marsh. "You know who that is, don't you?"

"No, but it's difficult to tell with this much facial damage. Should I?" Marsh asked.

"That's Noah Lofton, our prime suspect in the Black murder." Wilder said, slamming her palm against the door jamb before walking out into the hallway. "*Goddammit!*"

Just in front of the building a white van drove off down the street.

## V

"So now what do we do?" Mina asked.

The question sat there on the air, challenging any one of them to answer it. For another long minute, nobody dared to try. Then Alan got up from the couch with a sigh and moved to his bookcases, fingering the spines of the hardcovers there.

"Well," he said. "I don't know. That's the fuck of it. I really, honestly don't know." That was the truth, too. For all his desire to get to the bottom of what was happening, he didn't know what to do next. Being scared only made things worse.

"Well, can we stay here? I mean, are we safe here?" Mina pressed, eyes searching him. "The men who attacked you...I think they're the same men who killed Noah. If they know where you live, Alan, they..."

She stopped short as Alan raised his hand at her. "I know," he whispered. "I know."

"But..." Mina started.

"Just stop. For a minute, can you please? I need to think." He resumed staring at the books on his shelves, not reading the titles. He couldn't think of anything to do that might help. *The fuck of it is that, just like all those years ago with your mother, you're not in control here,* he thought. *You're not in control and that scares you more than anything.* He shook his head, and grunted in frustration. He turned and looked at the girls. "I need to go talk to my dad in Massey Bay, like I originally planned. I arranged for Parissa to stay with my friend Celeste while I'm gone, and I think it's best if you go with her, Mina."

"But..." Mina repeated.

"No arguments. Okay? I just need you two to do this for me. I can't risk leaving the two of you here in case someone decides to drop in unexpectedly. That's not going to happen twice."

Mina held her tongue and nodded, rising from her seat on the couch. Parissa followed suit, quiet as a mouse.

"I need you to call a cab for me, okay? There should be a sticker on the fridge," Alan said. "My cell is on the coffee table there. I need to go get dressed before we head out."

Mina nodded and returned to the living room to retrieve the cell phone. As she turned it on and brought it up to her face, she could smell the lavender faintly on her hands. She smiled a little. She walked over to the fridge and started dialing.

*　　*　　*　　*　　*　　*

"Wait here, all right? I just need to see these two ladies off and then I'll need you to take me to Harv's." Alan spoke with Mitch, the driver of the cab, before stepping out. Mina and Parissa already stood on the sidewalk. Behind them, towering three storeys into the sky, stood Celeste's apartment building. Alan came around to join them. "Come on, you two. Let's go."

*　　*　　*　　*　　*　　*

The cab pulled up outside Harv's Rental Cars just a few minutes later. Alan gave Mitch a twenty and a handshake.

"Thanks, and sorry for all the running around we made ya do." Alan said.

Mitch nodded. "Hey. T'weren't so bad, ya know. Busiest I've been all week." He lowered his voice. "Sorry 'bout yer shop."

Alan nodded back, but said nothing. He clapped Mitch on the shoulder and then stepped out of the cab. He jingled the keys that belonged to his totaled Tercel and then walked across the street to Harv's.

*    *    *    *    *    *

Harv talked Alan into a sparkling BMW that he had sitting right by the front door. Alan protested at first, but Harv was a hard man to say no to.

"Lookit, I'll charge ya the same as I would if you was gettin' the Toyota, right? So stop worryin' about it, Al. Besides, it's the least I can do considerin' what happened to...well, you know. Deal?"

Alan agreed, and handed Harv another twenty out of his wallet. Then when Harv went to get the keys, he slipped a folded ten under his computer mouse. Harv had gone through a messy divorce that spring and had started chronically drinking away most of the profits his rental shop brought in, but Alan slipped it under just the same. In small towns, that's what you did. You played good neighbour and looked the other way.

"All right, here ya go!" Harv pronounced loudly as he turned back to face Alan. "Just make sure ya bring her back with a full tank and we're square." He reached across the desk to shake Alan's hand. He wanted to say more, Alan could see it in his face, but at the last second Harv decided to let it go. Alan relaxed a little inside. As much as he was grateful for the concern of everyone in the Cove, he was getting a little tired of the apologies left and right about *Bookends*.

"Thanks, Harv." And he walked out the door.

*     *     *     *     *     *

One thing Alan was immediately grateful for with the Beemer was the A/C. In the Tercel he was used to just cranking open the window and letting nature do the rest, but it was a real luxury to be on the road with the windows closed and still feel comfortable. Still, he felt out of place sitting behind the wheel, with more gadgets and buttons that did God knew what in front of him. But he needed wheels and Harv had insisted, even when they both knew the Camry would have served him just fine. He smiled a little to himself as the leather under him crinkled a little. The nice thing about BMW's was they didn't take long to get used to.

"No, they sure don't," he said as he turned onto the highway heading north.

*     *     *     *     *     *

Massey Bay was a lot like Shallot's Cove: quiet and idyllic. Even less happened in Massey Bay than the Cove, and that was saying a lot. Here the population dropped to double digits, and Alan had long understood this was likely the reason for his father's move eight years earlier. *Far easier to drink in peace when there's nobody around to nose into your business,* he thought, with grim acceptance. Edward Black was a good man. An alcoholic, yes, but a good man all the same. He slowed down as he passed the *Massey Bay Welcomes You!* sign; he'd missed his turn countless times before and driven up to a full mile past the trailer park where his father lived. He was not going to make that same mistake today.

Even with his caution, the driveway to the park snuck up on his right as usual and he slammed on the brakes, causing the Beemer to grunt to a stop almost immediately. He jerked forward against the seatbelt and shot a look in his rear-view to see if anyone was hurtling toward him. The road was empty. He fell back against the seat and eased the car off the road towards the driveway.

He marveled at the trailer park as he crept through it at five miles an hour. He'd never noticed any discernible change in the park's appearance in the eight years since his father had put down roots here. It was like it was frozen in time. *The more things change…*

He pulled up in front of his father's double-wide and killed the engine. He stepped out of the car and looked at the trailer over the top of the Beemer's roof. Ivy had claimed a fair portion of the trailer's front end, completely entombing the little raised garden his father had built just in front of the trailer the year after he'd moved in. The light green lattice fence and gate were falling to ruin, paint peeling in most places. To see the place decay like this made him sad. He spoke to his father on a regular basis on the phone, and did not think his father had increased his drinking. Either he was sober when Alan phoned, or the old man was getting better at not sounding drunk. With how the place looked, however, he suspected the drinking had escalated. God, he hoped he was wrong…

He stepped around the car and walked over to the feeble wooden gate. He pushed at the top of it with his hand and a piece broke off and tumbled to the ground. Another bad sign. He pushed again, this time near the middle, and the gate creaked open without much resistance.

He walked up the three steps onto the constructed patio and put his hand out to knock on the door. He retracted it almost immediately. On the door was a sign that read: *Gone Fishin', Fuckers!,* under which swam a cock-eyed fish giving the reader the finger with a single fin. Alan sighed and went back down the steps, heading towards the back of the trailer to where he knew his father was.

## VI

The elevator eased itself into a slow, cushioned stop as it reached the fourth floor of the 9th Precinct. There was a soft chime as the lit 4 button winked off and then the door slid open, grunting only once at the midway point before retreating into the darkness on Wilder's right.

The overhead fluorescents caught the glitter of her eyes as she stalked off the elevator into the bullpen. When she yanked out her desk chair, she could feel the eyes of the entire room glance her way even as she bowed her head and placed it into her upturned palms, elbows resting stolidly on her paper-filled blotter.

So close, yet so far. She'd let him walk and now he was dead.

"Fuck," she whispered into her hands. Now what?

She heard a squeaky rumble of casters as Det. Morris pushed himself over to her desk.

"Not now, Mo," Wilder mumbled into her hands. She lifted her head up and scrubbed her scalp with her fingertips. She looked over at Morris with eyes that were both weary and angry. "Every time we open this case up a little more, something else shuts it down hard. I knew it was a mistake letting Lofton walk. Damn it!" She thumped her fist hard on the blotter and then closed her eyes against the throb of pain which echoed up her arm.

"Let's go back to the top and work our way through it," King said, approaching her desk from the right. "Start with the gardener…"

"Landscaper," Wilder said.

"Whatever. I'm up for a little road trip across town. How about it?"

Wilder stood up. "I need you guys to stay here and focus on Lofton. His death is definitely connected and I want to know how and why. I'll follow up on Miss Khorasani." She watched her team move back to their respective desks before snatching her keys and bee-lining for the elevator.

*     *     *     *     *     *

Wilder's Crown Vic rolled into Parissa's empty driveway. She sat there staring for a long moment, her fingers drumming the steering wheel. She rationalized that there was nothing unusual about it, but no car in the driveway got her wind up. *Way* up.

She opened the door and stepped out, moving the corner of her jacket to one side to give herself easier access to her service piece. She didn't like that there was no car in the driveway. She didn't like it one bit.

She ascended the front steps and, as she approached the door, sudden movement caught her attention and she spun on her heel, lightning-quick. A purple-throated hummingbird darted back and forth between a cluster of flowers in a hanging basket, oblivious to all around it. A tiny smile pulled briefly at one corner of her mouth and she chastised herself for what she considered tantamount to "rookie nerves". *This is just another meet and greet,* she thought. *A follow-up. Relax.*

She knocked on the door.

*     *     *     *     *     *

A minute went by before she raised her hand to knock again. The thud of her knuckles on the wood echoed dimly inside. Beyond that, she heard nothing. There was nobody home.

She walked across the porch, past the hanging baskets the hummingbird had gorged on and tried peeking in through the window of the empty sitting room where she had sat with Khorasani and Black just a couple of nights earlier. There were no windows on the opposite end of the porch and, as she descended the steps again, she took quick note of the fence that spread out from the sides of the house and then away toward the back. She thought quickly of scaling it but she knew her limits.

She pulled out her cell phone.

"Morris, it's Wilder. There's nobody here. I need you to run a trace on two cell phones. One belongs to Parissa Khorasani. That's double S in the first name, K-H-O-R-A-S-A-N-I. The other is Alan Black. See if you can ping their GPS and figure out where they are. I'm on my way back to the precinct."

She cranked open the door of the Vic and tossed the phone on the passenger seat. She was a quarter of the way back to the precinct before she got her seatbelt latched.

\*　　　\*　　　\*　　　\*　　　\*　　　\*

She pulled up in front of the 9th and had just managed to fish her cell from the floor of the passenger seat when Morris and King came bursting out of the front door.

"Don't turn it off," Morris yelled, as King opened the rear passenger door. Morris piled into the front seat and shoved a piece of paper into Wilder's hand. "Alan's might be turned off because we couldn't raise him, so he could be anywhere. We got a lock on Parissa's though. She's up in Shallot's Cove."

"They're together," Wilder muttered grimly as she pulled the Vic away from the curb.

## VII

The grass was calf-high around the back of the trailer. Alan waded through it, frowning. The drinking *had* gotten worse, then. There was no other reason for his father to let the place get like this. At least the stone path that led to what his father called "The Massey Marsh" was still there, visible and clear of weeds. His father had built a little shack in the woods and an outhouse, a putrid thing which Alan refused to use.

He stepped into the clearing where the shack was just as his father came out of the outhouse, pulling up his fly and belching ferociously. He was shirtless, and Alan watched as the old man snuffed up a hefty booger and launched it into the bush. Alan groaned.

Edward Black turned in the direction of the sound and his face broke apart in a huge grin. He drained the last of a can of beer before speaking.

"ALAN! My boy, it's good t'see ya!" Edward bellowed. "What brings ya out here to my neck o' the woods?"

Alan couldn't help but smile. His father might be a drunk, but he was a jovial man beneath it all. The senior Black was a quintessential charmer, and could have sold ice to the Eskimos had he put his mind to it, instead of living off the meager welfare checks he received. Alan had offered once to send him a little money to help offset any costs his father might have, but Edward wouldn't hear of it. Pride ran rampant in the Black family, and ran deep. Alan understood what he meant, however. You stood on your own two feet in this family, or you didn't stand at all. Edward had tacitly bent that rule years ago by going on welfare, but like everything else the old man did, Alan simply looked the other way and said nothing. He couldn't help but notice the contradiction that seemed to define his father, but still he loved him. Oh, how he loved him.

"Heya, Pop," Alan said. "How's things?" He kept it light.

Edward scratched his small pot-belly and let out another monumental belch. "Oh, you know. Same shit, different day." He paused, and looked at his son. "How's that shop of yours keepin' ya?"

Alan weighed his answer. "Well, uh...not too good, Pop. Not too good at all." He watched as his father kicked open a cooler by his feet and pulled out another beer.

"Damn, son. That doesn't sound right to me," Edward said. "Thought you said that place was hoppin' busy. What'd you call it? 'A cornerstone of the community?'" He lifted the beer to his mouth and swallowed heartily. Another belch. "Is that why you're here?"

Alan bit his tongue. When his father was drunk he tended to show jealousy towards his son's success, and here he was, goading him. *Coming here was a mistake,* he thought. "No, it's not," Alan said. "I'm not here because of that."

Edward finished the beer and turfed it into the bushes behind him. This time he gave his mouth a rest and let his ass join in the fun. Alan frowned.

"Well, then," Edward said. "What'dja come here for then?"

Alan studied his father for a long moment, trying to figure out how to say it.

"Mom's dead," Alan said finally. Edward's face slackened.

"Damn," Edward said. "That old bitch died?"

"Pop, don't call her that," Alan said.

"What? A bitch? Well, I'm sorry to break it to ya, Al, my boy...but your mother was a Grade-A fuckin' bitch." Edward punctuated the last four words with his meaty finger, jabbing at the air with authority. "Ain't no two ways about it."

"Come on, Pop. Is that any way to talk?"

Edward's face reddened. "These are my woods and I'll talk any goddamn way I please! The way your mother treated you, and treated me..." his face sank. "I hated what she did to you for all those years. Never bothered to see you, never bothered to even fuckin' call...God, I hated her for that. Fuckin' *hated* her for that." He went to kick open the cooler again and instead knocked it on its side, the lid popping open and the lone beer rolling away under a fern.

"Pop, come on..." Alan said.

"Fuck her," his father muttered. "I'm glad the old cunt is dead. Serves her right, too. Fuckin' drugged-up bitch."

Alan watched his father struggle to his feet and lumber over to retrieve the beer from the underbrush. The old man grunted and another massive trumpet bellowed in the clearing as he bent over. When he was sober, you could dress Edward Black up in the finest tuxedo and showcase him to the cream of society. Get him drunk and he wasn't worthy of...well, much more than this, actually.

"How long since you were sober, Pop?" Alan asked.

Edward looked at his son through slitted, wary eyes. "Why?"

Alan took a deep breath before taking the plunge. "Because everything you own either looks like shit or is falling apart," he said. "The grass hasn't been mowed in ages and your fence out front is rotted through, for a start. I can't imagine the state of the inside of your house. How long?"

Edward took a large swallow of his beer. Last thing he wanted was to sit here and be grilled by anybody, especially his son. His house, his rules. "Who the fuck do you think you are, asking me questions like that? Huh?"

Alan felt his gut slip to somewhere around his left testicle. Getting Edward Black mad wasn't a mistake most people made more than once. He took a deep breath and tried his best to placate his father. "I...I'm just concerned, Pop. I came to tell you some bad news, and I find you looking like this. It breaks me up inside, seeing you like this. That's all."

"My son," Edward muttered to himself. "My son...he's *concerned*, is he?" He turned to face Alan. "How long since you've showed your *face* around here, huh? Too busy to see your old man? Or too *embarrassed?*" He rose from the old lawn chair he'd been sitting in, the rubber straps sagging pendulously. He threw the empty beer can into the dirt as he advanced, his jowls set in a vicious snarl.

"Pop..." Alan stood up, backing away warily.

"Too embarrassed to see his own father! Can't show his face! Almost lost my eye four months ago when the lawn mower threw its guts up all over the lawn, didn't I?" Alan took a closer look at his father and saw that there was indeed a nasty scar just below his left eye. How he wasn't blind looked to be a miracle. "Not that you noticed," Edward continued petulantly. "You're far too busy living the easy life down in the Cove! Couldn't even spare the half hour drive here to see his old man as he bled all over the lawn like a stuck pig! Huh? *'How long since you were sober?'* You come here, all high and fuckin' mighty, askin' *those* types of questions? HUH? I oughta fuckin'..."

Edward's right foot sank into a pocket of mud and in his inebriated state, he toppled over on his face like a rotten tree. He couldn't bring his hands up in time to brace himself as he fell and he roared in pain. He just lay there, snuffling and whimpering into the dirt. Alan stopped retreating, and instead took a small step forward to see if his father was okay.

"Pop...?"

Edward launched himself off the ground with astounding agility, firing a wild roundhouse through the air at his son. Alan jumped out of the way just in time.

"Get the *FUCK* off of *my property*, you little dog-fucker." Edward's tone had adopted a sinister, almost snake-like quality. "Get out. You little whelp. You shitting dog-fucker."

Alan stood numb as his father slowed his advance, his muscles tensing. There was no joviality in his father's eyes now, despite the fact that he was grinning. Alan tried to speak, but nothing escaped his lips but the tiniest of squeaks.

"I'd start moving, boy," Edward said, his grin widening. "If you don't, you'll suffer. Oh, how you'll *suffer*."

Alan bolted.

# VIII

It wasn't until he was beside his rented BMW that he stopped for a moment to catch his breath and see if his father was on his heels. There was a heart-stopping moment in the back yard when he slowed only a little as he passed the split chassis of the lawn mower which sat in the far corner closest to the trailer, and he swore he could feel his father's yeasty breath on his neck. The sight of the rotor blade buried in the wood frame of the trailer got his feet going again, and he rushed headlong past the front door and burst through the gate, shattering it into half a dozen pieces.

He turned as he reached the driver's side of the car, and saw no sign of his father. His breath was hot in his chest and he hung his head down a little to catch it. When he looked up again, he swore he could see a hulking shadow on the far side of the entrance to the woods. He blinked and it was gone. But then a rasping laugh breached the air between them, followed by a slew of drunken profanities. He needed to get away from here, away from his father.

He pulled open the door and slid inside, hardly waiting until his seatbelt was buckled before turning the ignition and gunning the engine. He almost spun out as he forced the car into a heavy U-turn and roared out of the park.

His nerves were shot. Edward Black was the sort of man you didn't want to offend. For several years, Edward was the bartender for a local pub. That is, until he beat up an unruly patron so badly the man was in a coma in the hospital for six months, his face so damaged he never ate solid food again for the rest of his life. Edward was damn lucky to have avoided jail on that one. Strangely, his father's boss had backed Edward up on the incident, citing the patron as blind drunk and "looking for trouble." In truth, all the patron had done was smack a waitress's backside as she'd passed, and Edward had caught him in the act. A simple toss-out at best, but Edward took it too far. His boss smoothed everything over with the police, but it didn't stop him from firing Edward the following day. Edward avoided prison, but not unemployment. That's when the drinking had begun in earnest.

Alan pulled into the parking lot of a Dairy Queen just off the highway and rested his head against the steering wheel, the engine idling. This was it. He was alone now. His mother was dead, and his father had turned him out like a crippled stray into the dark. He had no family left to turn to now. All he had was Celeste, Mina and Parissa.

Parissa…

He reached for his cell phone. He needed to call Celeste and check up on the three of them. He needed to make sure everything was at least somewhat normal on their end. He got Celeste on the second ring.

"Hello?" Celeste said. In the background, Alan could hear muffled voices.

"Celeste, it's Alan…you guys okay?"

There was a pause as Celeste pulled the phone away from her ear and said 'It's Alan' to someone. Then she was back.

"We're fine. Okay, not really. Parissa slipped into some kind of trance and we can't get her to come out of it. Mina and I are taking her to the hospital in Waterford."

Alan's heart sank. One was bad enough, two was worse. "I can meet you there. Right now I'm about halfway between Massey Bay and the Cove, but I can meet you in Waterford. Can I talk to Mina?"

A pause. "Sure." Then the clumsy sound of the phone changing hands in Alan's ear.

"Alan?" Mina said.

"Hey, Mina," Alan responded. "What's going on with 'Rissa?"

"We were all fine at Celeste's place, just sitting and talking, when Parissa just slipped away into another trance. She isn't speaking or anything. She's just sitting here staring at nothing and she doesn't seem aware of what's going on around her. It's like when I first got to your house, Alan. Exactly the same."

"All right," Alan said. "I'm going to meet you at the hospital, okay? I'll be there soon."

"O-okay." Mina hung up the phone.

"Mom's been killed," Alan muttered to himself as he pulled back out of the lot. "Pop's gone nuts, my cat, my shop; now Parissa's going into fucking *trances?* What the fuck is going on here? I could really use some goddamn good news right about now."

He was just passing his driveway on the left as he headed out of town when he saw someone walking around his front yard.

## IX

"Can I help you?" Alan said as he stopped the car and got out.

The woman stood there looking at him for a long moment, her vibrant green eyes searching his face from under a swath of raven-black hair. She extended her hand hesitatingly.

"Alan? Alan Black?" the woman asked.

"Depends on who's asking," Alan responded. "Who might you be?"

Her face flushed a little with embarrassment. "Sorry," she said, dropping her hand. "The last couple of days for me have been a little a topsy-turvy. My name's Adele Watkins." She tried for a smile that mostly succeeded.

Alan closed the door of the BMW, pocketing the keys. "Well, Miss Watkins. I can't say as I know you. Should I? I haven't had the greatest week either."

"No, I guess you haven't," Adele said.

His eyes narrowed, giving him a suspicious look much like his father. If he could have seen his face right then, he would have hated what looked back at him. Hated and feared it. "What does that mean, Miss Watkins?"

Adele flushed even harder. "Look, I'm sorry. I shouldn't have come here." Alan frowned a little and turned to get back in the car. "But I had to," she said, the words tumbling out in a rush. "Noah Lofton begged me to."

His hand froze on the door handle, and he looked back at her over his shoulder. "Who?" he said, incredulously. "Who begged you?"

Adele swallowed hard. "Noah Lofton. Just yesterday."

"How do you know Noah Lofton?" His suspicion was growing by leaps and bounds. "Tell me honestly."

"Is…is there a place we can sit down? I have a lot to tell you."

Alan released his grip on the door handle and pointed the way around the house to the patio overlooking the ocean. Adele mumbled a 'Thank you' as she passed him.

*    *    *    *    *    *

When they'd settled into their chairs on the patio, Alan was the first to speak up.

"Now tell me what's going on," he demanded.

Adele fumbled in her purse and brought out a pack of cigarettes. She pulled one out with a shaking hand and stuck it between her lips. She held the pack out to him, and he raised his hand and shook his head. She tossed the pack back into her purse and pulled out a lighter, drawing in the first puffs of smoke with short, practiced pulls. She exhaled a cloud and then coughed, her eyes watering.

"Tried to quit, you know?" she said to Alan while considering the burning cigarette. "Stopped smoking for almost three years. This week *totally* fucked that up." She took another drag.

"Why are you here?" Alan prodded. His patience was wearing thin.

"Right," Adele said. "You haven't had the greatest week either. I can tell by your face." She pressed her lips together, thinking of how to begin. "First of all, I assume Beverly Black is your mother?"

Alan nodded. "She's dead. This week started on that delightful note."

"I suspected as much. Noah Lofton came to see me at my office earlier this week with a document of hers."

Alan shifted forward in his chair. "What?"

Adele nodded, taking another drag off her cigarette. "He wanted me to get him money that was bequeathed to you. It was a fair amount of money. Held me at gunpoint. Lovely man."

Alan shook his head. "That's a lie. My mother was poorer than a church mouse. She lived by herself in a house not much bigger than this place, down in Waterford." He rose to leave. "I think you must have me mistaken for someone else."

"I don't think so. Your full name is Alan Thomas Black, yes? Your mother's is Beverly May Black?"

Alan sat back down. "Yes..."

"Then I think I've got the right man. According to the Will, anyway."

Alan shook his head. "Will? What Will? What are you talking about?"

"Your mother's Will. You...you didn't know?"

Alan laughed, a short, mad cackle that fell harshly on his ears. "My mother and I didn't speak for ten years leading up to her death. And not once in *thirty* years did she ever mention any Will. If she had one, that surprises me on two levels. One: that she had one. Two: that she left anything to me in the first place. Like I said, she was dirt poor. What was there? A trunkful of goddamn hydrangeas?" He scoffed. "Jesus Christ," he muttered to himself.

"So you didn't know," Adele said, watching tendrils of smoke rise up from the tip of her cigarette. "But she had one all the same." She looked up at him. "And she left you more than just hydrangeas."

Alan looked at her out of the side of his eye. "I don't suppose you have it with you?"

"No. Noah took it with him when he left my office. He probably still has it. How do you two know each other?"

Alan ran a hand through his hair. "He dated a friend of mine a long time ago. He was a bit of a loose cannon, to be honest with you. Between you and me, I don't think he was wound all the way tight." He tapped his forehead with his finger.

"Was?" Adele asked.

"Yup," Alan nodded. He made a gun with his fingers and pretended to fire it at her. His face bore no humour at the childish action, and Adele flinched. "His girlfriend got here in a panic this morning."

"Oh my God…"

Alan nodded, and paused, thinking. "Did anyone know about this Will other than you and Noah? Think hard."

Adele's hand shook even harder as she took a final drag off her cigarette and looked for a place to put it out. Finally, Alan found an old scallop shell half and handed it to her. She took it gratefully and butted out her cigarette, thinking about his question.

"Adele?"

"No. No…he gave me the impression he was the one holding all the cards. He even said at the beginning of our…meeting…that he'd already killed two women and that he didn't mind making me number three. He seemed so *in control*. But then yesterday, he rushed into a restaurant where I was having dinner, and he was a mess.

He looked like someone had run him over with a Mack truck. The biggest difference in the second meeting was his attitude."

Alan smiled inside to himself at that. *So Celeste really did run him through the wringer. Shit.* He kept his poker face steady. "How do you mean?"

"The first time I saw him, he was dressed sharp and totally in control. He held a gun to my face and demanded I do this job for him. Demanded that I get him money that was supposed to go to you. But the second time, he was beaten. I mean physically *and* emotionally. Someone had raked him over the coals, Alan. He wasn't making a lot of sense in the restaurant, but he did say two things. One, that he was out; that things were different now. I can't even begin to guess what he meant by that. The other thing was like I said. He begged me to find you. *Begged* me."

Alan furrowed his brow in puzzlement. "Did he say why?"

She shook her head. "They threw him out of the restaurant before he could explain. That's assuming he was going to explain. Like I said, he was a mess."

Alan leaned back in his chair, totally at a loss. He brought a shaking hand of his own up to his forehead and rubbed it, the beginnings of a monstrous headache creeping in behind his eyes. He tried to imagine someone like Noah, a man who always seemed to be out for only himself, beaten down and humbled in front of a total stranger. Especially when he'd displayed such classic Noah arrogance in front of this same stranger earlier that week. His death seemed to confirm in Alan's mind that Noah wasn't running the show, although he would have liked you to believe so. Someone else was pulling the strings after all, and had the further capacity to cow a total alpha male such as Lofton. Someone far more dangerous than any of them realized. The headache thumped once against his eyelids, and he let out a shaky sigh.

"So you've no idea where the Will might be now?" Alan asked at last. Adele shook her head. "That's what I thought," he continued. "Which means it could be anywhere. Are you sure he wasn't carrying it when you saw him in the restaurant?"

Adele shook her head a second time. "He was wearing nothing but a torn pair of slacks and a bloodied dress shirt. The very same that he wore in my office, in fact. The only thing missing was his sport coat. He put it in the inside pocket of his sport coat when he was in my office. That's the last I saw of it."

"Then we need to find that coat. It might still be in there," Alan said. "It's worth a try, anyway."

Adele's cell phone chirped inside her purse, and she pulled it out, frowning. She checked the display. "Sorry," she said. "My office ringing. I need to take this." Alan nodded, and Adele moved past him toward the big willow by the BMW. He got up out of his chair as well, and went inside the house.

He walked up to the big picture window, feeling again the totality of his solitude. The house was eerily silent, with the ocean beyond not even rippling. Misfit was gone, her pillow on the sill still indented from when she last lay on it. His nose tingled and the tears came all at once, drowning him in his loss and his sorrow. He felt violated, his entire being injected with a massive, sick poison. Worse than everything else, he felt trapped. He was cowering in the corner; could almost see the axe as it came whistling down to end everything forever.

He was still sobbing when the cloth drenched in sweet oblivion descended on his face and blackness consumed him.

*      *      *      *      *      *

Adele snapped her cellphone shut and walked back over to the patio to where they'd been sitting. Alan wasn't there.

"Alan?" she called, looking all around the patio and down the path to the ocean. She walked around the side where his barbeque was and saw nothing. The side door was open and she entered the house, calling his name once again. "Alan?"

She heard a car door slam and she started at the sound, only jogging to the front door as she heard the BMW's engine start up. She struggled with the lock on the door for a moment, and by the time she opened it and stepped out onto the front deck, the Beemer had already turned and was racing out of the driveway in a cloud of dust. She ran to the edge of the deck.

"Alan!!" she cried.

But the car was gone.

# X

Darkness. Darkness everywhere.

He blinked once, to make sure his eyes worked, and the darkness remained. His body jolted a little and the sound of the BMW's engine broke through the fog in his brain. His headache was amplified by the sickly sweet aroma still lingering in his nostrils.

He was in the Beemer's trunk, with no memory of how he got there.

*What the fuck?*

The engine softened and he felt the car slow, and then the whispery crunch of the tires as they hit a patch of dirt. His body shifted a little as the car turned to the right. Beyond that he knew nothing. His eyes began to adjust to the gloom, and he glanced around, trying to see what might be in here with him.

The car hit a pothole, and he bounced up, striking his head on the trunk lid. He fell back, groaning loudly, and felt a tiny trickle of blood start to wind its way across his forehead. His vision muddied for a moment. His headache throbbed.

The car came to a gentle stop, and he heard the driver get out and slam the door behind him. The car rocked a little on its springs, and he heard footsteps coming towards him. He tensed; he was not going to go down without a fight.

The trunk popped open and his face was blanketed in sunlight. He hadn't counted on that, and was blinded by it and flinched. It was all his abductor needed to bury his face in that cloying sweetness once more, and the bright sunlight faded to black.

*     *     *     *     *     *

Alan woke up a second time and for a long time, his eyes couldn't focus or tell him where he might be. His nose knew, however, and the smell of ammonia and human shit was overwhelming. A combination of the chloroform and excrement set his stomach into knots, but he willed himself not to throw up; he couldn't deal with more unsavoury aromas.

His vision cleared and his eyes confirmed what his nose already knew: he was in his father's outhouse. The cut on his forehead was still bleeding, but slowly, and the tickle of the blood on his skin was maddening. He went to lift his hand to wipe it away and discovered his hands were bound together behind his back.

"Lovely," he muttered.

He looked down at his feet and saw that they were bound together as well. *So much for a daring escape,* he thought. A single droplet of blood fell onto his jeans and spread out in a tiny bloom. He looked around at his surroundings and tried to decide what to do. Outside the tiny structure, he heard someone clear his throat and spit. He drew a breath to holler, but at the last moment he clamped his teeth down on the cry and swallowed it hard. Outside the outhouse, death was waiting. That he knew with absolute certainty. In here he was relatively safe, at least for the time being. Near his feet he saw a moldy pile of shit that had long been abandoned by the flies that buzzed incessantly around his head. In here he was safe, and alone. Just him.

And that stink. That fucking *stink*.

He shot a glance at his jeans again, and saw the outline of his cell phone in his pocket. The keys to the

BMW, which he'd put in the other pocket, were gone of course, but the cell phone was still with him. If he could only get free, he might be able to send a text or something. Send for help.

He started to shimmy his wrists together, tried to get the bindings loose. His fingers brushed something as they moved, and then he froze as something light and feathery caressed the back of his hand, moving.

He was deathly afraid of spiders, ever since he was a little boy. He remembered seeing a large specimen – a wolf spider, his father had later told him – perched on the wall above his bedroom door, legs spread and menacing. It was easily the size of a golf ball, but the shadow thrown by his night light made it appear three times larger. He held his breath and stared fixedly at the grotesque thing sitting on his wall, and for what seemed like an eternity boy and spider were frozen together in time, neither moving a muscle. Then a moth (or it could have been a daddy long-legs, he had long forgotten now) brushed up against the spider and the thing had shot across the wall with such lightning speed that he had screamed in absolute terror. Screamed loud and long, until his father bolted through the door with his own eyes wide. His father asking what was wrong, what happened to make him scream like that, and Alan pointing a shaking finger at the wall. It was motionless once more, and for a moment his father didn't move, and Alan thought that maybe his daddy was scared of spiders too. He thought maybe his daddy and him would stay frozen like that forever until the spider came down and had himself a meal fit for a king. Then his father had grabbed one of Alan's comic books and brought it down hard on the spider, and it had fallen to the floor, amid another scream from Alan. His father had grunted with satisfaction, and began to turn to Alan, started to say, *look I didn't wreck your comic even a little*...and then the spider had started to shudder across the floor toward his father, slow...but moving.

He shut his eyes to the memory, but it was just as vivid behind his lids. In the end his father had brought down one of Alan's rain boots on top of the spider with a spectacular squishing crunch, but it was dead at last. They had gone out to buy him new rain boots the next day, hadn't they? Yes, he seemed to remember they had.

But the spider never really died, did it? No, no it was still alive, and now it was crawling up his arm, set to finish what it had started all those years ago. The sensation of its legs on his arm was unbearable, and he fought every instinct inside him to scream as loud as he had back in his bed when he was five. He looked straight ahead in a frozen panic, and saw a second wolf spider, as large as the one on his bedroom wall, sitting on the inside of the outhouse door. Its legs were spread and its tiny mandibles waved in the air, as if to say hello.

The spider on his arm was past his elbow now, and advancing. Soon it would reach his shoulder, and then from there...Alan was terrified beyond the capacity for rational thought.

He caught movement from its waving legs out of the side of his eye and he turned his head just a little, enough to give him a modest glance at the creature. It was huge, nearly twice the size of the one on the door, and Alan watched it breathlessly as it crested his shoulder and progressed downward toward his chest. He could feel the tips of its legs through the fabric of his shirt, hot and pointed, and it only stopped when it reached his midsection.

Then it turned around to face him.

Alan's eyes threatened to pop out of his head and he pressed his lips together hard enough to draw blood, which then trickled out of the corner of his mouth. The wolf spider started crawling back up toward him...toward his face. Alan couldn't breathe. The tiniest of whimpers struggled to escape him, but they came out like tiny gagging noises. Outside, the throat cleared and another glob of spit landed in the dirt. The spider advanced.

His head was pointed down at the spider, his chin buried in his neck. It stopped just at the collar of his shirt, its onyx eyes reflecting his face back at him like a mirror. Alan couldn't look away, couldn't even move. If it bit him now, he would have done nothing to prevent it. He just stared into the spider's eight glittering eyes...

...and saw maddening intelligence there.

The minutes ticked by with agonizing slowness, and then the spider extended one foreleg out in front of it, slowly. Alan was almost cross-eyed, watching every move it made. At last, its leg brushed his nose, as if to gauge how big this prey really was, and then retracted it. Small beads of cold sweat broke out across Alan's forehead and lip, and his breath came in short, shallow gasps. He would spend all of eternity drowning in the inky blackness of the spider's eyes.

At long last, it turned away from him and slowly marched down his shirt to his jeans, then down onto the floor, where it crawled under the door and out into the forest. Alan remained frozen in place for an hour afterward.

\*　　\*　　\*　　\*　　\*　　\*

243

The sun was beginning to sink behind the trees when his stomach really started to growl in earnest. His terror-induced paralysis had long ago abated, and he shifted uneasily on the greasy toilet seat, his legs going numb.

He looked up to the outhouse door, but the wolf spider that stood guard there had slipped away to other places beyond. Dusk was coming; now was the time to hunt. He listened hard, but didn't hear anyone outside either. He shifted on the seat a little, took a furtive look behind him to see if there were any more surprises waiting there, and saw nothing. Then he leaned back against the wall and brought his legs up, preparing to try and kick the door out.

The flat of his feet cracked against the door, but didn't budge it even a little. He brought his knees back to his chest and then shot them out again, slamming the soles of his shoes flat against the door once more. The impact jarred his knees and hurt his feet, but the door stayed shut, tight and firm. He brought his feet down to the floor and sighed, frustration mounting. His stomach growled again, and his legs started to jitter a little. *Weak,* he thought. *I'm weak because I'm hungry.* A dawning realization. *Maybe that's what he wants. Weaken me so I can't escape.*

The light was fading fast, and spending the night in this shithole with wolf spiders and God-knows-what else roaming around did not appeal to him in the slightest. He set to work on removing the binds on his wrists in earnest.

*   *   *   *   *   *

The light was all but gone, and he had gotten no further than bloodying his wrists in his struggle. He stopped at last, and leaned back against the slimy toilet lid, closing his eyes for a moment. That's when he saw a flash of light from somewhere outside, and the sound of footsteps coming through the underbrush. Coming toward him. He sat up, ears twitching, and waited.

"Go hang those from there, there and there!" one voice barked. Alan recognized it instantly. It was his father. But who was he talking to? He watched as the light seemed to spread and grow outside and guessed it was lanterns being hung from the trees around the clearing. Then he heard the jingle of keys in a lock just outside the door.

"Christ, I can't see to open this fuckin' thing. Bring that shit back here a second!" His father again, barking orders. The light swelled as it was brought to the door, and then he heard someone jump a little and then the sound of a heavy foot planting itself in the dirt.

For the third time, his father spoke. "Hah! Fuckin' spiders! They crawl all over this thing like they own the goddamn place. Not that one! Not anymore!"

Inside – and to his surprise – Alan found himself whispering a word of thanks to his Pop. Then the lock snapped open, and fell into the dirt. The door was wrenched open, and Alan stared up into the bright light of a lantern. He couldn't see who held it, but a dirty hand grabbed him by the collar of his shirt and yanked him out of the shitter and into the dirt in the clearing.

# XI

Alan rolled over onto his side and watched one of the men take his lantern and hang it from a nearby tree. The sun was just a sliver on the horizon now, but the trees held their own twilight. He looked around and saw four men standing near him, his father in the middle, and tried to sit up.

"I'd save my strength if I were you," his father growled menacingly.

Alan blinked some dirt out of his eye and lobbed a spit of his own onto the ground. He looked up at his father with fear and anger.

"Why are you doing this?" he asked.

His father stopped in his tracks and laughed, turning to look at the men with him as he did so. The men laughed right along with him, a grotesque sound in these peaceful woods.

"Here," said Edward. "Give me that, and start digging over there. You too, over there and help him. I don't want to be here all night waiting for your sorry asses. I've got shit to do." He took the semi-automatic that one of the men in black was holding and watched them pick up two spades that were leaning against a tree. Alan started to realize what was happening.

"It was..." he began, but then Edward knelt down by Alan, pulling a syringe out of his pocket as he did so. In this close proximity, Alan's nose detected the faint scent of his father's cologne and his throat closed in fear. His eyes never left Edward's.

"Me?" Edward said, jamming the syringe into Alan's shoulder. The pain was only cursory; Alan felt himself go limp and his world start to collapse in on itself.

Edward sat back on his haunches and regarded his son. "I have no idea what you mean."

*        *        *        *        *        *

His father stood up and brushed the dirt from his jeans. Alan watched him; it was all he could do. Whatever Edward had injected him with was affecting his thinking as well. He tried to shake his head clear, but his body was totally unresponsive. Even more terrifying was the way his vision tunneled to pinpoints in front of him. He tried desperately to focus.

*IT WAS YOU!* he screamed inside his head. But all he managed was a small grunt in the back of his throat; even his mouth had seized up like a rusted hinge.

Edward chuckled to himself. "You're not up to talking, are you? That's okay. Let me clear things up a little. I've injected you with a mild narcotic called ketamine. Something I got from a friend of mine. On the street they call it Special-K. Now, I don't expect you to know that; you wouldn't know the difference between a baggie of coke and icing sugar. I've come to accept that from you. You shitting little dog-fucker." His father turned away from him a little, gesturing. "In the meantime, allow me to introduce you to my little helpers."

He walked over to the two men dressed all in black who were digging furiously. He put a hand up to stop them and they paused, resting the tips of their spades on their shoes. Edward reached up and pulled the black masks from their heads.

"Alan! Meet my friend Mitch, and my other friend Harv," Edward shouted triumphantly. "I'd go with a more elaborate introduction, but I think the three of you are well acquainted, am I right?" Alan stared at his friends incredulously as they resumed their digging.

"And over here," Edward continued, "is the man I've assigned to be my look-out. Alan, meet Officer Holby. Officer, you remember Alan, don't you?" Holby nodded with a smile and shifted his weight on his feet, his hand resting on top of his Sig. Alan could do nothing but stare.

Edward regarded his son with interest. "What's that look for? Don't pout. Not when things are just getting good."

Edward dragged his aging lawn chair close to Alan and sat down, grunting just a little from the effort. "Holby, bring my cooler over here, would ya please? A man gets thirsty with all this talkin'."

Holby dragged the cooler over to where the old man sat. Edward yanked the lid off the top and reached inside for a beer. He held one up in Alan's direction. "You want one? I feel I was rude, not asking you earlier," Edward said. He cracked the tab on it and offered it again. "Come on. Take it. All that time in my facilities must have made you *plenty* thirsty." Alan rolled his eyes up at his father; it was all he *could* do. Edward shrugged and said, "Do I have to feed it to you like a little baby? Do I?"

Alan closed his eyes as the cold brew came pouring down over his face. He felt his spirit breaking, and his ears burned with humiliation.

"Won't even drink my fuckin' beer when I offer it," Edward muttered to himself. "Just like you to refuse me. Shitting little dog-fucker. Shitting little crybaby." He kicked Alan high on his forehead with the sole of his shoe. "Why did I take care of you all those years, huh? Wanna tell me that? Or do I have to answer for you too?" He kicked a small cloud of dirt in Alan's face.

Alan whimpered into the dirt, completely helpless. *Hope lost*.

"How we doin' over there with that diggin'?" Edward called over his shoulder. He turned back to Alan and leaned in close. "'Scuse me a second, my boy. Just need to take a little look-see on their progress. Sit tight, will ya?" He reached out a hand and patted Alan on the cheek, and then got out of his chair. He kicked it as he went to move past it, and it collapsed in on itself. Edward regarded it for a moment before flapping his hand at it and muttering under his breath. Alan watched his father walk over to the two men as beer dripped out of his hair and into his eyes. Holby shifted his weight again and Alan turned his attention to the cop, who seemed focused on something off into the woods somewhere.

Another drip, right into his eye, and Alan jerked his head in instinctive response. His breath caught in his throat at the movement, and he furrowed his brow a little. He focused hard, and moved the fingers on his right hand ever so slightly.

The drug was beginning to wear off.

He looked back up at Holby. The cop was still focused on the darkness, and had not noticed Alan's little discovery. The sound of his father turning away from the dig site caught his attention again, and he made to lie as still as he could as his father walked back over to him and sat down.

"Where were we," Edward said, conversationally. "Oh yes..."

"Did you kill my mother?" Alan whispered.

The affable glitter in his father's eyes died in a heartbeat and he looked down at his son, his face slackening. Alan watched him in fear, knowing that there was little he could do from his current position, drugged up or not. Edward shot a look over his shoulder at the diggers. "Get a move on with that hole!" he shouted.

Alan's eyes moved from his father to the two men over at the far end of the clearing. A wave of anger and betrayal throbbed through him as he thought of the easy smiles on their faces just this afternoon. Thought about how they apologized for his shop. How they'd looked him in the eye and lied to his face. *Was it all for nothing?* he thought. *Have I truly got nobody that would stand and defend me?* The desire to rise up and murder the four of them overwhelmed him momentarily; the fingers on his right hand twitched in response, and that movement, slight as it was, brought him back to reality hard. There was nothing he could do in his current state. The best he could hope for was to ride out the effects of the ketamine and pray that he was still alive when they wore away.

A movement from Edward, as his hand reached into his pocket for another syringe. "I brought extra," he snarled. "I just didn't think I'd need it." He pulled the cap off the needle and lunged at his son.

Alan took a sharp intake of breath and threw his body clumsily out of the way just in time, and Edward drove the needle straight into the hard dirt, snapping it off at the base. The movement caught Holby's attention and he whirled around, drawing his gun and firing it wildly in Alan's direction.

"NOOO!" Edward screamed, grabbing his own gun and firing three slugs into Holby's gut. The reports were deafening in the clearing and a small flock of birds squawked somewhere before flying off into the distance. Edward marched over to Holby as he lay twitching on the forest floor. Mitch and Harv had dropped their spades in shock and were reaching for their own guns when Edward turned in their direction. He fired four more rounds, two each into both men. Harv and Mitch collapsed where they stood and Edward stood swaying in the middle of the carnage like a drunken Angel of Death. His breathing was raspy and ragged. "Nobody kills my boy but me," he said to the darkness.

He turned back to face Alan, who had backed up to the base of a tree and was fighting against the paralysis in his muscles as he rubbed his bonds against the rough bark.

"Go on. Break free," Edward goaded, sitting back down on the dirt in front of Alan. "Break free and I will kill you where you sit before you've had a chance to get your hands out from behind your back."

Alan paused, his eyes focused intently on his father. "Why are you doing this?" he repeated.

Edward threw his head back in a roar of laughter. "It comes to that, does it? You want to know why! Despite the fact that you won't live longer than the story takes to tell?"

Alan's mouth hung open. Looking his mother's killer in the eye – his own father! – seeing him laugh at his question in the pukey green-white glow of the clearing, made his stomach lurch. He had known, of course. Had known probably since he walked through his mother's office earlier that week. Edward reached over for another beer, and Alan took his chance to covertly resume cutting his bonds.

"Close that fuckin' mouth of yours," Edward said. "You look like a goddamn retard." He popped the top on the beer but did not drink.

"Why, Pop? What did she *ever* do? Sure, she was never there for us! That doesn't give you the right to..." He couldn't bring the word past his own lips. He took a small breath, closing his eyes. His voice softened. "For all your anger, surely you see that?"

"If there's anyone who deserves to be angry at that delusional cunt, it's you, Alan. The way she fuckin' played you for a chump all those years. Toyed with me. I don't understand how you can just sit there and take it. My God, you're even *defending* her, it sounds like!"

Alan turned away, his face sullen. Was his father right? He heard a light snap behind him; one of the strands had broken apart. Almost there…

Edward raged on. "Never even paid fuckin' child support! All those years I struggled, and she never gave me a fuckin' dime! And you're okay with that? You're okay with how we lived?" Alan watched a small vein in the middle of his father's forehead start to throb.

"Mom was *destitute!*" Alan shouted. "She never paid anything because she *couldn't!* What the fuck, Pop? You can't get blood from a stone!" Alan took a breath, and tried to calm the fury inside him. "You're insane," he whispered.

"Am I?" Edward said, suddenly calm. That jovial smile that seemed so out of place here danced briefly again on his lips. "Am I really? Suppose it will interest you to know that your mother was not as poor as you might think."

Alan puckered his face in confusion.

"I did a little…digging, if you'll pardon the expression. Found out some *very* interesting things about dear old Mommy."

"I don't understand," Alan said. He heard the second strand snap and knew he was free. He kept his hands still behind him, however. He could play a good hand of poker when he had to, and he was set with the hand of his life. Or so he hoped.

"MONEY!" Edward screamed, leaning in close to Alan, flecks of spittle landing on his face. "All those years that she never kept in contact? Never bothered with a single cheque to help me out? She was sitting on a PILE of money!" Edward shot upright out of his chair, collapsing it once more. "That cocksucker she dated. You remember? When you were six?"

Alan thought hard. "Dougie?"

Edward slapped his hand on his knee and began to pace. "Douglas Windermere liked to gamble. Roulette, poker, craps, you name it. Anyways, I'm sitting playing a couple hands of five-card stud a year ago, and Windermere sits his ass down next to me. We got to talkin' a little later over drinks, and he tells me his mother's some kind of fuckin' *multi-millionaire*, but never cut him in on any of the family fortune. That honour, it would seem, had already been bestowed years ago upon Mommy Dearest. How do you like *that?*

"'Course, he didn't know that I knew who Beverly Black was, that she and I were married once upon a time. He was just in a mood to bitch about old wounds and I provided an ear. At least that's what I figure. I also didn't know what to believe, and I figured him to be totally full of shit. I mean, this was quiet, dim, delusional Beverly Black we were talking about. And Windermere seemed to be just another arrogant rich brat with too much time on his hands. So I just waved it off as so much fluff, and sour grapes."

One of the lanterns winked out, dimming the clearing a little. Edward turned to look, and Alan took advantage by adjusting his seat. His hand was going numb, and he shook it gently. Edward turned back to his son and continued speaking.

"So I ignored it for a long time, except it kept naggin' at me, and soon I couldn't stop thinkin' about it…what if the bitch really *was* holdin' out on me all those years? So finally I figured, hell, couldn't be half bad to see what's up. So I went to her place." He drained his beer. "And guess what?"

"What…?" Alan said tonelessly.

"Somebody had beaten me to it!" Edward sputtered. "Her office was trashed, but no sign of her or anything interesting. When I went outside onto the verandah and saw the garden torn to shreds, and an *unnatural* mound of dirt under that jagged old apple tree, I got out of there. *'Prudence is the footprint of wisdom'*, as the saying goes."

"You didn't…" Alan began, trying to figure it out. "If it wasn't you, then…"

Footsteps crunched the underbrush, and both men looked up to see a man in a dark double-breasted suit enter the clearing. In his hand was a 10mm.

"Mr. Black," the man said. "Remember me?"

Alan was silent, struggling to place the face. Just as he thought he had it, recognition faded into a fog. He chased after it in his memory, but it danced just beyond his reach, frustrating him intensely. He glanced over at his father who appeared, for a moment, to share his difficulty in recognizing the figure who stood in front of them, and then an evil smile broke casually across his father's face. As the seconds drew out in an infinite pause, Alan took advantage of the distraction and began to untie the bonds around his ankles as swiftly as he dared.

"Well," Edward said as he rose to his feet and adopted an attitude of congeniality which Alan found repulsive. "What brings you to my neck of the woods?" In the silence that blanketed the clearing, Alan could almost feel the tension as it crackled in the air between the three of them.

Douglas Windermere pulled the hammer back on his 10mm as he aimed it at Edward, his face like chiseled stone. "It's remarkable," he said, "how much the sound carries through the trees from here. It's remarkable, also, how foolish you've become in your old age, *Ed*." He advanced on Edward, and the old man took an instinctive step backward. "You play a terrible game of poker, my friend."

As the last of the knots fell away, Alan suddenly recognized him, and he struggled to his feet. "Dou..." he began. Lightening quick, Windermere pivoted on his heel and fired, just as Alan's legs caved out from beneath him. Later, he would recall in stories that the ketamine – the very thing that aided in his mother's death – would be what ultimately saved his life. The bullet, intended for his heart, buried itself deep into his left shoulder. Alan screamed in agony, nearly blacking out as he hit the forest floor.

The shift in Douglas' attention gave Edward almost enough time to galvanize his nerve and fire his own gun at Windermere, but Douglas reacted violently in anger to his missed shot, and skidded out of the line of fire just in time. The bullet from Edward's gun droned past his ear, and Douglas snapped his head aggressively back in Edward's direction, his eyes blazing.

"YOU FIRST!" he roared. From within the haze of black pain, Alan watched in silent desperation as Windermere took a single step forward and put a bullet between his father's eyes. A spray of blood, brains and small chunks of skull flew away from his father in a haphazard cloud. He closed his eyes too late, and the image burned in the blackness behind his eyelids. Fear and anguish filled him in a suffocating wave. Edward sagged to his knees like a drunken marionette before what remained of his scarred left eye rolled back in his head and he collapsed into the dirt.

Windermere lowered his gun a little, smiling at what he had done. *Good things come in threes,* he thought as he listened to the laboured breathing of the young man lying against the base of the pine tree. The shoulder of Alan's t-shirt was almost black with blood, and he looked up at Windermere in agony, sweat blanketing his ashen face. The pain within him throbbed with each beat of his heart, and his breathing was shallow.

"Your father was very useful," Douglas said to Alan, without taking his eyes off the corpse at his feet. "Clever, even. But not as clever as he thought he was."

Alan fought to retain consciousness, which threatened to slip through his fingers with each breath.

"He was innocent, of course," Douglas continued. "Well, except for this little charade." He gestured with his empty hand at the dying light of the clearing. "One thing I've learned from your family is an appreciation for dramatic flair."

"Please…" Alan whispered. "Please…everything I have left is yours, if you want it. Just please…don't kill me."

"Don't kill you? Of course, you know I have to kill you. You know far too much for me to let you live. You're a liability." Douglas looked down on Alan, his face softening as if with fraternal affection. "Don't worry. I'll make sure everything is taken care of, even that little Iranian princess of yours." He smiled, showing a mouth full of nicotine-stained teeth. He aimed the barrel at Alan's forehead.

## XII

"WPD! HANDS IN THE AIR!"

Douglas stopped in his tracks but did not comply with the directive. His eyes never left Alan's, and Alan saw in horror that he was still smiling.

"HANDS IN THE AIR, I SAID!" Wilder shouted again, her blue eyes crackling in the lamp light. Morris and King sprang out from behind the detective and jogged across the clearing. Alan looked up and watched Windermere lower his weapon just as Morris reached him.

"Douglas Windermere, you are under arrest for the murder of Edward Black, and for the attempted murder of Alan Black," Morris said through gritted teeth, as King wrenched the 10mm away. "You have the right to remain silent. Anything you say can and will be used against you in a court of law. You have the right to an attorney..." The two detectives turned Windermere around and marched him out of the clearing in handcuffs, Morris's voice fading as they left.

"Father...?" Alan whispered, his hand reaching out into the light of the clearing.

Wilder ran to Alan, Dr. Marsh right behind her. His eyes watched her intently as she came towards him.

"Detective..." Alan managed. "How bad is it?" He began to shiver in shock.

Wilder squatted down by Alan. "You took a bullet in the shoulder, Alan. But Dr. Marsh is here, and she'll make sure you're all right." She shifted her weight a little, and her face softened. "I'll talk to you soon, once we're sure you're going to be okay." She smiled a little and rose to her feet, and Alan watched her go, yellow police tape already being stretched around the perimeter of the clearing.

He drew a breath and began to cry. Whether it was from the pain, or the fact that it was all over, he couldn't tell.

*Epilogue*

Alan woke in the recovery room of Waterford General Hospital several hours after shoulder surgery to see two familiar faces smiling back at him. He tried to raise his left arm in a wave, but a flood of pain soared through him and he let it fall back on the sheet.

"He's awake! Go get Mina!" Celeste said. Parissa dropped her book in her haste and flew out the door.

"Hey," Alan croaked. His mouth felt dry and papery, his tongue too thick.

"Hey..." Celeste replied, reaching for his hand. "How are you feeling?"

Alan brought his too-thick tongue out over his lips, and tried to answer, with no success. "Water?" He finally managed.

"Oh!" Celeste said, reaching for a paper cup and filling it from a pitcher that sat on a small table next to the bed. She handed it to him and he took it with his good hand, drinking as quickly as his throat would allow. Still, some of the water trickled down the corners of his mouth.

"Ahh. That's good," he said, finding his smile at last. "Surgery. Always gives me the worst cottonmouth. Bluhhh."

Parissa came back in with Mina and a nurse in tow. The nurse, a cheerful woman with rosy cheeks, slid in between the bed and the separating curtain and began discreetly checking his vitals. Parissa nudged in next to Celeste and smiled at him. Mina hung back, nervous and small.

"Hey you," Parissa said quietly. "Feeling okay?"

"It's not an experience I would go through again, if I could avoid it. Hurts like hell, but otherwise I'm fine." He looked at Parissa with barely veiled concern. "What about you? What happened?"

Parissa rocked back and forth on her heels, and bit her lip. "Doctor said it was probably just too much stress. I've never been any good at dealing with a lot of discord, and they think I just..." She sighed. "Like a defense measure, you know?" She looked at him with big eyes, hoping he would understand. Alan nodded.

"Well, Mr. Black," the nurse said. Alan saw her name tag read 'Lall'. "Your vitals look fine and barring any questions, I think you should be able to go home in about an hour. Okay?" Alan nodded and the nurse took the little clipboard with her out of the room.

"An hour..." he repeated, bringing his hand up to his forehead and rubbing gently. The last twenty-four hours – hell, the last *week* – seemed like a terrible dream. Celeste was the first to stand up.

"I'll go sign the release forms or whatever they need. Let's get you out of here, Alan." She shivered. "I don't like hospitals much." She turned and left the room.

"I'm going to go check...on our parking pass," Mina said, shadowing Celeste out the door.

Parissa and Alan were left alone together, the only other occupant in the room snoring softly in the opposite corner. Parissa leaned over and kissed Alan gently on the lips, lingering there for a long moment, and then she pulled away with a sigh.

"I'm so glad you're safe," she said, her fingers tracing the air above his shoulder delicately. She hesitated. "Did you mean what you said the other night? When you told me you loved me?" She bit her lip.

Alan nodded carefully. "I meant every word." And he pulled her into another embrace.

\*     \*     \*     \*     \*     \*

With Parissa's help, he got himself dressed, and he was just tidying his hair as best he could when Det. Wilder came into the room. The couple looked up in surprise at her arrival, and then Parissa gave his hair a final fluff and kissed him on the cheek before leaving the room.

"Detective. Good to see you again," Alan said. He adjusted his arm sling and grimaced.

Wilder nodded, quiet and reserved. "Good to see you up and about. That was a hell of a shot you took last night."

Alan looked down at his shoulder. "I thought he killed me. I really did." He looked at her with a puzzled look on his face. "How did you know where I was?"

She smiled. "Well, funny you should ask that. I distinctly remember asking you not to leave the jurisdiction when I first questioned you. So imagine my surprise when I went to Miss Khorasani's house to follow up and found nobody home. That's when we tried to track you via the GPS on her phone."

"Ah." Alan dropped his eyes.

"That was an intensely stupid and foolhardy thing you did, Alan. I hope that when your shoulder heals, it offers a reminder to you every day about how close you came. I really do."

Alan nodded. He tried to think of a way to explain what happened, when Wilder raised her hand at him.

"But, despite all of that, I completely understand *why* you did what you did. You sought justice. This case and your actions remind me of why I became a cop in the first place." She smiled at him. "I'm not here to lecture you, Alan. I really just wanted to make sure you were recovering and also to let you know a couple of things."

"Oh?"

"Mr. Windermere made a full confession once we got him back to the 9th. He was behind not only your mother's murder, but Noah's death also, even though technically that was a suicide. There was the bombing of your shop, too. He said Officer Holby was the man behind that one. Although, with him dead, that'll be impossible to corroborate. Then there's the attempted murder of you and of your friend, Celeste DuMont. I doubt there's a jury in the world that *wouldn't* convict him at this point. Not with that laundry list of charges."

Alan nodded, processing it all. "Good..." he said.

"The second thing I wanted to do was this." Wilder reached into the inside pocket of her jacket and pulled out a dark blue envelope. Embossed on the front were the words *Last Will & Testament*. Alan took it with a shaking hand.

"How...where?"

"We were in Noah Lofton's apartment investigating, and found this on a side table by his front door. As it rightfully belongs to you, I'm making sure you get it back."

"So, it's true," Alan said, mostly to himself. Wilder looked at him questioningly. He looked back at the detective and spoke again. "My father spoke of a conversation he had with Douglas. I didn't make much sense of it, but..."

Wilder pressed her lips together in thought for a moment, nodding, and then turned to leave. "Oh, one other thing, Mr. Black," Wilder said, stopping to look at him over her shoulder. "I would suggest you don't read that until you are back at home." With that, Detective Wilder left the room just as the three girls came back inside.

"What's that?" Celeste asked, pointing at the envelope.

"Nothing," Alan replied, tucking it into his jacket. "Nothing at all."

*　　*　　*　　*　　*　　*

Alan stood at the picture window of his little beachfront house, gazing out at the ocean as the waves washed over the sand. Celeste had offered to take Parissa and Mina back to her place, and give him a little time to recover on his own. He had accepted almost too quickly.

His shoulder throbbed under his jacket, and he shifted his arm gingerly in its sling to try and relieve the pain. With a sigh, he turned away from the window, sat down carefully on the couch, and pulled the envelope out of his jacket. The navy blue of the envelope, with *Last Will & Testament* embossed in gold in the center, evoked a sense of peace, of innocence. It seemed like such a simple thing, something not worth killing people over, but in the end several people *had* died as a result of this envelope's existence. His mother, Noah, Kimberly, his father...even he had come within an inch of dying.

He shook his head in disbelief, pulled the paper out of the dark blue envelope, and unfolded it.

He scanned it. She'd named him executor of her estate, which surprised him, but the real shock came a line later:

*I, Beverly May Black,*
*hereby bequeath my estate and all my belongings*
*to*
*Alan Thomas Black,*

*A sum total worth $350 million…*

There was more, much more, but Alan couldn't read it. His breath had caught in his throat and his mind spun in futile disbelief. So there it was, in black and white, confirming what his father had said. There really was the possibility of some story there about his mother, and millions of dollars that had somehow come into her possession. *His* possession. He let out a huge sigh. Perhaps one day he might find out the whole truth behind what happened. For today however, it was enough to be alive, here and now, in this moment. He mechanically picked up the envelope without looking to replace the Will inside, but it was upside down, and a slip of paper fell out of it. He picked it up from his lap and began to read.

*Dearest Alan,*

*I am writing this note to you in the hopes that you will understand at last why I did not remain in contact with you for all those years. If I could take back all those years we didn't speak, I would do so in an instant. For reasons that will hopefully become clear to you, I've done what I hope will make up for all those times I wasn't there for you, not only as a mother, but also as a friend. Please forgive me all that I have done, and remember one thing: a mother's love for her son is absolute, and undying. Remember that those who do not recognize the monsters within are doomed to be consumed by them. May all your journeys be blessed with happiness and comfort.*

*I will always be there, if you need someone to talk to.*

*Love always and forever, Mom*

Alan read and re-read the note a dozen times, his breath shallow in his chest. In the end, she *had* loved him. She had *always* loved him. And in the end, she had made the ultimate sacrifice for her son.

He turned to look out the window again, and saw something move from the corner of his eye. There, on the arm of one of his patio chairs, was a flower pot. Inside, a marigold and an iris fluttered in the breeze. He looked at them and smiled.

Grief and hope.

# ACKNOWLEDGEMENTS

I fell in love with reading and books at a very young age. There was no world I couldn't conjure up within the pages of a book. No battle I couldn't win. No agony I couldn't suffer. It was all there. Books were my first love, and the first to love me back.

I remember being about three years old and lying in bed, breathless and wide-eyed, as my mother sat on the edge of my bed and read "The Raven" by Edgar Allan Poe before I went to sleep. The imagery and the words both terrified and excited me like nothing else I could imagine. Something about it drew me in, even at that young age, and held me fast. "The Raven" soon became a nightly ritual, and it didn't take my mother long to be able to recite it, start to finish, from memory. Inevitably, she began trying to give me alternatives; options to choose from instead of Poe. Every time without fail I chose to lose myself in that room. The dying embers, the Night's Plutonian shore...the bust of Pallas. All my soul in a single word: Nevermore. The darkness called to me and I was powerless to resist. A bit of that darkness follows me everywhere, even today. In quiet moments it will show me what lies in its murky corners. Showing me and beckoning with an eagerness I can't convey. But I don't fear it. I never have.

Words are powerful, more powerful than most people realize. The ability to transport one into a fictitious world for any length of time is nothing short of a miracle. It's magic...magic in its truest form. Words can bind you, captivate you, make you laugh, make you cry. For anyone who has finished a book and needed time alone to say goodbye to the lives of those they'd just met, this is for you.

This novel is my first attempt at such a miracle. The people within these pages reflect souls I've met along the way; characters that have made my journey more interesting for being in it. It is here that I wish to say Thank You.

First, to my mom and dad, Joy Carlé and John Law. They have always supported me in every venture I chose to set my hand to, regardless of whether I saw it through to the finish.

To my grandmother, Peggie Law. A vibrant woman with a heart full of youthful exuberance, she and I have discovered we have much in common through our writing. Encouragement of each other has become the order of the day, and I'll always cherish this unique bond.

To Shanna and Peter Abrahams, for the laughter, the drinks and for making me part of their family without hesitation.

To Lisa Kell, who helped me with any medical questions I had along the way. For what I got right, thank her. For what I got wrong, blame me.

To Mary Morris, who has been there through good times and bad, and always helped me find my footing when I wasn't sure of my path.

To Dori and Petra Dueck, for always keeping things fun and interesting.

To Dan Paunovski, for his friendship and support while I struggled to balance my work life and this book.

To Diane Cliffe. Your edits and insight helped make this novel far better than I could have ever hoped.

To Ashley, Kelly, and Zoe Duff at Filidh Publishing. These three ladies have offered so much support and enthusiasm as we got closer to publication. I wouldn't be here if it weren't for you.

Finally, to you, the reader. What is a storyteller without a captive audience? Without you there is no me, and for that I will be forever grateful. With luck, my magic will keep and guide you for years to come.

Keep the candle burning...

-K.L.
January 24, 2015

*Photograph © 2015 by Andrew Britney*

# ABOUT THE AUTHOR

Kristoffer Law grew up surrounded by books and learned to read at the age of three. He has one other published work titled "Happy Anniversary" which can be found in the collection "The UnValentine Anthology", published by Filidh Publishing. He is currently working on the second book in the Alan Black series, titled "The 4th Wall".
"The Jagged Tree" is his first novel.

Kristoffer lives in Victoria, BC with his cross-eyed tabby Jana.